Michael Meehan grew up in north-western Victoria, and was educated at Monash, Adelaide and Cambridge universities. He now lives with his wife and son in South Australia. This is his first novel.

THE
salt OF
BROKEN
TEARS

MICHAEL MEEHAN

VINTAGE

A Vintage book
published by
Random House Australia Pty Ltd
20 Alfred Street, Milsons Point, NSW 2061
http://www.randomhouse.com.au

Sydney   New York   Toronto
London   Auckland   Johannesburg
and agencies throughout the world

First published 1999

National Library of Australia
Cataloguing-in-Publication Data

Meehan, Michael. 1948– .
  The salt of broken tears.

 ISBN 0 091 83913 0.

 I. Title.

A823.3

Designed by Yolande Gray
Typeset by J&M Typesetting
Printed by Griffin Press,
A division of PMP Communications, Adelaide

10 9 8 7 6 5 4 3 2 1

To my parents, Francis and Sheila

Well I remember how she blew in off the track that windy day more than a year ago, borne in like a thistle seed on the hot winds that beat in from the north, clothed in nothing but the green cotton dress that flicked and chopped about her, a patched and faded relic of some other person's life, and she carrying nothing, bringing nothing of her own but her taut bare freckled body and sandwhipped hair in auburn streaks that ran before her in the wind, a smile of impertinent white teeth and an improbable tale about a wagon on the road and a farmer gone suddenly unhelpful, a ragged tear in her dress at the waist and a broken wheel and a recommendation—no paper, mind, just her own account, such as didn't make much sense in the telling anyway—from a Lutheran pastor over at Rainbow who might for all that we knew never have existed at all.

Well I remember how she landed in on us that day and the whole place ablow at the time, the screen doors crashing and no-one ready then to push her back out onto the track again in that kind of wind, no-one going into town that week and she offering as soon as she could walk again to stay on and help with the children or down at the shed or just

1

about anything we could want, and we—both my husband and I—feeling that it was our duty before God at least to feed her and put some decent clothing upon her back before setting her off back down the track towards the no thing from which she had come, no family she could speak of and her only past the fading voice of some unknown pastor of another creed.

Well I remember, too, how she made her way slowly up the track towards the house with the children calling me wethanded from the copper to watch a thing unlike we had ever seen before, a bareheaded and barefoot girl making her way up along the track alone, with the nearest town twenty miles distant and not to be walked by man or beast in the heat and wind and the sand toiling hot between her bare toes and the sandflies piping and teasing at the flapping hem of her skirt, with the farm dogs bounding and snapping in play about her and the men whistling as she limped hatless past the sheds, the ragged dress blowing up over her legs and half up around her woman's waist and she part blushing and part seeming to be loving it, half crazed and half excited by fatigue.

Up along the track she came, with Old Tollie and Joe Spencer bent over the twisted plough, unbolting parts gone rustfixed long before, the last stump too high in the ground for the spring to save it, one horse down and all the side pulled over and no plough to take its place this side of the town. Old Tollie made as always for the shade and a shovel or a crowbar to lean on and Joe Spencer hammered away at the bolts, thinking that if they can't be fixed then they can be broken proper, thinking that if any busted up old stump can break it so must he, the weakness and the anger growing about him in the heat and the sweat coursing in gleaming rivulets across his bare moving shoulders while he beat away in a toil of anger with the hard bolts ringing, the sweat running and the sandflies teasing away at him and at that busted but ungiving share.

Up through the broken beat of sledgemetal she came, with no-one even thinking then to lend a hand, as though anyone who walked through the sun on that day must have a power beyond helping, along the track and in with the dust and the breeze. Joe Spencer did not notice for a time with all the sweat and anger that ran about his eyes, until Old Tollie touched his arm and toothless grinned him over to that green flapping figure blown up across the sandy rise that led past the sheds and the hoots and whistles of the others, on towards the house where we stood silent now and waiting with the waterbag. Joe watched her pass in silence and caught the look of someone that had passed through it all somewhere down there along the track, the dry look of dying in her eyes.

And I remember how she could scarcely speak when she arrived at the verandah, slipping and stumbling upon the steps, how without a word but only a nod she grabbed with two hands at the waterbag as I offered it to her, and took the dripping canvas to her lips. She took it and drained the half of it without letting it fall, one part straight down her gullet as if she never needed to swallow as other people do, and the rest down the front of her dress and around and over her breasts with the watered cloth clinging to her and she laughing and lifting the cloth away from her body with a dusty laugh like the croak of a fading crow. Then she raised the bag above her head and showered herself in the

last of it, the best of it working down her front, over her
skirt and through the ragged tear at the waist and down
around her knees bared by her arms raised high, the water
running in dusty rivulets around her calves and over her
bare feet as she showered herself right there and then on the
verandah with the children won over to laughing with her.
They laughed, it seemed to me, without really knowing
why, as if there were nothing but cool tankwater on this
place awaiting to be poured about, our world all but
blowing away on that day had she cared one moment to
see, as if we had no thought on our minds but to admire
these obscene gambols borne in upon us along with the dust
and the rolling tussocks of lignum that had worked loose in
the wind, the best part of the soil, on that day I do so well
remember, strung out across the reddening skies and
coasting far and away from us on that hot northern wind.

Well I remember how she showered herself from the
waterbag in a laughing waste of cool water, and how the
dress came apart as she raised the bag above her head. I
quickly sent the boy from the verandah, the girl then falling
into the wicker layabout, her hair lying in wet and muddy
lanks about her shoulders, her torn dress awry and the
whole world gone still as she trudged in out of the scrub
and over the lakebed and up to the house, the men shuffling
in unease at having greeted what might be a form of
dying with cries and hoots and whistles. Old Tollie and Joe
stood fingering their tools, Tollie leaning heavily on the
crowbar and Joe Spencer caressing the hard blunt head of
the hammer and picking at its splintered wedge and staring
up at the girl up on the layabout and the movement of
women about her as at some new thing he'd never seen

*before, as though he too knew that the unexpected would
no longer come to us in the simple form of flying axeheads
or a fall from a horse or the wrenching of an arm in a
machine.*

Hannah I remember watching, Hannah not much younger
than the girl, my daughter still almost a child but growing
and now trying to help perhaps for the first time and not
standing back with a shy lank of hair drawn across her
mouth, her dry and straggling locks now dragged back and
tied in a ragged stook behind her ears, her freckled skin
and thin arms still raw from the burrs from the sheep we
marked the day before and her yesterday's dress still shot
across with long fine arcs of dried lambsblood. She took
water in twisted handfuls in the flap of her own skirt and
raised it to cool the girl's forehead, sitting to one side of the
girl and mopping her brow with it and looking across to her
brother, watching her brother to see how he would watch
the girl, to see how he would see the forbidden tangle of her
legs splayed out across the layabout and the wet shape of
her body moving in long gasps against the dampness of the
torn green dress.

Not quite leaving he hovered at the verandah's rim,
watching me as always, setting as always in a sullen violence the post between himself and my command, gawking
at the girl as she fell upon the layabout, gawking from the
depths of his cuffed and castoff clothing always too large
and tied about him with lengths of bindertwine, with his
painful stretch of wrists and ankles and spider hands ticking
at the lanks of hair that spiked from underneath his hat, or
fumbling in the long pockets of his peajacket, his thin
shoulders slumping low to meet their bagging depths,

clasping at the post with mittened pockets, glancing from the layabout down to the plough, down to the plough to catch Joe Spencer's face, looking always as a doting puppy to Joe Spencer, looking up to the girl and back down to Joe again to see how he should see this girl.

Perhaps the strangest thing of all was old Auntie Argie leaving her silence for one moment to sit next to the girl, Auntie Argie with not the sense left to her to push a mosquito away or come in out of the sun, moving across from her rocking chair such as she never quitted without the help of others and with a kind hand bringing her crocheted rug to cover the girl. She sat next to the girl and placed with a smile her hand upon her burning hand, holding her hand that was banded in ribbons of water and dust, as the girl clung to the wheeling rim of the wicker layabout with the whites of her eyes rising and her whole breast moving against the clinging wetness of her dress.

Finally Joe Spencer wiped the taste of it from his mouth and went back to his work, striking a noise to set the world amoving yet again but knowing as did all who watched her arrive and even Old Tollie in the broken toil of his slow thinking that this shred blown in with the dust was something that no-one had told us could ever happen. Nothing had prepared us for this unnamed girl with no other garment, nor shoe nor bag nor hat nor anything but that insolent smile she carried as she trudged up along that track and out of a likely death in all that dryness, through the heat and the midday sun and the distances that lay between us and the nearest town. Well I remember the rhythm breaking out again of iron upon iron down by the shed, and Auntie Argie's rug in the name of common decency thrown over her as she lay upon the layabout, the untalking boy still staring from the edge of the verandah and passing down all that he saw in looks to Joe, and all our minds touched with wonder by the sight of a young woman coming half naked from the dust, our minds moved by something that now ran beyond even the things that Cabel Singh had told us around his evening fires; even Cabel Singh who knows each living insect and can trace the movement of the drifts, in all his stories had not told of women, had never told us of a girl who walked across the drifts and ridges, as Eileen had walked, alone and blown and hatless, and uncovered to the wind.

Thinking of the torn and bloodied dress amid the straw and dung, the boy moved through the darkness of the cooling house. He heard nothing but the crack of iron cooling in the chill night air, the motion of bodies moving restless in the night and the rising sound of turkeys gobbling from a farm far distant to the east, moving in faint waves through the dark and through the thin walls of the house. He crept across the creaking boards, thinking always of the bloodied dress, laid out as though about to be put on, laid out as though with care and neatness across the tousled heaps of straw and fragrant horsedung, the crumpled cardboard of her borrowed suitcase and the scattered remnants of all that she possessed flung out across the stable floor.

Wearing still the heavy garments he had worn the day before, for hours he waited in his hessian leanto, the waving fabric of the walls admitting bands of moonlight, waiting for the last of the lamps to fade. He waited for the last mumblings of dispute and the creaking of the beds and the sound of Hannah's sobs to ease. Then he rose and drew from beneath his stretcher the things that he had prepared to take, all that he had prepared in secret through the later part of the day, after Lonnie Cooper had gone and the last of the curious neighbours had followed in his dust; Lonnie Cooper, sweating heavybellied over him, struggling with the mystery of the torn dress and scattered oddments, kneading the fabric of the bloodied dress between his fingers, the old green dress mended and now torn again, as though he could tease from it some special knowledge. Easing his heavy thinking around all that they had told him, Lonnie Cooper had picked up clues where there were no clues and fitted them into stories where there were as yet no stories, stories that made sense of everything except the stable, the emptiness, and Eileen.

They had sat about the evening table in the dying of the light, in silence apart from the stifled chatter of the younger children, all sitting in silence like Auntie Argie, and Auntie Argie only different from the others in her secret and unchanged smile. His father and Old Tollie had talked of nothing, not even of the work of the day to come, and even Joe Spencer had been dark and silent and for once unboasting in his eating, chewing silently in his corner and starting at each alien sound. The boy's mother and the younger children were subdued and solemn amid the crusts and pools of tea, with no-one daring to mention the name of Eileen, as though Eileen must now never have existed at all, as though the very speaking of the name Eileen might serve to bring her back, and some wondering in hope and some perhaps in dread that the flywire door might shriek and crash and that her noise and laughing insolence might fill again the spaces that had opened out between them.

When they were done with eating, Joe and Old Tollie had taken the lamp and stepped into the night, with all the doors of the house left open to take in whatever breeze might crease the still night air, all the rooms left open to each other but with nothing flowing between them, no sounds of Eileen restless, with calls and whispers and sleepless curses following her about the house.

He took the things he had prepared, the black woollen jacket that had been his father's, which would protect him in the nights, and two heavy cotton shirts and a rolled blanket and his boots. His boots he carried with him, creeping barefoot through the broken flywire door that led across the back verandah and into the shack of weatherboard and iron that was the kitchen, thick with the smell of fat and trapped heat and charred woodsmells from the stove. From there he took matches, a pan and metal pannikin, a tin opener and as many tins of food as he could carry, and a cold leg of lamb that stood in the dank Coolgardie safe that dripped softly beside the door. These things he placed in the canvas haversack he had brought, and carried them back into the sleeping house, lifting the scraping door on its hinges as he closed it so that no-one would wake, moving down the long passage that ran through the house and out onto the verandah at the front.

He looked into the room where his sister Hannah had cried through the rest of the day and far into the night, his sister Hannah who had slept in Eileen's arms and talked and laughed deep into the night, weeping long after the others had all gone to sleep. He had waited below the waving hessian and listened to the sobbing until it faded, to be followed only by the sound of turkeys, the sound of distant gobbling rising and falling, and now and then the restlessness of dogs down at the yard, the yelping of the pup and then the howling of the other dogs into the night, howling as they always did when they felt his father slip from them and into sleep. His thoughts ran with the howling, beyond all the questions of Lonnie Cooper that he could not answer and all the easy wrongness that Lonnie Cooper was intent to seize upon. His thoughts moved again upon the sounds beyond the dogyard, of the nighttime cries and the weeping in the dirt beyond the dogyard, of Eileen quietly sobbing as she fumbled with her torn clothing and limped her way in darkness to the house.

He looked into the room where his parents slept, another flimsy sleepout like his own, tacked against the western wall of the house and walled with flywire and heavy wooden screens now raised to catch the cooling air. The room was dark but with the moonlight sifting through the screens, and the boy could make out the shapes of his father and mother on the bed, his father facing the far wall and sleeping deeply without covers in pyjama trousers and an old and torn white singlet, his shoulders hunched and the thick odour of sleeping mansweat coming to him with the filtered breeze that passed through the rusted flywire and carried on into the house. Closer to where he stood his mother lay, close so that he could reach out and touch her if he chose, his mother clad in a long and heavy cotton nightshirt which had rucked up about her knees. She lay with her long dark hair let out in oily lanks that coiled across her face and shoulders, her legs and knees lying towards him, but her right shoulder turned back and her arm flung towards her husband, as though to restrain him from some sudden and intemperate act, as though she might keep him from creeping from that bed and roaming out into the darkness, for hours moving in silence and pain across a country that he seemed to prefer in darkness than in the necessary labour of the unforgiving light.

She was turned back with her arm across him so that her body was slightly twisted and her chest pushed forward, and the boy saw as for the first time, as he watched her taut and in discomfort even in sleep, that it was still the body of a young woman and that in her sleeping she was not unlike Eileen. And then he saw too that she was watching him, that her eyes were open and she was staring at him, or perhaps just sleeping with her eyes open and that the moonlight was catching a tear or some other motion, though still it seemed that her sightless eyes measured him intently, as though knowing that he was seeing as for the first time, as though he knew that the girl had gone off with Cabel Singh, as though knowing that he was leaving to seek out Eileen and Cabel Singh, beyond Wirrengren Plain and far up past Windmill Tank, and out into the wastelands to the north.

'It's Eileen's dress. Come quick, it's Eileen's dress.'
'Look! It's all bloody!'
'Move away from there! Come away!'
'Has Eileen got no clothes on?'
'It's all smelly!'
'Come! Come away from there!'
The torn but neatly set out dress had lain amid Eileen's scattered things, the borrowed cardboard suitcase trampled and broken, and falling from it her clothes and a metal clock and cheap perfume and scattered underwear. The same green dress it was that she had worn a year before, torn at the time but mended since, and now laid out upon the straw,

with hat and shoes and stockings and even the gloves she never wore set out in place as though in some dry mocking echo of the way she never was, mocking except for the tear in the frock and a run of dried blood across the breast and to the waist, the dress spread out across the horsedung and the odorous tangle of straw.

The stable was as always cool and dark, even in the high heat of the day, but with the heat and sweat and light soon growing in an air that was thick and close with smells of dung and dustcrusted grease from old machinery parts mingled with the dry hard smell of old and cobwebbed harness hanging in the shadows, harness that had warped and stiffened in ancient horsesweat and hardened long ago in rocklike forms, now moulded deeply into the cobwebs and shadows of the pinesplit walls.

His father still told of how this had once been his home, and that the forks and roofing timbers were all that had been left after the dry of 'fourteen, after the luckless previous settler had torched the lot on leaving. He had arrived and slept out in the open beside the black ruins of the stable and had patched it on three sides with new pine slabs and covered the roof with fresh loads of straw. He built up the tangle of yards and cattle races from piled stumps and tongue and groove, and they had all lived in the stable for a time, he and the children and their mother, before the first parts of the house arrived, and for a time it was the only space for living, the stable still cluttered here and there with clothes and bedstead wreckage and parts of a toppled iron stove.

The dress of Eileen was laid out before the long manger, the flat unmoving fabric spaces that might have been Eileen set out below a deep trough formed from mallee stakes and fencing wire and a curved sheet of corrugated iron, set out below a frayed and familiar rope that dangled from the beams, a frayed rope now moving gently with the movement of air through the pine slabs of the stable, swaying with the movement of the children, turning amid the sound of the flies attracted by the blood and dung. High above the boy the crossbeams creaked under the thick roofmound of broom and straw and windborne dust, pushing upon the timber forks which bowed as though they felt again the weight of a turning girl, and Eileen squealing with joy again as at those times when she had swung and turned and toppled for them in the dripping darkness. She filled again the dim and odorous spaces, Eileen swinging from the roofbeams on a crude trapeze made from a stick that had been twisted and tied in that same rope, leaping from the manger and coiling around and swinging back, tucking her legs up and twirling in the air, and then flailing for a toehold on the iron.

On wet days in winter they would all go down through the mud to the stable, to the close dampness and the dark and smelly water that leaked down through the roof, the dampness drawing memorable odours from the pine slabs and the straw. Eileen turned on her trapeze, her dress tucked in her knickers, flying in monkey arcs across the straw, with the beams creaking with the weight of it, and the wisps of straw and falling dirt showering her and the children below, Eileen stopping with a wicked splinter in the ball of her thumb, but falling still in laughter to the straw below, upside down and falling in a crazy tangle of legs and straw and matted hair, and all the children, despite Eileen's nasty splinter, calling for their go.

He pushed the younger children away, now roughly as they

tried to play with Eileen's things, and the tears and protests began. He hauled the yelping pup away and forced his sisters to the narrow door and back into the stable yard. Fixing the squirming pup with a length of twine, he bid the children run up to the house, to fetch their father or their mother, or Joe Spencer or even Old Tollie, to come and see what they had found. They jostled each other and strained against his shepherding arms to peer one more time into the darkness, to see the scattered things. He hauled at their clothing, dragging them away from the door, yelling at them now to keep away.

He appealed to Hannah then to move, to do something, to find help, and Hannah broke from her daze and ran out of the yards and up towards the house, beginning to yell as she ran for someone to come and see what they had found. The little ones then followed at the run, and he entered again and alone into the darkness of the stable, moving carefully in the half darkness that met his return from the outside light, edging his way again through the sharp points of farm wreckage that had built up through the years, the broken engines and dumped and tangled harrows and rusting coils of fencing wire, to make his way back to Eileen's scattered things, the gloves and hat and stockings set out in the shape of a woman who could never be Eileen.

Taking off his hat, he waited in the growing light and heat, with the sound of the flies and the creaking beam, hearing now in the distance the ceasing of the beat of a hammer upon some metal part over at the forge or the machinery shed, and up at the house the slamming of doors and the beginning of an older woman's calling, and the high pining of a child's voice. He stood before the dress in the close and darkened air, able to bend down and run his hand across the fabric and touch the mark of blood running across the dress which was the same dress that she had worn unbuttoned on their way back from Windmill Tank just days before, that she had worn as she clung to him on the bench of Cabel's cart as they rolled north together, that she had worn in the hours that they had spent together upon the track as they trudged back to the Ridge, amid the crickets and the evening mosquito hordes.

He ran his fingers down the crust of darkened blood and wondered if it turned on what they knew at Windmill Tank, on the long afternoon they had passed in the heat and in the green waters of the tank and on the long walk back to the south, both knowing that there would be trouble when they arrived, both knowing that the sunburn and the mud and signs of washing in her hair must mean a scolding, both hungry and blown about with evening flies and then mosquitoes as the dark began to fall, his body aching with a new kind of fatigue and Eileen with some wild spirit still brimming in her eyes. Eileen singing cheerfully to the onset of the night, refusing to do up her clothes properly until they came up to the house, the two of them reeling still as they moved through the first netting gate and low fence which now span and coiled about them as they passed, and the boy had clung with hands like claws to the strainer post for just one steady moment. They trudged on in the evening darkness through the gates and over fences and towards known things run unfamiliar, and there was no reassurance in the outline of the Ridge, or the high palms and patter of falling water, or the sound of the windmill spinning in the wind, or the noisy bounding welcome of the dogs.

*

He crept through the sound of moving crickets, beyond the sleeping house and down to the forge where he took two waterbags from the wall and filled one from the rainwater tank, knowing that he could fill the other in the morning from the mossgreen waters that dripped from the pipe up at Windmill Tank. He took his rifle, the old .22 single shot with the front sight gone and two packs of bullets that were not his to take, pliers and his father's marking knife, because it was the one knife he could find. He crossed down to the stable, finding his way carefully through the strewn machine parts and rubbish and not looking at the scattered baggage of Eileen left strewn in the straw after Lonnie Cooper went, his mother not wanting perhaps to touch them and the men and the children feeling it was not for them to gather up the scattered underthings of Eileen.

He took his bridle from the walls and his light saddle with the pommel split and weathered, and another rope and halter and a set of hobbles, and went out again into the night to find, somewhere in the timber housepaddock to the east, the horse that was called his. The horse, which was in fact a large and shaggy unshoed chestnut pony of indeterminable breed, was standing as though waiting by the fence that was nearest to the house, and he bridled it in silence and led it to the saddle, brought it over to the stable with the dogs now beginning to stir and bark at the pony and at the stray sounds of the night. He gathered as much as he could carry of oats and chaff from the manger and stuffed it into an old chaffbag, and then found a way of roping all the pieces to the saddle or around his shoulders so that the tinkling of the hobbles would not ring out in the night.

He adjusted the girth and the length of the stirrups, and

without mounting the pony he set off to the north. They walked past Old Tollie's leaning shack, past the snoring of Tollie or perhaps it was Joe Spencer, and past the high wheeling of the windmill and the slow patter of water into the tank, the water falling loudly in the night. He stopped briefly at the dogyard, risking the yelping of the dogs. He let the pup out, his brown mongrel kelpie twisting and coiling with excitement and its eyes bright in the moonlight, for this was not the first time he had taken the pup for a secret stroll in the night. He tied it on a long lease of bindertwine and drew it away from the other leaping and excited dogs that ran up and down the length of their yard, and he crept with the horse and the pup across the ridge and down towards the netting gate.

The gate was an unwieldy tangle of wire and stakes and a crude straining lever formed from a fork of mallee that the boy had never moved without Joe Spencer's help. He found now a special strength to open and even close it behind, to let the horse and the pup pass through, leading them out onto the sandy tracks and along the line of the fence that could scarce be seen in the half darkness of the night, and along the cart tracks that would take them through the few cleared paddocks to the north and out into the open lands beyond.

The boy had often travelled this way, but always in daylight, for when it had been time for Cabel Singh to go, for almost as long as the boy could remember, he had pulled himself up on the wagon when Cabel was finally packed and ready, the horses harnessed and the spare horse tethered behind. He would wave to the others and sometimes Cabel had let him take the reins, and they would lead the cart out through the netting gate which Joe or Old Tollie would open for them. Up they would ride through the cleared lands and past the sand drifts that marked the furthest fence, off upon the tracks that soon led to where there were no tracks at all, along the western reaches of Lake Wirrengren which no-one had ever known to be a lake, and deep into the seas of blue mallee scrub beyond, blue seas that opened into pine country, and then beyond, the lands of salt and desert to the north.

When they reached as far as Windmill Tank, which lay amid a patch of shade at the northern edge of the first vast stretch of open country, long after the tall palms and spinning windmills of the house were out of sight and miles to the south, Cabel Singh would set him down upon the track and give him a drink and cold johnny cakes, and they would shake hands and say goodbye until the next time. The boy would then sit in the shade of a tree and watch until Cabel's cart was finally out of sight, far across the open plains and into the huge belt of gums that marked the northern rim of the ancient lakebed, waving now and then to Cabel's dust and the unsteady rolling shape of the wagon as it rumbled to the north. As the day began to fall, he would find his way slowly back towards the Ridge and to the routine jobs that led to the end of the day, of bringing in wood and helping with the milking, and he would soon begin again to watch for another visit of Cabel Singh, living the slow weeks of farm and the long trudge to school for the end of whatever story Cabel had been telling and for the beginning of some new tale to take its place.

But the last time they had gone, just three days before, Eileen for the first time had come running alongside the cart, which had set off as always at a lively pace once the netting gate was passed, with Cabel's horses fresh and Cabel's dog and his father's and Old Tollie's dogs still fighting their last battles around the cart and tripping at Eileen. She had bunched her skirts up in one hand and held out the other, to be lifted up, running alongside the cart and begging to come with them, with the sharp voice of his mother lost somewhere behind them in the dust. He had let out a hand to help her, clinging to Cabel with the other, and she had jumped up next to him on the rocking cart, hatless and barefoot and her long auburn hair awry, laughing back towards the figures which emerged from the house on the cry of his mother, looking back through the dust towards the netting gate and the palms and the windmill on the ridge.

They sat unsteadily on the narrow seat beneath the welcome shade of Cabel's flapping canvas, the boy feeling the powerful body of his friend Cabel Singh next to him and his firm hand knotted in the whip and reins, the smell of Cabel Singh not the smell of his father or Joe Spencer, and Eileen rocking and squirming next to him as she struggled still for her unstable edge of seat, her arm clenched around his shoulders and her hair in his face and the odour of her happy perspiration mingled with the green smell of toppling horse-dung and the leather and the dust. Cabel had smiled happily at his rolling jamboree, knowing that in taking Eileen he was risking his welcome on the next round that brought him to the Ridge, but all looking only onwards towards the track and the adventure and the sun gleaming upon the sand drifts and the soft and gateless tracks that lay ahead.

They went down to his camp in the summer evenings, even the little ones, down to the familiar place beside the machinery shed in the evenings when it was fine. There, Cabel would be expecting them, would give them coloured jellies to eat and have them sit about his fire. He would sit among them and smoke his bubble pipe, and the little ones would call for old stories, stories that were now familiar, though never less than strange.

Cabel would laugh with them as he sat before his fire, sometimes drawing on his bubble pipe, and sometimes stirring at a curry, which he would also share. He would share with them his johnny cakes, the thick flat pads of fried dough that he dipped for them in a simmering curry, and they would tell their own stories to Cabel, tales of birds' nests and rabbits and the long trek with Hannah down to Baring school. Sometimes Cabel would join in to tell them stories of his own childhood, so long ago and far away. He was far younger than the other hawkers they had seen, and younger, it almost seemed, each time he passed the Ridge. But they could not imagine Cabel without his dark beard and his cart, could not see the ageless Cabel as a child like themselves, and always preferred the tales that Cabel told of the wastelands to the north.

'What did I say? What did I tell you, the last time I was here?'

The children would begin to tell him in a rush of bits and pieces the outline of some story he had told, and finally Cabel would seize upon some detail, some fragment that reminded him of another story, and he would begin to talk. Then they would settle into silence, the boy's eye catching sometimes the eye of Hannah or of Eileen, and they would smile to each other the smile of deep immersion, of a profound and familiar pleasure as Cabel began his tales.

Sometimes he told them stories from his distant childhood and of places far away, but mostly he told stories from the country which lay about them, a country scarcely to be known as Cabel told it, a country bare and featureless to view but which in Cabel's stories took on a motion and a life where one bare and vacant stretch of scrub peeled off into another and threw his wanderers together in new and fragile combinations. He told them always of the far country, of the wastelands to the north, of abandoned towns out in the desert, and of the river that ran through the country to the east, and of the green lands to the south. He told stories of travellers like himself, and often like Eileen, wanderers who came in off the road from nowhere and who lived in the luck of chance, where the next track they chose might be a track leading only to another track, and to a death beyond luck among the soaks and sandy ridges. All ran into worlds they only knew when Cabel spoke, when Cabel's voice ran softly out into the falling darkness, with the night creeping in upon them as though to listen, clinging to the fading rim of the circle cast by the fire.

Cabel sat in the half darkness of the night but always nearest to the fire, always at the centre and in the special shirt he would put on in the evenings, a shirt of a whiteness they never saw elsewhere, and sometimes with a turban of a brighter colour and sometimes with nothing on his head at all but with his long hair falling free about his face and down his shoulders, or sometimes just tied behind. His skin was dark against the white but no more so than those who worked in the sun. He had once been a soldier, the boy had been told, and was said to know more of horses than anyone. Even as they sat about the fire, Cabel would sit erect, crosslegged but with his back and shoulders straight, as though sitting at attention even as he told his tales. Even the boy's father, who had little to say of anyone, admitted that he was a fine stamp of a fellow, after Cabel once saved a team of horses that had got into the wheat. And as Cabel talked, the boy would watch always the colour of his eyes, deep black, unlike the soft brown eyes of Eileen whose eyes so quickly took on the glow of the fire and the light of the sun. He would watch Cabel's eyes as they looked deep and black into the glowing of the fire.

The boy would watch Eileen as she sat crosslegged in the dust, her hands bunched in her lap and her eyes shining as she stared into the gleam of the dying ring of fire, as the soft voice of Cabel teased them away and into worlds that lay beyond the world that dropped away as they sat about his fire. He watched the motion of the flames about her eyes as she sat crosslegged by the fire, as they listened to the stories that reached far into the night. He would watch Joe Spencer too, Joe Spencer always sitting back a little and busying himself with sticks or piles of stones, but drawn despite himself to Cabel's fire, scarcely seeming to follow Cabel's stories but always there to watch Eileen, watching Eileen draw her knees up in her arms or brush away the insects on her skin.

They would watch his gaze and listen, and the boy would watch the face of Cabel Singh as the moving light ran up across his beard and face and magnified the deep gleam of his eyes. As he spoke they would all move closer to the shrinking embers, listen ever closer to his stories, and look now with the eyes of Cabel Singh, look deep into the lands of Cabel Singh. They listened as his stories ran out through the flickering of the fire against the drooping fringe of pepper trees, as they reached out to shape the sand drifts, the ridges and the dark fringe of the retreating scrubland, stories with no real beginnings and no endings, of strange and ancient godlike beings who moved across the country in an eternal wandering and at every moment held their whole fate in their hands, where the river goddess Ganga and Arjuna the archer and Bhishma the warrior who lay upon his bed of arrows mingled freely with the wandering trappers and shootcutters, channel dredgers and bagsewers to the north, all characters who in some of Cabel's stories vanished or came to grievous and untimely ends, but who would always come back later in another time and place and on another of Cabel's visits; and all his stories were of people moving across an open country upon which all things might come to pass.

He spoke too of the land about them, of the northern deserts and the vast saltpans and low and trackless forests that they would one day cross together. They learned of the dry country beyond the high drifts to the north, the green lands and open flowing rivers to the east and south, and of Cabel's journeys that took him always up through the seas of low forest that lay beyond Wirrengren Plain, and out across the drifts and vacant plains, and on towards the silver lakes that lay far to the north, great lakes where you could walk across the surface of the waters and never once get wet, where all the water was made of air and faded and blew about you as you crossed. They learned about the dry flat lands that lay beyond Monkeytail Tank and to the east, and Pheeny's Rise and Rocket Lake and the tank at Last Chance, where they would ride with him one day, before moving out across Raak Plain and towards the solid earth of

Carwarp Downs. From there they would ride on through taller forests to meet the river on one of its crazed foldings as it wound out beyond Kulkyne. There they would meet a vast and rolling river with more water than they could ever imagine, sweeping through the dry country with nothing but dust and thirsting trees and dry and yellow country to either side. Beyond the river they would ride into the swamplands, where trees grew upon the waters and strange birds lived like fish beneath the surface, of giant stranded seabirds that had stayed so long as to lose the art of flight, and of bright banded snakes that sped like thoughts across the brink. There, Cabel said, they would sleep on broad beaches of crumbling bark and soft damp sand, and they would stay for as long as they pleased, and live upon mussels and duck eggs and riverfish and rabbits and wild honey.

'Joe?

'You all right, Joe?

'What are you going to do, Joe?'

Because the boy knew that Joe must do something. He watched but from a distance as Joe shuffled from foot to foot, beating his fist from time to time against the slab walls of the stable and threatening violence to the trees and to the blank heat of the day, and then retreating in misery to the shade of the pepper trees, to sit and splinter sticks and kick aimless patterns with his heel amid the dirt, glancing back now and then to check on the others, the boy's father and Old Tollie, who stood about the gateway to the stable, scratching their elbows and stroking their chins and gazing helplessly out across the lakebed and the spaces that lay vacant to the east.

Joe Spencer had lost his high ruddy colour and his cocky smile when he was told, and finally he was taken by Old Tollie even gently to the fallen log that lay beneath the shade of the pepper trees, on the place where the hawker's cart had been. He sat with his shoulders hunched over an enamel mug of tea that Hannah brought, alone until the boy approached, sitting with Joe for a time in silence and, like him, just fooling about with bits of stick.

No-one had talked to Joe Spencer for a time, for it was known that he spent more time than anyone with Eileen through the recent months, taking her with him in the Ford collecting stumps, and sometimes playing cards in the evenings up at the house, and more often just sitting with her on the wicker layabouts on the verandah, Joe in his armless and unbuttoned shirt, blowing his smoke rings off the verandah and out into the night, teasing and joking with Eileen who would rarely simply read or sew as the boy's mother did and who it seemed could never be without some other person, even silent smiling Auntie Argie, to banter and provoke. Eileen would lie on one of the layabouts, laughing and teasing with Joe, placing her ankles over the rail and spreading her knees and raising the fabric of her dress to catch whatever cool breeze might filter up the ridge, and she and Joe would pass hours in the falling darkness, ribbing and poking at one another and sometimes with ancient Auntie Argie still quietly beside them as though she were not there at all. And when it was time for Joe to amble back down past the dogs, past the netting yard that had been coiled about a clump of mallee, his passage was marked out for the girl and the old woman who lingered on the verandah in the rise and fall of the red glow of the last of his cigarette.

'Joe?

'You all right, Joe?'

But Joe dismissed the idea that things might not be all right with a harsh snuffle, wiping his bare forearm across his face as though it were the sweat of work that he was clearing, pitching a stick over towards the pup, who leapt and yelped with the joy of it and then came back with the stick for more.

'Bastard! Bastard, bastard, bastard!'

That was bastard for whatever had happened to Eileen and bastard that his feelings about it were so strong and bastard that the boy and his pup should see him in this way.

'What're you going to do, Joe?'

'Dunno, yet.'

'What do you reckon happened, Joe?'

'Dunno, yet. Jesus, kid!'

Why did you hit her, Joe?

Which was the question that he did not ask, and he did not ask about the sounds that he had heard, of Joe arguing with Eileen in the night and the sound of the dogs restless and the pup yelping as he crept down past the dogyard and the sound of the blow and the weeping in the dirt. He was silent for a time, knowing not to push Joe too far, not wanting to leave Joe because of the questions the others might ask, his talking with Joe a refuge from questions and silences and strange looks of the others, with Joe slumping forward with his elbows on his knees, his chin pressed against his clasped fists and cracking knuckles, staring with a concentrated gaze of anger down across the vacant spaces of the lakebed.

'What do you think, Joe? What are you going to do about it?'

'I reckon we ought to talk to the Indian, for one thing. That's one thing we gunna do. That's one thing we need to do.'

'Why Cabel Singh, Joe? Why talk with Cabel Singh?'

'I reckon he knows something. He told her something, when they were on the track. Give her funny ideas.'

'What sort of ideas?'

'Just stupid bloody ideas. That's all.'

And Joe Spencer's shoulders began to square again with the growth of an idea that might mean some kind of doing.

'I'd like to have a bit of a yarn with this Cabel Singh. That's all. That's what I'd like to do.'

'He's gone up to the north, Joe. You saw him. Days ago. He won't be back for a couple of months. That's what he said.'

'He knows this country. He knows this place. He lives out in it. He told us once that he hasn't slept under a roof for ten years. He knows every inch of it, every damn twig and rock of it, like none of us do. He knows things we don't. He even watches the sand drifts move. He told us that once. He remembers where they were, ten years ago, and he watches them move and cover things, bushes, trees. He knows the place.'

'Doesn't mean he done anything, Joe. Why would he hurt her, Joe?'

Why did you hit her, Joe? Why was she crying?

And neither did he ask about the blood that was on Eileen's dress, not asking if the blood was from the blow that he had struck her beyond the dogyard, not asking about Eileen as he had seen her, as she had limped past where he was hidden, sobbing and trying to fix her dress and stumbling up towards the house.

'What was it that he told yers anyway?'

Joe turned on him.

'What did he tell her? What did he say to the two of yers, out there by Windmill Tank? What the hell were yers all doing out there anyway?'

Joe turned back and gazed out to the dry lake.

'He could come and go without any of us knowing it. Without leaving a track. Better'n an abbo. Maybe she seen him in the nights. With none of us knowing a damn thing about it. I'm going to find him and talk to him. Just talk to him, that's all. That's what I'm gunna do.'

Joe thumped his fist against the palm of his hand and snuffled and spat, and gazed out again across the lake and steadily cursed it all in a soft and steady stream, cursed Eileen and Cabel Singh and the cleared country and the country still to clear, the boy for his questions, and the pup that would not shut up, and all the empty spaces and dark ideas that rose before him off the empty lakebed, of Eileen stealing naked out to meet the darkness, this time to greet the smile and secret knowledges of Cabel Singh, who crept back in silence from the north, leaving no mark as he moved across the moonlit plains. Joe's eyes gazed sightless into the heart of it, and he coughed and spat at the reek of what he saw, turning now and then to glare down at the stable and the boy's father and Old Tollie still shuffling about.

'In and out like an abbo. None of us knowing a damn thing about it. Not a damn thing.'

They sat about in silence, until Joe was released by the boy's father, who called him over and told him to get the stumps off the truck and take it into town to fetch the policeman from up at Ouyen, though no-one rightly knew if it was a police matter at all, if scattered clothing and a girl of her age gone off meant anything at all. He might have a chance, they thought, of raising someone who could open up the Exchange on a Sunday and get word up to Lonnie Cooper in Ouyen, to see if maybe she had taken the main road and turned up there.

Joe leapt to his feet and whistled to his dog and cranked the truck and brought it across in seconds in a great jolt of smoke and whining metal and ground gears, leaping into the rear and tearing the black and tangled stumps from the tray, the stumps that he and the boy had collected the day before, and piling them in a dusty and unsteady stack below the pepper trees, toppling them across the hawker's ring of stones, across his tracks and the mark of his pickets in the dirt.

The boy sat on Joe's log, watching the rage of Joe's labour, watching Joe's anger spill out into the thankful violence, watching him raise the larger stumps above his head and pitch them in the air to crash and topple, the anger running out into a rage of muscles heaving as he flung the roots upon the pile, kicking the last of the stumps from the tray with one heavy boot and then the other and slamming the tailgate closed with a shriek of grinding iron. Without a word to the boy, and with another harsh assault upon the gears, he set the truck bucking and jerking off upon its way, ignoring the boy's request to take him along and moving off down the track in clouds of dust and oily smoke, the old Ford straining and bucketing as he tackled the furrows by the gate, setting out over the dry lake in a low billowing stream of dust and towards the pine clumps and scrublands that lay between them and the town.

In the heat of the day he would sit on the edge of the oat-stack, hiding in the shadow of his broad felt hat, watching as Joe took oats up from the wagon, his muscles taut and the sinews standing out upon his arms, and he would watch as Joe's legs took up the weight as the bags toppled and his body staggered and then held. He watched Joe's body take on strength and balance as he straightened and shifted his feet and locked his back into a steady hold, then lumped the bag across the unsteady footing of the stack and dropped it, with a last grunt of delicious effort, precisely in its place.

He watched him at other times, too, when he worked nearer to the house or around the garden with his shirt stripped off and his muscles firming and easing to the steady thrust of the shovel delving at the clay, the driving of the pick-handle into the knotted roots of old rosebushes, or oleanders to be grubbed out. And the boy would watch with a pleasure that was like the pleasure of his own body when he saw the straining arch of Joe Spencer's back and the force of his legs driving down into his heavy and workmoulded boots, fixed hard against the beaten earth.

He watched him as they swam together naked in the dam or washed together after work, and he would see the white skin tight across Joe's chest, the thick curly hair that was beginning to appear there, and the thin line of hair that grew from his loins and his navel upwards, the sharp acidic odour of stale filth and oil and mansweat that rose from him as he began to wash, and the long rivulets that the brown water made as it coursed down upon his back and stomach and clung in soapy froth about his groin. He watched the thick contours of Joe's back and shoulders as he stooped to dry his feet, and the turn of the muscle and the darker hair that he saw when Joe raised one arm and then another to slap roughly at his body with the thin towels that his mother would leave out for them, slapping with harsh affection at his own body as he slapped the necks of his horses after a day's hard work, flicking and cracking the thin wet towel about him like a whip.

When they worked together, the boy would place his spindlebody next to Joe and try to learn Joe's rough and careless way of moving, exploring the spaces of his own ungrown body and speaking in a voice that was like Joe's, speaking only in words and through thoughts that he knew to be Joe's. He slapped roughly as Joe did at his own bony frame, and lumbered about as though under the rich weight of muscle in the way he saw Joe do, because he knew that one day he would need to know how to care for and move within a body that would be like Joe's body, with its thick flesh like the flesh of a horse that rolled and strained beneath the skin, with its own dark coils of thick and secret hair that stored the heat and odour of the sun and work, with arms burned red and brown against the whiteness of his body, with a deep red vee at his neck where the sun would beat in, where his shirt too would fall open, as Joe's shirt always fell open, as he laboured in the sun.

He tore at the sleeves of his shirts in the way Joe always tore the sleeves from the shoulder of each new shirt that he put on; and when he saw how the gaping holes mocked his thin arms and flapped about his bony chest, he wrapped himself in his father's heavy peajacket and wore it even through the high heat of the day, and had worn it from that day since, as he wore each day the battered army slouch that Joe had given him, and the heavy boots that were not boy's boots at all, boots that needed the aid of rolled newspaper and bandages just to stay upon his feet.

For years he had clung closely in this way to Joe Spencer, with his ragged blond and curly hair, his face cut about and always poorly shaven, his movements brute and awkward unless heaving and straining in some mindless test of strength. Joe Spencer never seemed to ask for more of life than a tough job to do, a clean shirt at the end of the week, a trip into town and a beer at the Patchewollock pub, and some daily labour, some daily resistance to bring back to him his power, something to move or bend or break, to keep his blood quick and his ready spirits chanting. Joe Spencer was a good straight shot, whether in the bush or at bottles behind the Patchewollock pub, and a good straight lumper too, with a name for it on stacks as far away as Speed and Tempe.

Joe seemed not to give a damn where he had come from, or where he was going, but gloried only in the name of a damn good toiler who could last from sunrise to sundown at the plough or the shovel without complaint, who could always get an acre or two more from his horses than even the boy's father, who had worked them all his life. Joe seemed to know the thoughts of dogs and horses and had a feeling for the insides of machines, the oily bowels of the neighbour's tractor and the endless trickling cogs that spilled from the truck's gearbox one day when Joe had taken it all apart, and worked all day through the silence and curses of his father, to put the whole thing back together again without the loss of so much as a drop of oil, and it working perfectly from that day to this.

The boy's clinging never seemed to bother Joe, because Joe was still half a boy himself and had grown up in this way within the shapes of other men. He laughed at this splinter of a boy who was his skinny echo, and ruffled his hair and teased him, but always with rough kindness, and he showed the boy that he understood, every time he twisted his arm or knocked his hat off and ruffled his hair and cupped his hand behind the boy's neck and sent him twirling in the dust. Sometimes in the evenings, or when wallowing in the dam, or out collecting stumps, he would wrestle with him and let the boy feel the strength that was in his back and arms. He taught the boy lots of things before his time, and many things that boys his age could never hope to do, and even, once or twice, had told him of Eileen. And when Eileen herself leaned over the boy, as now she often did, and caressed him still as a child, but always with her eyes and hands roving about him in a mocking and intruding way, he felt the starts of desire and found he hardly knew whether it was his desire or just a knowledge of the desire of Joe Spencer. When Eileen smiled at Joe as she moved about the table and Joe grinned back and his father scowled at them and caught his mother's eye across the table, the girl would be sent scuttling from the kitchen on some useless errand and the boy would watch Joe's eyes follow her.

Then Joe would turn and wink at him, and he wondered at these times how much they knew of his nights amid the bushes past the dogyard, wondering about these winks of Joe and the gentle hands of Eileen, and what they told him of the movement in the nights beyond the dogyard; and in thinking on it he slipped yet further beyond the silence and the dark looks of his parents, beyond all the chatter of the other children and the last of his childhood world, of nests and jacks and rabbit traps, to cling more tightly to this secret life of Joe Spencer and Eileen.

He moved in silence far beyond the house, following the fenceline that faded close ahead into the darkness of the night, the darkness lifted by the moon which hung above the drifts, the silent nighttime spaces theirs alone. They moved through the bands of cleared country and past the open reaches of low stubble that led out towards the drifts, where the cleared country ended and the high drifts and pine country began. The moon threw long shadows across his path, and the sound of distant turkeys and the fading yelping of dogs only told how far he had left the familiar world behind.

For miles he moved through familiar places made unfamiliar in the darkness, opening and closing gates for the horse along the tracks that led towards the eastern edge of the vast Wirrengren Plain. They climbed the low hills and over the tall sand drifts that lay just to the north of the ridge, and soon they broke into the unfenced country, moving out in the half light of the night on to Wirrengren and following the dim outline of a winding track that took them north and through the thin and waving grasses towards the centre of the low expanse. For hours they walked through the open heart of the country, through the bed of the lake that had never, in anyone's memory, been in water. They walked in silence along the looping track which ran off towards the north and the west, the pallid speargrass drawing low the light of the moon and gleaming off into the distance towards the rim of scattered timber that marked the boundary to the east and, far to the north, the sight of moonlight on the low slopes and sand drifts that lay beyond the rim of ancient gums that lay along what was once the sandy shore. The boy trudged alongside the horse and the pup padded softly behind, and they walked this way until they saw the first signs of morning light.

He stopped at Windmill Tank, where he had been just days before with Eileen and Cabel Singh. The sound of the spinning vanes came to them from the distance, long before they were near, before they could see in the faintness of the early morning light the dark patch of low timber and the scatter of troughs and farm wreckage, of rusted iron tanks and old car seats. The boy filled his waterbags from the water which slowly dripped as always from the buckled overflow. He released the horse in hobbles to graze on whatever it might find in the low fringe of grasses that lay about the troughs and amid the tufts of saltbush that lay a little further out. He built up a small fire with scattered windfall timber, and he and the dog lay down and away from the dull glow of the fire, so they could watch the last of the stars. They listened to the crickets singing in the bush, and to the distant moaning of an owl somewhere towards the north. He wrapped up as best he could against the early morning chill and curled up with the warmth of the pup, and they listened together to the sound of the wind in the trees and the sound of the horse's hobbles and the trickle of water from the tank, to the steady rattling sounds of loose paperbark against the trees and the beating of floating strings of

flaking bark that ran out in the wind. They listened to all the
sounds of the windmill patch of scrubland, which creaked
about them as though it were creeping from them in the
night, as though all the world that was familiar to them to
that moment was now flaking and peeling and breaking
away in sheets like ancient paper and coursing off upon the
winds.

'What did you hear last night? You must have heard something.'

'Nothing. The dogs were restless, but they always are.
Nothing apart from that.'

'How did she seem, when you last spoke to her? Did she
seem all right to you last night?'

The boy would only tell her that the girl had seemed well
enough last night, sitting as usual under the light of the lamp
in the living room, playing a game of cards with herself, not
trying to talk to anyone but sitting quietly under the light of
the big Colman lamp. He had passed and looked at her
reflection in the oval mirror, had watched her game of
patience inverted in the mirror that hung upon the wall
of the living room, had watched the tip of her tongue
between her teeth as always when she played with care,
watched the freckles on her nose and her nose wrinkle in
annoyance when she made a fault. He often watched her
in this way, watching Eileen in the mirror so that others
would not see that he was watching, and she had looked up,
Eileen's sleepy eyes catching his eye as he looked at her. She
smiled secretly in the quiet of the room, smiling at his secret
admiration, at perhaps his knowing that she was waiting for

the world to sleep and for her time to slip down yet again in the darkness to the dogyard.

He watched her reflection in the mirror, Eileen at the centre of the room's reflection, her tousled auburn hair softlighted in the Colman's glow, and she smiled her warm and always halfsleepy smile at him, happy that he should admire her in this way. She seemed to know his thoughts of her much better than he did himself, seemed in her smile to carry some special knowledge of him, and her smile moved always about him like the touch of a kind hand. She ran her hand through her thatch of hair that was loosely tied behind but straggled out around her ears, her large brown eyes taking in the mirrored room, the children lying and playing on the floor, and the backs of the heads of his parents as they sat silent in their chairs, his father's hair pasted in a rim about his ears by the sweat of the day, his head nodding, almost sleeping, and his mother buried deeply in a book.

'What are you doing?' he would ask, though it was always clear what she was doing, and yet it pleased him just to ask, as he knew Eileen would then grin and reach across and rumple his hair, run her fingers through his hair and roughly shake his head, and then go back to her cards. Then Hannah would drop her book and come also to the table, and she and the boy would force Eileen to take up the cards and deal them out a hand. This, he told his mother, was all that had happened, that last night, as on a hundred others.

At times throughout the day his mother had taken him aside, measuring always his resistance, knowing that he knew more than he said, knowing that Eileen had talked to him, as she had talked to Hannah, talking to them of adult things, of things that might explain. She knew well enough that they had listened, and too often, to those wild stories of Eileen, her one consolation being that, however wild the stories were, the truth was surely worse. When he would not answer, she ran a worn hand through her hair and gazed out into the glare at the stripped and naked plains that lay about them, as though what had happened in the stable, and the boy's knowing, and all the boy's stubborn resistance were rooted in that glare and emptiness.

'Did she tell you anything? Did she say anything to you when you were out with her last week?'

The boy moved deeper within his hat, lowering the brim so that he could not see her eyes.

'On the way back from the tank? Anything else you should have told Mr Cooper? Is there anything else that we should know?'

'Well,' she murmured finally, when she failed to provoke him, 'I'm not surprised. I can't say I'm surprised. The way she carried on. But I didn't think that this would happen, in this way. I didn't think that it would happen just like that, on our place. Not in this way.'

Thinking that it would come, but slowly, as all fate came to them slowly, like the dryness that crept on day by day, or the slow dust of the Debt Adjuster's car as it crept towards them from far across the lake. She furrowed her hair with nervous fingers and looked again to the men fanning flies away in the shade by the stable. She looked at Hannah too, a sad little figure throughout the afternoon, in her yellow pinafore and ragged fuzz of hair, now pallid and silent underneath the pepper trees, sitting with her head in her hands on Joe's log, staring into the pile of stumps that Joe had left, staring deep into the pile of stumps and to that hidden place where Cabel had kept his fire.

She was aware that some special thing was needed, that someone needed to attend to the grieving girl, who now neither cried nor spoke, but it was not in her now to offer that thing. It had not been in her to offer that form of kindness for some years, except in flashes to Auntie Argie as she dazed about the house. Instead of looking to the breaking girl, she moved over to the stable again and backwards and forwards from the house, looking for some relief in blaming, blaming the flies, blaming that rude and inconsiderate hussy who had brought them so much trouble, cursing the grieving and the relief and the confusion that she had left behind, scolding the pup who grew louder on the excitement of a scolding, and the son who had fallen upon some secret female obscenity displayed in this obscure way and who had spent she knew not how long dwelling upon it, alone in all the monstrous depths of whatever it was that happened there. She blamed this ditherer of a son who was determined to be no help at all, who let her know in his silences that he knew something, sheltering from her beneath his slouch hat, setting himself and his silence against her in this business and taking up all that he knew into whatever cloudy and resenting incommunicable world in which he passed his time.

'Go and talk to Hannah,' she said finally, but in a softened tone.

'She's finding it all very hard. Go and help your sister. Tell her something. Just see that Hannah is all right.'

She moved at last to go up to the house.

'You can do that, at least.'

The boy did not speak to his sister but only gestured to her to come with him. She rose from Joe's log and they found their way together down to the gateway that led out onto the lake, down to the clump of trees that stood about the gate, that gave out onto the lakebed and the track that led through the spare forests of scattered native pine that lay between them and the town. She climbed upon the strainer post and the boy climbed the dead tree by the gate, and there they simply waited, whispering now and then to each other, their voices softened by the sight of adults still milling about and talking in muted voices over by the stable, and by sad thoughts about Eileen.

They watched the last of the dust that followed Joe Spencer rise slowly and disperse in the air, and they waited still, knowing that long hours and the heat of the middle of the day must pass before Joe Spencer would return, before they would see another cloud of dust in the distance and then the sound of motors, and then perhaps Joe Spencer with Eileen laughing by his side, as she had driven back with Cabel Singh not more than a week before, waving to them as she rode through the gate and saying that this was all a mistake and just another kind of joke, and that she had come back to stay with them, that she had changed her mind, and that now she was back, they would do things as before.

The boy left the tank and rode again across the open plains and through the yellow fields of waving grasses that led to the north. At the furthest edge of Wirrengren Plain they climbed up through the heavy gums and over light sand drifts and into the low seas of dense blue mallee that would lead, Cabel had once told him, onto the tracks that led up towards Linga and Underbool and Boinka Town, and across the threechain road that led off to the west.

He travelled slowly with the horse and pup, sometimes riding and sometimes walking ahead and leading, because of the chafing of the saddle and the biting of the ropes he had strung across it. At times he carried the pup which soon tired of the long slow route along the tracks and exhausted itself with chasing after rabbits and distant mobs of wild goats, with tearing at the entrances of rabbit burrows and sending flocks of grazing galahs and Major Mitchells into shrieking clouds of flight. By the late part of the morning the pup had settled into the length of the journey, simply padding alongside, its tongue lolling and a smile upon its face, or so it seemed, as they made their way in silence through the rising heat of the day. And when they rested now and then in the shade of a native pine, the boy would take one of the canvas waterbags and give the dog a drink from his hat and the horse some cocky chaff and oats and a long drink from the pan.

They came upon a belt of open country in the late part of the day, an open plain between two seas of bushland, with a sparse cover of grey blasted grass and the splintered hulks of broken trees with here and there a clump of native pine. And in the distance the boy saw movement and a flash of white, and knew that it was wild goats, running from a tank. He tethered the horse and pup to a fallen pine and took his rifle and loaded it and crept slowly from stump to fallen tree in the hope that he might even with his front sight broken get close enough to shoot a young goat; but the goats seemed to catch wind of him from more than a quarter of a mile off, and scattered to the scrub.

He crept on slowly towards the tank and scrambled up the western bank, peering over the edge and at a fragile pool of greenish water surrounded by its wide midsummer rim of cracked and broken mud that held, well back from the water's edge, the blackened ribs of two unlucky sheep. He fired among the flock of feeding waterbirds that he knew that he would find there, the ducks and dabchicks and ibis, and he wounded a brown duck. Then he went back for the pup and horse and, hauling off his clothes, he waded in after the duck, leaping and sinking in the deep sucking mud, with the three of them soon plunging in the mud and plying the green soup of the stagnant water with the pup swimming round and round and tormenting the thrashing bird and the horse drinking and retreating, shying and foundering in the mud and pulling back but then returning, after a time, to the mud and the water's edge. The dog finally took the exhausted bird in its jaws and brought it to the boy, who had now coated himself from head to toe with the cool black mud, and he wrung the bird's neck and flung it up the bank. He then lay naked in the cool dark mud, which dried and cracked upon his skin, and he let his mind run out into the silent scrub beyond the tank, run out through thoughts of Eileen, and Joe Spencer bending to his work, past all that he had known of at the Ridge, to shape itself for the spaces to the north.

He watched her as she smiled at Joe Spencer, the warm and almost sleeping smile she passed always to Joe Spencer, even across the table in the kitchen when they were sitting at their tea. He would see Joe's muscles tighten and the veins net out across his forearm and his shoulders take on a strength from Eileen's special smile, which seemed to flow in warmth like gold about his body when she turned to him, and even and perhaps especially in the midst of others. Joe's eyes followed every movement of the girl as she moved about and leaned across the table with plates of food, as she moved about the table in the baggy shifts and heavy cassocks that the boy's mother had flung upon her. When she finally came to the table and sat at the end of the long stool with the younger children, to see that they were fed, Joe would sit up from his plate and bread and begin to brag and banter with Eileen or indirectly through a joking with the boy, and tell in great mouthfuls of food of all he'd done that day, about gigantic feats against posts and sheep and stumps and falling tracts of green mallee. Eileen would smile in open happiness at these tributes and his mother would scowl and give her things to do to take her from the table and the room.

At times Joe brought his work up to the house, taking machines apart or stitching harness in the shade by the woodheap, and Eileen would amble over with water or a mug of tea. The boy watched them as they spoke together with Eileen holding her straggling hair out of the way, in a long lank across her shoulder, and leaning across Joe to see what he was doing. Sitting on the stump pile or sometimes helping Joe with his work, the boy would watch as Eileen looked with happiness at his labour, on a bung windmill pump or a broken tine or some rusted fragment from the combine.

At times he caught the face of his mother behind the dull glass of the lacecurtained kitchen window, his mother peering out and watching the movements of Eileen as she passed the mug to Joe or simply held it for him while he worked, her hand clasped around the mug and the hot tea slopping, with Joe working intently and then stopping work for a moment and squinting up at her as she stood between him and the sun, protecting him from the worst of the heat, her arms sometimes caressing and enfolding her body against the heat and all the white light of the yard and against all the empty spaces of Joe's concentrated silence as he finished the mug of tea in a gulp, and wiped his forearm across his mouth, and gave his attention back to a resisting bolt. Eileen would move in closer, interfering with the light, with Joe saying nothing about it but working stronger within the warmth and shade and intimacy of her stooping curious form and the soft musky odours of her body and the motion about him of her blowing skirt.

The boy watched from his perch upon the stumps as Joe reached for a larger spanner to attack a rusted bolt on a broken pump that he brought for no good reason up to the house, and he watched as the girl held again her unpinned hair with one hand as a snake over her left shoulder and leaned over Joe, the two of them with rapt attention locked upon the bolt that would not move, and all of them, and even the mother shrouded by the dusty lace of the kitchen window as well, passing backwards and forwards past the lace of the window and then stopping to watch intently, watching his forearm strain and lift. Joe began to heave and groan and the bolt seemed to creak and fight and give, and then they saw the spanner spinning out across the dirt, with Joe's scraped arm showing a deathly white then blue then red, dripping along its length as the dark blood began to flow.

'T'arn't so bad,' the boy heard him say after a moment of loud then muted cursing as the girl crowded in upon the arm and upon the growing stream of blood, pulling his hand away so that she could inspect the graze, answering with her closeness to the man's sudden need and pain and the sight of spilled blood by lifting her skirt and using it to wipe away the first flow of blood, which quickly came again in thick red gouts along the wide line of the wound. The boy watched as Eileen then ran back towards the house, bunching the bloodied part of her skirt in one hand and not looking to the face that she knew to be watching her from the kitchen window, though all the while, or so it seemed to him, performing to the kitchen window. She returned in moments with a black three cornered bottle and a length of old striped shirt, and in that time Joe had gone back to wrestling from another angle with the bolt and the pump, the blood now running down his hand in grimy rivulets and out upon the pump to mingle with the grease and crusted dust.

She knelt before him in the dust and forced him to drop the spanner and took his arm and turned it so that the palm faced upwards, the hand hovering awkwardly palm upwards and quivering with the pain. She moved forward so that he would lay it on her breast, the back of his hand resting upon her breast as she knelt before him. She wiped the wound along the inside of his forearm with the scrap of shirt, now smiling and laughing at something with Joe who winced and laughed between clenched teeth but still protested at the fuss and tried in play to draw his arm away. Soon the arm was clean but with the beads of dark blood beginning again to appear and force their way up through the scraped and broken skin, and the boy watched from his perch upon the stumps Eileen stooping down over Joe's arm, Joe crosslegged now in the dust before Eileen, but even he looking over now and then to the watcher at the kitchen, as she raised herself from her haunches to bend over his outstretched arm. She ran her tongue along the length of the wound, her wet tongue running through the flow of blood which ran about her lips and chin, with Joe's outstretched hand still drawn up for solace deep among the billowing folds of her blouse, her eyes glancing up at those of Joe from under halfsleeping lids, as though sleepy with the pleasure, to smile at him in a way that stirred some other memory that took him now beyond the knowledge of the watcher in the kitchen or the boy who perched upon the stumps. Joe glanced uneasily to the kitchen, and Eileen smiled further as she licked the crimson beads again.

The boy watched as his mother broke noisily from the house as he knew she would, watched like some withered sage from his perch high on the stump pile while the screen door scraped and slammed and she strode towards them with her skirts flapping against her round hard knot of stomach and her thighs striding against all the outrage of what was happening there, and her voice pitched high in indignation from the moment that she left the kitchen.

'Get on back in here, you little whore!'

She strode over to Joe and forced him to his feet, grabbing the cloth from Eileen who had started back and stumbled to her feet, dousing his arm in dark gouts of the thick liquid from the bottle, and twisting it around his arm and tying it with rough protruding rabbit ears, all in a moment and with a force that made Joe gasp in pain.

'We don't pay you two good money to get up to your tricks out here, in full view of everyone. With the boy looking on and all.

'Just you get back to your work. A scratch like that!'

Joe looked at her sheepishly and then, with a smirk flung to Eileen and a flexing of the muscles of the injured arm, began to look about him for his spanner.

Eileen retreated towards the kitchen, discovering again the blood upon her dress and seeking to bunch it together, as though to hide it in her hand but with the hidden blood squeezing through her fingers as she waited for his mother who then strode over to her and grasped her by a handful of her hair and began shaking her roughly and slapping at her with her other hand, tugging fiercely at her hair and striking at her with wide and useless slapping blows.

'In front of the boy and all! Can't you see the boy is watching?

'Ragamuffin! Look at your skirt! Little hussy!'

The girl shook herself free and, clutching at her injured hair, just blushed and grinned and cast her still halfsleepy look back at Joe who, with a helpless smirk over to the boy, had gone back to wrestling with the pump. Eileen moved herself out of reach of the anger and the clawing and slapping hands of his mother, who had finally decided not to be led into some squalid chase around the yard and was making for the kitchen. From a safe distance Eileen peered back insolently through her tousled locks at Joe, who only looked up for one awkward grinning moment, and then to the boy who did not move from his position on the stumps, who did not raise his eyes or move or in any way show that he had seen anything other than Joe working at the pump, who simply watched as the bodies moved and the dust lifted and the sounds of work broke out again. The girl then moved off to find a tap, to rinse Joe's blood from her skirt, the boy's mother calling as though after her, though more in a voice to reassure the boy about the nature of such things.

'Never seen the like of it, I haven't. More like a pack of wild animals. Not seen the like, I haven't.'

He rode north through the late part of the day on tracks hacked years before, through the low and undulating forest, through coarse grasses that clung with exposed roots to the yellow sands and past miles of stunted trees in bluegreen and grey and copper, a forest so low in places that the boy could see across the tops of the trees, which gave sight only of further waves of dense and distant scrubland exactly like the bush through which he passed. He goaded the horse up the slipping sandhills that traversed the track, climbing to the top of each low sandy peak in the hope of finding some break in the repeating seas of wiry leaves and flaking bark, but only meeting another view just like the last, a sight across the indifferent scrub towards the scrub ahead. He rode on slowly, taking his direction only from the rising and falling narrow rift that ran to the north and to the east, hoping on the word of Cabel's stories that the track would bring him out again on open country, beyond Underbool and Linga, and the last of the government sustenance camps, and onto the main track up to the salt mines, where he would surely meet up with Cabel Singh.

When the darkness came, he built a fire in a clearing and sat with the pup by his fire and listened to the sounds of the night, with only the moaning of the wind through the pine needles and the movement of crickets and the clinking of the horse's hobble chains to disturb the deep silence. He thought then of the one time when he had been far into the depths of the scrub with Cabel Singh, the time when Cabel had taken him up to O'Sullivan's Lookout, a sandy mound that rose high above the mallee bushland, far to the west of Cable's usual route. The mound rose like a barren island from the dense seas of low and sprawling scrub, and he and Cabel had taken the wagon as far up the sandy mound as the horses could manage, for Cabel wished to show him all the lands beyond. They struggled with the horses in a slow and heavy winding that brought them towards the peak, but only with the fall of the sun, and at a time when it was too late for the boy to return.

At the top the sands grew level, with the hot northern winds teasing the clinging bushes and skimming sheets of sand across the rim. In a few deft motions Cabel had set up his camp, staking out a hessian windbreak, recovering from the blown sand a small circle of stones and a nest of coals, piling together handfuls of sticks and shreds of mallee and broom and lignum that the winds had trapped against the brush. Within minutes he had lit the fire, at first in clouds of white and then in a darker smoke, with blackening pans soon cracking and spitting oil against the glow, with the dog sitting, its ears uplifted and its eyes catching in flashes the motion of the flames.

Then Cabel unwound the long and dusty cloth from his head, untying and unwinding his hair and shaking it loose and letting it flow about his shoulders, and he, the boy and the dog sat down beside the fire. From a drawer beneath the cart he fetched his bubble pipe, and added to the embers some dry cowpats from the crate in which he carried his chaff. The pats took fire and smoked and smouldered and teased away the insects that rose up with the cooling of the day, and together they watched the sun go down, and saw the red lights flicker and run out in rivulets through the dust that hung in the west.

They sat and watched the brightness fall away, in a silence broken only by the keening of insects drawn in hordes from the wilderness, and the soft ripple of air through water as he drew upon the bubble pipe. Cabel threw the boy a blanket, and slipped deep into the rhythms of the pipe, into the glow of the embers and the ripple of water running through the warmth and silence, through the sounds of the papery leaves and the flaking bark of the surrounding scrub. He drew the cool smoke in, and eased it out to mingle with the smoke from the embers and the raw fragrance of the glowing cowpats, and together they watched it waft out from the peak, into the darkness all around.

The boy smiled at his friend Cabel across the embers and Cabel smiled in return, at the warmth of the silence and even the company of the insects that moved within the light, and they talked far into the night of the lands of the dead and the lands of the living that lay ahead. The boy recalled how he wished that night to talk to Cabel not of strange lands and reckless wanderers and of demons with strange names, but just for this time of Cabel himself, and even of his own life back at the Ridge, of Hannah and Joe Spencer and Eileen. But Cabel told him that when he moved into this country, he left all such things behind. The boy had just seen how they had struggled in the sand, and how dangerous it was, in these vacant lands, to carry too much baggage, and when they moved into the wastelands they should leave all they could behind. Cabel had then winked at the boy and laughed, and the boy laughed too, and he kept Cabel's words close by him, in the thought that one day he might know what those words meant.

As he lay alone in the darkness, which eased with the dying of the fire into the soft half light of night, the boy thought again of the story that Cabel then told him, of being lost for the first time in the heart of these vast seas of low and viewless forest, where there were no sights and no changes in the shrieking birds or stunted trees or the grass that scraped at you like wire as you passed. He told of how he learned to take his bearing from the sun, and to live within the simple motions of breathing and sweating and placing one foot before the other. When you first rode into these trackless and interminable wastes, and the sameness of the next mocked at the sameness of the last, you risked a slow and special form of madness. After hours of moving straight but seemingly in a circle, or moving in a circle while seeking a straight line, you would begin to fling your name and all your familiar achievements in challenge at the cruelty of mute blue above and at the dumb and repeating seas of flaking bark and listless eucalypt—'Cabel Singh, I'm Cabel Singh'—because everything that was there began to tell you that you were not, and that time and place and direction were not, and that all the familiar seams that lay across your thinking were fraying with each sightless ridge you passed. And Cabel told him that until you began to bend your understanding to the forest, until you learned to move amid the forest like the water in the sea or as a wave across the stream, you would answer to its menace with thin curses and in such feeble incantations as would just run out like spilt water into the thickness of the sand.

'**C**ome with me, Hannah,' she would say. 'Come to my bed,' and we would creep along the passage and warm into each other's arms. There Eileen would speak to me, the two of us often whispering far into the nights, whispering and laughing until they called us down the passage to let them get some sleep, and then Eileen would sigh and, with a final hug, I would slip off to my bed.

'Is this like Joe?' Sometimes in the evenings I would ask, 'Is it this way, with Joe Spencer?' Eileen would only laugh, though sometimes she told me secret things about Joe Spencer, about her and the nights and the strong arms of Joe Spencer, and I wonder now if she was with Cabel Singh as she had been with Joe, if one day Eileen would come back to us and take me in her arms again and tell me secret things of Cabel Singh, as she had told of Joe. For Eileen had told me much that was for older ears, just one more reason, as my mother always said, why she should in the very name of charity itself have been sent back to the place she came from, which meant no more than the track itself, this naked girl who had blown in out of billyo and would one day just blow off to billyo again. And when she went, there would be no more talk of her and Joe Spencer in the evenings, or while out collecting stumps. No more talk of it, she said, but only the memory of it and the foul secret of it and the slow blight of all such talking as there had been.

Within Joe's pile of stumps, within the tangle of roots and dark spaces and scuttling spiders and still coiling filaments of dust, I found more shelter for sad thoughts than in the dry spaces of my mother's thinking and the lake that stretched beyond. Grieving for Eileen, the loss of Eileen from my arms in the nights, I found my space for thinking, amid the nodes and splinters and deep in the dark hollows, of those days together when we would watch for Cabel Singh, for the highloaded cart of Cabel Singh to come unannounced as always up the track towards the house, the pots and pans aclatter as the cart pushed over the bumps and furrows by the gate.

We knew for miles off by the three horses when it was Cabel's cart and not Old Sally, the two horses in harness and the third walking beside. We would watch and sometimes help him as he set up his camp beside the shed, placing the cart so that it formed a break to the wind, and setting out the harness on hooks on the side of his cart in the same way every time. Sometimes, in winter or when the wind was high, he would throw up a break of split wheatsacks over a frame of pickets thrust into the dirt to protect the tiny fire from the wind and blowing dust. We helped him set up his camp in minutes, the hessian windbreak and the small fire in the circle of stones that no-one ever touched when Cabel was away. We gathered about him for the chance of some small gift, and Cabel would let us rummage through the painted baubles from his bottom drawer, the *rings and pictures and bangles and coloured stones and boiled sweets and silken scarves.*

Even my mother would come with us at those times. Her voice took on another tone when Cabel Singh arrived, bringing with him tales of happenings on other farms and news that filtered from the south, when Cabel arrived with his cart laden with things we could not afford but which sometimes might be haggled for, with oats or vegetables and chaff. She was keen always to talk to Cabel of the world through which he passed, and we would watch her take a pleasure in wandering down to Cabel's camp in the afternoons and speaking with him there, sometimes taking Auntie Argie down to sit and listen in the shade beneath the pepper trees.

Cabel Singh would never eat with us, despite the invitations, never came inside the house, and had not, as we were told, entered any shelter but the canvas of his cart in many years. He always prepared his own food in the open, the aromas drifting up towards the house, the sweet jellies and fried johnny cakes and the pots of curry that bubbled on his fire. Long before Eileen came to us, my mother would go down through the day with some gift of meat or a cabbage or radishes or with something for Cabel's dog. She would talk with Cabel by the hour, as he cleaned his harness or rearranged his stocks, or simply sat under the shade of the pepper tree and smoked his bubble pipe.

Cabel Singh would smile and talk to her, and sometimes she would send us back to the house and sit and talk to Cabel as she talked to no-one else. We could later smell upon our mother the sweet odour of burning tobacco and smoke of dried horsedung and the tang of Cabel's curries hanging about her clothing as she came back to the house. Sometimes we stayed and watched as well, while Cabel mixed his curries, and we would see the care with which he measured and mixed the spices, the seeds and leaves and pods which he would take from little tins from drawers beneath the cart. He would grind them together with a small mortar and pestle, the fragrant dust encircling us and taunting us with hints of things that took us to the boundaries of all we ever knew. Cabel talked to us of each, and took us off into his dark and unknown places, telling of each coloured powder, each dried leaf and pod and seed and the tree or bush and the place from which it came.

We watched him as he heated the griddle and mixed and beat and shaped his flat and rounded johnny cakes, and fried them slowly in his blackened pan, the oil spitting and popping in the heat, and with Cabel warning always not to let our shadows pass across the food. All was done with a slow and cautious care that we never understood, until it was our own turn to take a johnny cake and dip it in his curries and then wonder at the layers, the strange separating smells and flavours that seemed to come one upon the other, and not all at once as other flavours did.

We would sit and eat with Cabel, and sometimes stay down in the summer evenings by the fire, with Eileen and often even Joe, who sat beyond the ring of light, watching Eileen as she sat crosslegged by the fire. I saw my brother as he listened to Cabel Singh, my brother muffled always in his foolish clothes and hat, but with his eyes gleaming in the fire, his face in his hands and his elbows on his knees, his eyes always alight with the things that Cabel told us, stories that seemed to grow up with us as we grew older, and *always Cabel himself seeming ever younger, more youthful with each time he passed the Ridge.*

One day Eileen brought me down to watch him, creeping with me to the stable and the two of us watching Cabel Singh through the cracks between the slabs. We watched Cabel as he removed his coat and the dusty light silk neckscarf that he always wore. He then took off his shirt, and taking off the coil of cloth he always wore, he let out over a large enamel basin his long black hair and combed it out to its full length, black hair that fell down to his waist. He combed his hair carefully in long even strokes through its dark and oily lengths, singing to himself and combing with a care that we had only seen in young women or with each other, as in the nights Eileen and I would sometimes brush each other's hair. He splashed his arms and back and shoulders with water from the rusty kerosene tin he always used, and we watched together the smoothness of his skin, the soft brown skin without the break of white and sunred of my father and Joe Spencer. We watched together as the water ran quick like oil across his shoulders and down in streams that ran about the spaces of his body, over his shoulders and under his arms, broken by the black hair into smaller streams that ran down to his waist. He washed his limbs with that same slow measured pace with which he cooked his meals, still singing always in a low and chanting voice, flicking his long dark hair about him and then drawing it over his head and soaking it before him in the tin. And we then saw a thing that we had not imagined, that he was marked by savage scars, his chest and upper arms, with jagged tears and punctures that ran here and there across his chest and stomach, and I felt Eileen start and felt her fingers tighten on my shoulder as we watched.

When he had finished and was dressing again, we turned away and crept towards the house, behind the shelter of the stable, no longer laughing and both feeling in shame and silence that we had stumbled on some secret and sacred thing, like Father Mullins robing in quiet prayer for the mass. We crept together but not speaking, away from Cabel Singh and up towards the house. And it was when we came up to the verandah that we met her, and saw she had been watching us as we watched Cabel Singh. She looked at me and at Eileen as we passed, and then down to Cabel Singh, still singing softly and moving about amid the tinkling of harness and the yelping of his dog, the whiteness of his new unbuttoned shirt moving in flashes amid the deep green of the pepper trees.

They broke from the edge of the scrub towards the late part of the day and came out upon the threechain road that ran beside the railway line that led towards the wheatlands to the west. The boy filled his waterbags from a vast iron tank beside the railway line, a tank that was kept filled by passing trains. He stripped his clothes off and he and the pup drank their fill and showered and played about together in the flood of water that he pumped down from a hose on a derrick that dangled from high above. They sat in the fringe of timber just back from the road until they were dry, and fed on the leg of lamb that the boy still carried in a damp hessian roll upon his back.

He crossed the road a little to the east of Underbool, the boy not wishing to take the horse and pup through the town, where someone might have heard something, where word may already have gone out that a boy had gone missing from the Ridge. They moved through the stands of uncleared timber that circled the town, keeping to the north of the wheat and oatstacks and well away from the stores, away from the sight of the early morning trucks and carts that moved about the main street, and the sound of men's voices over by the oatstacks. He kept well hidden from the weather-board and iron stores and houses that nestled in the timber around the railway siding, moving almost within the shadow of the huge oatstacks that lay along the edge of the railway line, but circling the town as he knew that Cabel often did, and moving back onto the road well to the west, yet curious still to know if word had gone out about the girl and Cabel Singh.

He rested with the horse and the pup by the side of the road through the late part of the day, and now and then a laden truck or cart would roll by, carrying stumps up towards the rail at Underbool, or bags of seed or loads of hay towards the west. Occasionally a car would pass, beating up from the distance through a cloud of dust and approaching in a sliding motion across the loose gravel, or a buggy or a cart with a family on board would move slowly by and the children would turn and watch as they passed, with racks of jostling children perhaps on their way from school turning to watch this boy of their own age in men's clothing, standing half hidden by his hat with a yelping pup and an old pony, waiting in the thin shade of the trees that lined the road, looking after them and drinking in their dust. Once a load of stooked hay went past in an open cabin truck with two kids perched upon the load. They pelted a store of brinnies at him and the pup as they rattled past, and the boy touched the stock of his rifle lying before him on the saddle and thought for a moment of how he might make them jump.

A farmer with a load of stumps in a spring cart stopped to talk to the boy for a time, and his dogs circled and snarled and sniffed at the pup, which covered and licked at their chops. The man asked the boy where had he sprung from and whether he had enough water to be out on the roads on his own with the heat of the day coming on. The boy showed him his waterbags and told him that he was from the south, and that his parents had seen to it that he had plenty of water and they had just gone on ahead, and that he was travelling to work for his uncle who had just taken up a big block further down the line.

Then they left the road and moved up to the rails, up to the line with its banks of grey stone rubble that ran into the distance, like waves that rolled up and down the sand drifts, with its long sleek rustcoloured rails polished silver along the top. The boy looked up and down along the tracks which vanished in both directions into watery pools of moving light, and he knelt down and tried to place his ear to the line because he had been told by the kids from over at Speed that this was how they knew whether or not a train was coming, but the rail was too hot with the heat of the day.

He drew the horse up onto the rails and they walked for a mile or so, picking their way over the sleepers and surveying the cleared lands and the fields of burnt or standing stubble and the patches of timber and the belts of low mallee scrub that lay on either side of the rail. Then they left the rails and rode instead along the winding bush tracks that led up towards the north, tracks that he had been told would lead him towards Clay Lake and the salt country and, much further on, Nowingi and Raak Plain, up past the last of the cleared country and the last of the sustenance camps, and on to Cabel's deserts to the north.

They passed through belts of uncleared timber and new blocks cleared by settlers working up from Linga and

Underbool. They passed the first of the scattered humpies and the new weatherboard cottages and the broom and corrugated iron and wheatbag shanties that the new settlers built on the edge of the wilderness. A little further to the north they passed a humpy set well back from the road, a heap of hessian and pine slabs and iron, and the boy saw amid a spread of green which turned out to be cactus, a young woman with a naked child on her hip, the young woman pointing him out to the child as he moved in broken flashes through the fringe of spindle timber that marked the edges of the track. The boy waved to her, but neither she nor the child waved back or acknowledged the pup who raced over to bark at them, but merely watched him from amid the cactus until he and the horse moved down the road and out of sight. He remembered the tales Cabel told them when they were younger, of a young woman like the one he had seen amid the cactus with the naked child, who had lived for years with her crazed husband chained in a hole in the ground at the back of her house, somewhere out amid the flaking trees to the north, feeding him with bones and scraps and living in this way for so long and waiting with such a desperate patience, as it seemed, for the husband who would never return from some place in the south, that after a time no-one ever asked about him, and so no-one ever knew.

She had been waiting for them by the netting gate. They became aware of her as they came nearer to the house, the dark fabric of her dress moving in the evening breeze. She had remained silent as they approached, with Eileen bracing herself for what she knew must follow, and the boy dropping back, casting about in his mind for some excuse or explanation to offer to the woman who waited for them at the gate.

'A fine time,' she said, 'to be coming home.'

They let themselves through the gate, and neither said a word.

'With all the jobs to be done. All the jobs now done by others and the two of you off, gallivanting around the country half the day and night.'

The boy could only mumble that they had to wait, that it had been too hot to walk back from Windmill Tank in the middle of the day, and that they had waited in the shade. She ignored his poor excuses and, as they came up to the house, put all her attention to the girl, while his father and Auntie Argie sat in silence, with no show of anger or even of interest at their late return.

'Your dress,' she went on, and still in a subdued voice. 'Look at your dress.'

Eileen said nothing, but looked down to her dress where the buttons, which she would not touch until just before they moved up towards the netting gate, had been put together all awry, with a gaping stretch of bare skin at her waist. She turned away, rebuttoning, and still without a word.

'And your hair! The mud—and on your legs as well.'

'It was hot,' was all Eileen could say.

'We had to wash, to soak ourselves. Out in all that heat.'

'Wash? Wash? Running around with no clothes on, more likely! Out there, in the middle of nowhere. And with the boy!'

Her voice began to rise as she turned her attention to the boy, to the marks of dried mud still upon his face, and the mud caked in his hair.

'What were you doing? What did she do to you?'

She grabbed him firmly by the ear, the boy yelping loudly with the pain, and his mother struggling to maintain her hold as he writhed away and pushed against her grip with all the strength of his bony wrists.

'Go wash!' she yelled. 'Go wash it off! All of it. I'll talk to you later. Don't let me see you till you wash it all off. All of it. Little brute!'

The boy managed to struggle free, nursing his injured ear, his eyes brimming with tears at the sudden pain of it, and yet he did not leave.

'And you!'

She turned her attention to the girl.

'This is the kind of thing we've come to expect. This is the kind of thing we're now expected to get used to. Wandering the country like naked savages. Without your clothes on. And in front of the boy!'

Her voice rose to a shriek as the blow fell, a heavy slap which took the girl full on the side of her face, followed by another, harder than the first, which sounded clear and sharp in the evening silence. Eileen stumbled with the force of it, but then stood her ground, her eyes filling with angry tears, tears from the shock of the sudden blow, and yet she did not move, holding her head high and her hands straight by her sides, as though inviting yet another blow, as though it would be beneath her to protect herself, as though now eager to provoke. The boy could hear sudden noises down at the shack, and now he saw a light, as Joe and Old Tollie made their way out to listen to the disturbances on the verandah, the boy aware of Joe's eyes upon them, though Joe was scarcely visible behind the lantern's light.

'What happened there?' she shrieked again. 'You and the boy together.'

She turned back to the boy.

'What did you do? What has she been telling you? Has she been talking about all her shenanigans? About what she's been up to?'

She threw a look of violence towards the light down by the shack. The boy was still nursing his damaged ear, but still he would not answer, and neither did he leave. His mother scowled at them, from one to the other, from the shrinking boy with his eyes full of tears to the girl who stood tall and insolent before her, as though demanding yet another blow, as though demanding that his mother lower herself, to strike her one more time.

'You must go,' his mother said finally. 'You must leave. You must pack your bag—not that you ever had as much as a bag—and go. There's no place for you here. Tomorrow, you go. We've had enough, the children and all. Tomorrow, you pack your bag and you go!'

The girl merely smiled at her. It was, the boy could see, a smile without insolence, a simple smile of amusement, despite the red weal on her cheek and her eyes still tearful from the blows.

'I'll go,' she said. 'But it won't be tomorrow. I'll go now. I'll pack my things and leave now.'

'No, you won't! Walking out like that, at night, leaving us all … upside down and inside out. The boy, all of us! You'll not go as easily as that.'

Without paying, in some way.

'You can't, you won't just go off like that.'

The girl just smiled again as the woman looked to the boy

with his brimming eyes and his injured ear, to her husband, who simply looked away, and to Auntie Argie, rocking in silent pleasure by his side. She pushed up against the girl, as though wanting to take her in her hands, in the same way she had taken the boy, hissing in her ear.

'What did you tell him? What have you told them, all of them? What is it that you said?'

He moved beyond the forests of stunted trees in the middle of the day and came upon a wide and gravelled open track that led up from Linga, and as they rode the air took on the smell of smoke and boiling eucalypt, and clouds of hot and darkened air rose up against the sun. With the darkness of the smoke came a glow deep in the scrub to the west and to the north, the clouding of the sun bringing out the gleam of hundreds of small fires. The boy still moved northwards along the track, keeping to the east of the fires, amid the sharp smell of boiling eucalyptus floating in the air. As the air thickened about him in dense white folds of green mallee smoke, he tied his handkerchief about his mouth and nose, and he watched the leaves floating across the track, the sparks drifting in the air and wafting before him as he rode slowly along the track that led towards the heart of the fires, the horse tossing and flicking its tail, its eyes wide and nostrils flaring in the thickening air and the pup restless and yelping in the smoke and alien glow.

A little further on, he slipped off the main track because he knew that it led down to the sustenance camp and he took another narrower track that led off to the north. He rode on through the thinning trees that skirted the camp, and through the screen of smoke that blew about the trees he could make out the tents and humpies, the shelters of corrugated iron and broom and phosphate bags and flattened kero tins that ran along the side of a creek that might in some years have carried water in the winter season. He saw people moving amid the tents, fanning the smoke from their eyes and talking in excited groups and seeking out the shade of the tall creek gums and the open spaces of the creek, but he did not go down to greet them.

Ahead of him, in the half darkness of the blowing smoke, he saw a woman sitting by the side of the road, sitting on a bank of sand, erect and alert, with a basket with things wrapped in newspaper. She was young, perhaps twenty years old, a little older than Eileen, with the mark of smoke and ash about her face and arms, and straggling oily hair that whipped about her face. She nodded at the boy as he drew near, and he slid down from the horse to talk to her.

'Where are you going, boy? There's nowhere that way.'

The boy tethered the horse to a shoot of mallee and sat on the bank next to her. Together they sat and watched the smoke and followed the burning leaves that drifted past, and they looked along the track that led off into the smoke to the north.

'It will be night soon. Where will you stay tonight?'

'Wherever we get to.'

'You could stay at the camp. There's people there will look after you. Give you a feed and all.'

She told him that they had been burning piles of cleared mallee to the north, breaking and burning as they always did, and that the wind had sprung up and the fire had jumped the break and got into the scrub, and that men had come in

a truck up to the sustenance camp and asked for help, and
the people at the sustenance camp had told them just to let
the damn place burn, though some of the younger men had
finally gone off to fight the blaze just for something to pass
the time.

'How old are you?'

'Sixteen.'

'My eye! More like twelve, maybe thirteen. Where's your
people?'

'Packed up. Gone south. I look after myself.'

The boy told her of how his parents had gone broke the
year before, and that everything they had was swallowed up
by the Closer Settlement Board, that his father had torched
the crops last year and had taken his mother and the younger
children off to some nameless place in the south where they
could not be traced, while he had been left behind to fend
for the last of the animals. He told her that he had been living
on his own in the shell of the house for the past few months
and that now he was travelling to the north to meet up with
his friend Cabel Singh, who had perhaps been through not
long ago.

'My eye,' was all the woman said and laughed in a listless
way into the trees and smoking air.

'You should tell the truth, you know.'

'Why?'

'Well, you just ought, that's all. People ought.'

He saw that the woman was young and had a pretty
freckled face, even though it was masked by the smoke and by
a streak of soot, left where she had wiped her brow and the
soot had mingled with the sweat. Her features were fine, and
he noticed that her body was oddly large about the hips

and buttocks: a young girl's face, he thought, with freckles like Eileen, but on an older woman's body that looked as if it had just sat that way, beside the track and in the blowing smoke, for many years. There was a bright light in her greenish eyes which might have been a reflection of the fires that glowed around them.

'Are you hungry?' she asked after they had sat in silence for some time. 'There's some food here. Only a little, and it's cold. But you can have some, if you wish.'

She opened one of her packages of newspaper. In it there was some bread with meat fat spread on it, soon a little blackened with ash. There was also bread and treacle, together with some cold potatoes.

'The men didn't want it. I made it for those who went off to the fire. You can have it if you want.'

The boy took the bread and the potatoes and they sat in silence again while he ate what he could. She watched him as he ate, holding the bread in both hands and gnawing at it hungrily and she smiled at him from time to time. She suddenly reached over and pushed his hat down over his eyes.

'You're a daft little bloke, aren't you! Grubbing round on your own. Saying nothing and heading nowhere, with your crazy mutt of a pup and your poor old nag that needs its toes clipped.'

'Not going nowhere,' he protested. 'I'm looking for someone. I told you, I'm travelling to meet up with Cabel Singh. The hawker.'

'Cabel Singh came through here a few days ago. Just a couple of days ago. Never stopped, like he usually does.'

'Where did he go to?'

'Up north. But there's people down there, at the camp,

who can tell you more. Old Sally's just been through, too.
There's people there at the camp as can tell you a lot more
about your Cabel Singh than I can.'

The boy knew Old Sally, who sometimes came to the Ridge
from the other direction to Cabel Singh, with a tiny cart and
his single draughthorse and his dog. His mother usually
bought some small thing from Old Sally, but kept her larger
purchases for Cabel Singh. But he told the woman that he
would not be going down to the camp, not even for one
night, and that he would just keep on heading up to the
north. The woman told him again that he was daft, and that
only crazy people or people who knew the country like
Cabel Singh ever took the tracks up to the north, and that
once he got beyond the salt mines it would be days without
water before he got to anywhere, if he survived to get anywhere at all, and that a kid his age still needed looking after,
and what about his horse? But the boy just thanked her for
the food, and started to go, saying that he would rather die
out on the northern tracks than end up staying with the
sussos, because his father had always said before he went
mad and torched the place that this was where they would
end up when all hope was gone. He said that he would be
just fine, and that Cabel Singh was a good friend of his parents and was waiting for him, anyway, out in the scrub
and just a little to the north. The woman called after him and
asked him why it was that he wanted to know where Cabel
Singh was, if he knew that Cabel Singh was waiting for him.
The boy didn't answer, but put the last of the food in his
pocket and climbed up on the horse and waved goodbye,
and moved out into the smoke.

*

He sat amidst the bright light of the lake, the man they called the Afghan crosslegged at his side, and he watched and listened as the Afghan and Old Sally drew in cool smoke and sent it wafting in thin clouds across the salt. He sat upon the lake on a wide mat made of split wheatsacks as Old Sally tamped his pipe, and they watched the sky together as the sun came down and the pink hues ran like soft oil across the shining surface of the salt, and caught the silver fringes of Old Sally's hair and beard. He listened to the sound of the water bubbling in the pipes and to the sound of the insects that rose up, even so far out on the salt, and began to keen about him with the dying of the light. The Afghan threw another cowpat on the fire, and they huddled together in the fragrant smoke so that the insects would stay away.

They sat in the growing darkness and listened in silence to the distant tinkling of the Afghan's camels' bells, the clink of the hobble chains and the bleating of a tamed goat tied to a tree beside the Afghan's hessian and broom humpy, where there were signs of movement and the sound of children's voices, the dim light of a hurricane lamp showing gold against the hessian walls as the shadows lengthened out across the salt. From time to time the Afghan's woman would come out across the salt to bring them something, smiling at the boy with signs of genuine contentment at his coming, but never once speaking. She was a large woman, much bigger than the Afghan, with a shapeless cotton shift and a large ungainly body and straggling hair, and she moved backwards and forwards in bare feet across the hard surface of the salt. Some rumours said the Afghan had three wives, but the truth of it, Old Sally whispered to the boy, was that she was just a local woman who had left her brute of a husband

and had gone out to live at the lake with the Afghan and his camels, because the Afghan was kind and never beat her. It was said that she helped the Afghan mine the salt and could do the work of two men, helping him dig the salt in blocks and break it with a sledge and sieve it and pack it on the camels' backs, so that the Afghan could take it down to Linga and the rail.

When the sun went down, the insects fell away, and Old Sally and the Afghan began to talk and to stir the food that the woman had brought out to them in a pot which now sat among the coals. They ate a curry that Old Sally made of lambs' tails, picked up earlier in the day from a yard he had passed down towards Boinka where men had been marking, who knew Old Sally would gladly take the tails. Neither Old Sally nor the man they called the Afghan had even asked the boy what he was doing so far from home, or told him that he was a daft little bloke as the woman at the sustenance camp had done, or demanded a name from him, and no-one asked him about his family, or when it was that he was going home. He was a traveller and that was a good thing for a boy to be, and if he chose to tell them about his family, or why he was out upon the wild country on his own, then that would be time enough. They ate johnny cakes dipped in the curry, and talked of the road, and of other travellers, and the country to the north. They talked of Cabel Singh, who had just passed that way, the Afghan said, a day or two before, but did not stop as he usually did, and only waved to them, and kept on to the north. They spoke to the boy of Cabel Singh, and of his friend Mullah the Shootcutter, who sometimes travelled with Cabel, and it was mostly Old Sally who spoke, while the Afghan sat silently inside the rim of the light, his skin wrinkled like an old sheepskin, his eyes set deep in creases in his face, but burning bright against the moving flames.

Old Sally said that when first he came to these parts, almost thirty years before, he had carried all his things in a metal trunk on his head, and had walked this way for mile upon mile, with a large stick to help him across the drifts and to beat off taunting dogs. He told of how once he nearly died out upon the roads, along a track where the houses were too far apart and he could find no water, and how finally he had to stagger on without his trunk, and how a farmer had kindly brought him back to get it, days afterwards, with the trunk still sitting unopened by the side of the road. No-one had touched it, perhaps because no-one ever passed that way.

He told the boy that he, like Cabel Singh, had been a soldier, but in an older war and in another country, and that it was in China that he had learned to look after horses, and it was from China that he came to the boy's country. He spoke of a family back in his own country, a wife that he had married when they were children and before he even went to China, and how he had seen his family only twice since then, and how when he died it was his wish that his body be burned and the ashes sent home to his family, to spread upon the sacred river. He told of how he had helped to burn the bodies of many friends and fellow travellers who had died upon the roads, and that they had in various places, at Speed and Tempe and down in Quambatook, far to the south, made huge pyres of mallee roots and fragrant spices and butter from the local farms and dry switches of eucalypt. He told the boy that Cabel Singh had asked him once to be sure that when his own time came, his body would be burned out in the centre of the great saltlake to the east, and Old Sally had agreed, because he was old and Cabel Singh was still young, and he knew that it was Cabel Singh who would build his pyre first.

Cabel Singh had been a soldier, Old Sally said, and had spent most of his early life soldiering for others, moving from place to place and being told what to do, and who to fight and kill. Cabel had been taken across the seas when he was not much older than the boy himself, and had been given a gun and told to kill people whom he'd never seen before and whom he usually had less reason to kill than the officers who pulled them into line and sent them out to fight. Although the boy wanted to know whether or not Old Sally had ever killed anyone, he kept his silence and let the old man gaze out across the salt and into the darkness, and talk in his own way about dust and smoke and boredom, and a soldier's life being mostly a life of waiting, and of bad food. He told of how they had sometimes eaten horses, and mules and dogs and even rats, and there was some story of Cabel's, he said, where they had even begun to talk about eating one another. He said finally that he had never been in a real battle, but that perhaps Cabel had, and that maybe he had killed some people, though he had never seen them, and he told the boy whose eyes were shining that killing people was nothing that he or anyone should be proud of. The boy was able to tell him that Cabel Singh had spoken to him, just a week or so before, of his time as a soldier, that he had spoken of it to him and to Eileen on his way up to Windmill Tank, and Old Sally looked at the boy with a new respect because he knew that Cabel never spoke of it to anyone. Old Sally said that mostly Cabel Singh would talk to you of anything except of what he had done himself, that everyone he met upon the roads knew Cabel's stories, but none could ever really say that they knew Cabel Singh.

Then the man they called the Afghan spoke at last and told the boy that he should look for Mullah Singh upon the roads. He should watch for Mullah the Shootcutter, as he was known, because he often followed Cabel Singh and sometimes travelled with him, and knew his routes, and where he could be found. He went on to say that the story of Mullah Singh was a sad story, even in a place where there were many such stories. Mullah and Cabel Singh had come together to this country. They had been in the war and had come as sailors, and had worked on the sugar in the north and then made their way south. While Cabel had soon decided that he liked to move from place to place and had bought a wagon and horses and from that time had never stopped moving, Mullah Singh had stayed and worked hard in the first place they came to, and saved his money and took up a block a little to the south. He had even married a local woman who lived for a time out on the green block with him, and together they worked and cleared the timber and fenced the block and broke the earth and ploughed it and sowed a crop; and then the rabbits came and then the wild mustard and then the dry, and the woman cleared out and Mullah was put out upon the roads by the banks. Upon the roads he had stayed ever since, not riding high from farm to farm as Cabel did, but carrying nothing but an axe and a canvas waterbag and a long string of tales of misery that noone needed to hear because misery was the one thing of which most people in these parts had laid down too good a stock. Mullah still moved about the country in search of bagsewing and shootcutting, but somehow always out of season, and always with wild plans that he would tell to anyone and always to himself as he walked from farm to farm, mumbling sadness and anger and tales of revenge upon the earth that threw him off, and wilder plans to get back on his block. It was known, too, that the other hawkers and travellers and especially Cabel Singh kept a kind eye out for poor Mullah as he stumbled about the roads. Old Sally puffed at his pipe all this while and added that Mullah the Shootcutter had become known to them all as Cabel's shadow, long in the morning and long again at the fall of day, because he was the only person who had been known to travel with Cabel Singh, the one person who knew where Cabel had come from, and the only one who knew where he went.

Old Sally told the boy that if he wanted to find Cabel Singh, then he would have to travel to the north and to the east, into the deserts and far beyond the last of the houses and the tracks that led off to the north, up into regions where there were no outlying farms to visit and nowhere to sell his wares. Cabel Singh took these long routes up to the north because he liked to move through country where no-one ever went, because he loved the loneliness and isolation of the far bush tracks and the smell of the saltpans. He said that Cabel did not use the maps that were written by others, but had maps of his own that were written in his head, or that were marked out in the land in the lines of creeks and the position of soaks and peaks and sand drifts, and that he understood the maps that once were drawn across the country in the minds of those who lived there long before the place was mapped and charted and roads were run through it and fences strung across it by the Closer

Settlement Board. The boy, he said, must understand that Cabel Singh moved always in a vast circle that did not join up with itself but which coiled inward like a spring, coiled to a centre and then moved out again, and that he took no notice of the roads and fencelines that others had set out across the scrub. He ran his own path northward and out into the desert as the Closer Settlement Board cluttered his ways with their roads and rails and fencelines, and that as the fencelines moved, so Cabel said, he too would move again.

The boy listened carefully to all Old Sally said, and drew his blanket close around him against the night. He thought again of his night upon O'Sullivan's Lookout, with Cabel Singh. He thought of how, as the night fell and the sky lit up in waves of red towards the west, Cabel and he had looked out at the last of the light upon the sand drifts, and the dark seas of scrub all around, and Cabel had told him of the Afghan upon his frozen lake, of the wastelands to the north, and the deserted town that marked the furthest reach of the Nowingi line, run out into the wastelands and then rooted up again. He told him of the climbing winds, and of vast dead forests where trees ran up through the salt in twisted forms and clutched with splintered fingers at the skies, of places where snowpans boiled and glistened in the midday sun, where the ice opened out of the desert and crowned the distant hills. And he had promised yet again to take the boy one day over the country of his tales, the dead lands to the north, to a country where roads and railways were simply lost amid the deserts and below the drifting sands, a place of abandoned towns with doors and windows beating eerily in the desert winds, of dusty beds thrown back and abandoned, of clothes laid out but never donned, of food left uneaten on tables and the skeletons of animals dead in their pens, of skeletal legroped cows still waiting to be milked, of horses saddled and bridled and tied up to await their rider, and the fragile bones of patient chickens, nesting upon unbroken eggs.

When morning broke, he took his leave and kept on to the north. He rode onto the tracks where Old Sally and the Afghan had seen Cabel pass, and out into the low flatlands that lay beyond the salt, a vast and deserted stretch of open plains and blasted timber and low creeping drifts. The Afghan told him Cabel called this place the country of the winds, where the horizon stooped and shrank and fell away, and the boy upon his horse was all that broke the flat unfeatured surface of the earth.

He rode on into the middle part of the day, when the sun was high and the hot winds began to blow, and the boy began to scan the low horizon for some sign of shade or shelter. In the distance he could see the willywillies rise, hot coiling winds that grew up against the sky like fountains and licked across the plains, that took up dirt and twigs and the stray scraps of tin and weatherboard left by other roaming winds, papers and sticks and old bits of clothing and the whitened bones of sheep, winding them skyward in climbing coils towards a reddening sky that stooped lower at each moment with its load of coursing dust.

They stopped at last to watch a column rising to the west, a tall coil of spinning air that licked and whipped and turned their way, and the horse began to strain at the reins and to shy and pigroot as the high body of the willywilly kicked savagely from side to side but travelled fast their way. He slipped from the horse and put a rope to the dog and coaxed the horse down, and he and the dog sheltered at its side, waiting for the beating wind to pass. He pulled his handkerchief up over his mouth and nose and crouched close to the ground, his eyes slotted tight against the flying sticks and the biting of the sand, but now listening intently, trying to interpret the strange sounds that blew from the coil of approaching dust, as he clung with frightened fingers to the roots of dead grass and the loose betraying surface of the track.

Then he watched as they broke from the face of the storm, the plunging cattle and a rolling wagon that pitched through the waves of flying sand, the horses with nostrils aflare and the dogs yelping and harassing the fleeing stock which ran before the hurtling wagon, the children holding their hats and clinging to the sides and to the rear of the wagon with its streaming tarpaulin, gritting their teeth against the beating wind and hot flights of sand, which sang like iron splinters in the wind. He saw them run from the face of the storm, the cattle beating forward with noses running wet strings of snot that flicked like whips and ran in muddied streaks along their flanks, their udders heaving and tails flicking, beating with wide and terror-stricken eyes against one another and pounding away from the face of the storm, plunging and toppling through the turning earth.

He saw the driver's eyes, raw and bleeding against the beating sand, the driver straining forward as though to be ahead of the wind, the blood soaking into the leather as he fought with his hands the straining reins, plunging and stabbing with the whip to catch the cattle who ran to beat the storm, but also because the wagon ran, bucketing and flailing through the moving earth, and one wheel wildly spinning to the limit of its hub.

He saw the woman beside him, her scarf twisted about her face, her eyes bound tight against the flowing soil, the child clutched to her breast and bound in a thick blanket to break the force of the sand that would tear the new skin from its face, the child squirming and howling in the tight knot of her arms. They broke from the face of the wind, with two grown girls barely clinging to the sides and more children to the rear and struggling to hold on, their lips thin and gritted and their eyes squeezed tight against the abrading winds that ran the country around them, as the road became a sky and the sky a road, and past them drove in heavy clouds, thick shoals of laughing earth.

'Hoy! Hoy there!'

The shouting broke upon him and the cattle, the cart and the seared family upon it burst from the wheeling circle of earth, the horse struggling up and bolting, and the boy just managing with one great whip of his winded body to flick himself from the track of the wind to avoid the horns and the pelting hooves and the lumber of heavy cartwheels that ploughed the drifts of sand. He pulled aside in time to see the face of the man straining through the sand for the path of the bucketing cattle, to see the terrified cattle drive away harder, in time to see the withered woman beside him with one hand clawing at her straggling hair, to see the children clinging to the rear of the wagon, some in excitation and some in white dread and one looking back in all the flat and mute abandon of one lost in the heart of an unterminating madness as they span on at the core of the winding coil, as the pots and pans and tools and bundles in hessian and chickens in netting crates bounced about them and the dust churned past below.

In moments they were lost again in the spinning fountain of sand, and he watched the wagon slewing and ploughing with a wheel suddenly off its axle and the whole caravan yawing and braking and the children flung off, the wagon sucked out of the willywilly and slewing around in a half circle, the horses twisted and straining in the harness but settling down finally as the winds and flying fragments passed over them and far off towards the east.

'My husband,' the woman told him as they helped him to the shade of a fallen pine and felt his bones and wiped the dust from his grazes, 'was a surveyor.'

The boy propped himself up on an elbow and rubbed an aching leg.

'Before he came, all that you see around you here was empty. Just a wilderness.

'He was a surveyor,' she said. 'He marked out the land and put everything in its place. Small thanks he's had for it, I can tell you.'

He took in air in heaving gasps, enjoying the feel of the damp rag on his face, the warmth of the stooping woman now cradling him in her arms. He saw, further down the track, that the wagon had stopped and keeled over dangerously towards the front and to the lefthand side. He lay still as she wiped his brow and washed some of the dirt from the graze on his face, and the children circled around him and one of them brought back the horse which had bolted, while the girls calmed the pup which had taken off after the cattle and had been tormented by the surveyor's dogs. Her husband was bringing back the stock who were straggled out along the road for a quarter of a mile or so ahead. He looked now to his broken wheel, and the fetlock of one of his tethered horses, and to his crying children, beating the dust from his jacket and his dungarees and cursing, and keeping an eye to the cattle, now stopped and at peace and some even beginning to chew the cud.

They had arrived, she explained to the boy, on a block to the north in the middle of summer when the leaves were grey and the soil was red and the birds shrieked failure at them from the trees. Most of the stock they had brought with them saw that they were serious about staying in that place and just set themselves down in the dry crevice that the maps marked out as a creek and died there, under the green shade of inedible spikes that laughed at them from the bank.

They had arrived on the block and set up a canvas shelter over a fallen tree and that was their house for the first month or so, while they began to clear, until the winds came and took away their canvas and lifted the soil and covered all that they had cleared with a fine down of new thistle seeds. And this was not so bad because the wind that came was a cool wind and they worked in the cool of the day and were ready when the rains came. The rains came in torrents and ran deep red furrows through the loosened earth and carried away their canvas yet again, though this was not so bad because the floods carried away the carcasses of the stock that had died and so they were able to start again. They rolled and they cleared and they secured the title through a solicitor fellow who was an old friend of her husband's, a man, they were told, who was wise in the ways of this part of the world, who had come through here some years ago with wild dreams about how the creek was due to fill and how the country would green and thrive. The Debt Adjuster then passed through and peered into the washaways and counted the carcasses of the cattle and threw in a few more carcasses that were never there because the Debt Adjuster was not a bad sort of a bloke and would always round out the figures a little up or down to keep a battler on his feet. Then the summer came and the rain did not, and soon the cleared land began to rise up and sing around their ears and take its leave and course across the plains, and they took their things and loaded the wagon and followed the earth and from that day, as the boy could see, her husband had not lost a single head of stock.

Her husband soon fixed the wheel because a broken wheel wasn't so very bad either. The woman asked the boy to come with them, for he was only a child and had no place out on the plains on his own, but the boy only pointed them back in the direction of the sustenance camp north of Boinka Town, where he was told that life was good because at least they fed you, and you could sit about in the shade and make plans for whatever future you chose to imagine for yourself. They looked to the boy for a time and saw that he had whatever food and water they were able to give, and then climbed back on the wagon again, because they felt upon them the beginnings of a breeze, with the air becoming troubled and the dust starting to rise and a large coil mounting again in the west and kicking up the dust and the dead grass, which the man said was the very earth to which they held deed and title and had followed from the north. The cattle were again becoming restless and even the boy's own horse was beginning to fidget and twitch, and he raised the arm that did not hurt to say goodbye to the surveyor and his family from beneath the stub of the tree where they left him with food and water.

They began to move towards the cattle, with the cattle beginning to mill forward ahead of them, restless and now bulling at each other as they circled and stumbled back onto the track, their eyes beginning to rove in terror again and the snot starting to run again in wet strands as the whip cracked around them and the wind began to run between them and the sand began to rise and bite, the man shouting and the woman moving again to drape her shawl about the baby's face, the wagon moving again along the track at first slowly and the clinging children beginning to cry out against the rising of the dust and the chanting of the blown sand, and then all moving forward more quickly towards the heart of the lifting wind.

The boy saw as they drew away that they carried with them all that they owned and the whole stock of the farm, their bedding and eiderdowns and rugs and dusty sheets and pillows and covers and handcrocheted quilts and embroidered pieces and doilies and traycloths and tablecloths and duchess sets and the antimacassars and beaded milkcovers that like his mother she no doubt brought with her when first she came from the south. He saw patched army blankets and bolts of hessian, galatea and calico and scissors and a bouncing sewing machine, with thimbles, darning mushrooms and needles and mattresses and waggas and spread phosphate sacks and feather pillows, all drinking in the dust. They carried what remained of their unbroken plates and crockery and the tea sets upon which she had perhaps dealt out sandwiches made of the few fragile cucumbers and dry and cheesy tomatoes with green cores that might have managed to survive the sandy soil together with the bitter acid things, the parsnips and turnips and radishes that alone seemed to flourish in that place. He saw their flypapers and phenyl and Rinso and Bonami and metho and turps and kerosene and paraffin oil, their mangle and flatirons and Aladdin and Colman and hurricane lamps, their spices and soaps and biscuits and tins of flour which cluttered the wagon and beat about in the back, so that they could eat as they ran. They rode with their iron pots and cast pans, their churn and their separator with its shining shells and a tall Coolgardie stuffed with clattering condiments, and a toppling barrel of salted pig that was not tied down, the brine washing with the sway of the wagon and soaking the sacks of flour and salt and sago with which they had wedged it in.

They turned back into the wind, carrying the family photographs, the wedding pictures in their carved or cutglass frames, the mementos, the samplers and the Immaculate Conception with hands in supplication, and devotional pictures and studio prints, the crystal vases, mirrors with frosted designs, the candlesticks and glass ashtrays. They carried with them their books, their Bibles and their dogeared catechisms, their Imitations of Christ and their Billabong books and their Pilgrim's Progress and their Longfellow and Morris Walsh and all the works of Whittier and Tennyson and their embossed Palgrave and Whitcombe and Tombs and Arthur Mee and the Victorian League books, and Kiplings and Tuppers and Brosters with the mark of the Mechanics Institute still upon them.

They carried with them the axes with which they cleared the land and shaped the fences and the sheds and the stables, the shovels and spades and forks and hoes that had broken the soil and pulled back the weeds and all the tools that they had used to break the soil and cast it to the winds. They carried the files and hacksaws and vices and bellows, the anvils and mallets and spanners and pipe benders and straighteners, the strainers and pliers and cutters and unused coils of rusted eight gauge wire, and all that they used to constrain the land and mark those boundaries over which the dust now tumbled and the soil now flowed with the good earth leaping from field to field and leaving nothing but uprooted thistles interwoven with the wires.

And they rode into the wind, bearing with them all their deeds and titles, the papers of purchase thereby witnessing that the soil that carried them along, that mounted over roads and fences behind them and against them and their lives and dreams, was indeed theirs while content to lie upon the flat face of the earth, letting all men by these presents know what had been theirs before the roots let loose their hold and the soil began to rise and cruise off upon the winds. With them they carried bankbooks, letters and the wills by which they might give, devise and bequeath the dead land to the living, certificates of marriages and births and forebears' deaths and bills for buying and for selling oats and bran and horses, and all their deeds of charter, of loans given out and loans recalled and tallies from the Debt Adjuster and survey papers and IOUs and documents of deep regret from the Closer Settlement Board, the papers rising and scattering in the air and amid the flights of untrammelled earth which pursued them across the plains. The boy lay back and watched the last of the wagon as it slipped into the wind in pursuit of the cattle who ran on ahead, the surveyor chasing his soil and the soil in close pursuit. He lay by the stump of a tree and watched as the singing of the sand began to fall away, and he rested his aching limbs as the light began to filter back again, through the hot and yellow air.

He stood upon the open country as the sun rose to its height, riding across the vacant plains and through the surveyor's lingering dust, riding on into an unbroken heat that baked the earth and flattened the last of the grey yellow grass, and drew harsh silver from the distant folds of sand. They edged across the fading tracks of wandering wagons and thirsting sheep that looped and threaded the mapless lands that lay off to the north. The boy pushed his hat down further over his face and goaded the horse into the empty spaces that lay ahead, following long unused and wandering tracks that led them past dry tanks and the bones of cattle and abandoned fallen humpies made of canvas and of kero tins. They passed the last of the lines of downed fences and anteaten posts and strings of cut and rusted wire, and toppled cattleyards and loading ramps and old bedsteads and fallen rainwater tanks and the skeletons of old machinery, gathering drifts of sand.

They roamed across the tracery of tracks until they came upon the mark of a recent wagon moving north, and they followed it as it wound between the low drifts and now and then a stranded clump of low and windblown timber, past dry tanks with embedded carcasses and fields of tablet mud that caked and cracked in the midday sun. By the late part of the day they passed beyond the last of the abandoned farming country and out onto a further grid of aimless tracks that led into further open flatlands of blown grass and splintered pine.

Through the last heat of the day he rested, watching the heat rise in wavering air from the baked sands that ran out from them in all directions, ran out from the base of the shattered pine from which they took their shade. They had reached the foot of a low range of drifts that stood up in soft arcs from the plains, and when it was cool they clambered up the falling sands and rode along the shifting ridges that ran along the peaks, moving from plateau to valley and on to the next low peak, exploring the new secret worlds that lay high up in the belly of the drifts, the vast plains of pure and moving sand that lay secluded in hidden plateaus, with tufts of green cattle bush scattered in the crevices and troughs, and tobacco plants with their soft green and fleshy leaves stranded high up amid the sands.

They saw new worlds of craters and deep basins and hidden forests of stunted native pine that had managed to take some kind of fragile root amid the blown sands, only to slope and bow and crack before the beating winds. They saw the skeletons of ancient trees that may have flourished before the moving drifts arrived, their tips exposed above the shifting soil. He made a camp within the shade of a stooping pine, and before him, spread out across a sandy crater, he saw the bones of animals, of sheep or kangaroos or cattle that had died some long and unknown time before, uncovered by the passing breezes and soon to be buried again with the passing of the winds. He saw strange shapes like the roots and bones of trees, baked into a crumbling chalky stone that was still stronger than the sands about it, the bones of ancient forests thrusting into the air, exposed in fragile spikes and towers, and crumbling at last and falling in broken shards upon the sand.

They rested as the darkness fell, and the boy thought again of water, and of how they were now too far north to go back again, and how they must keep on through the empty country. He thought again of a place they had passed early that morning, a driedout tank with low whitish mounds of earth about it. As they mounted the banks they saw a deep crust of dried mud still at the centre, the crust encircled by the rotting carcasses of sheep and wild goats that had come there seeking the last of the water, drawn by the smell of water and trapped there by the mud. He saw again their carcasses scattered around the rim, their skins tanned by the heat of the sun, now wrinkled bags of bones, and their eyeless sockets still showing the confusion and the longing that had led them to their death, bleating out into the silence of the sand, struggling against the beating of dark wings and the plucking of their eyes, waiting blinded in the night for the heat and the thirst and the crows of the next day. And he thought for a moment of the three of them, he, the pup and his horse, lying like the goats and he with shredded clothing and perhaps still the hat that Joe had given him, the three of them lying like tanned bags of wrinkled leather high up in the drifts, watching with empty sockets out across the craters and the high mounds of unsteady sand.

Cabel Singh left them both together by the side of Windmill Tank, where they leapt down from the cart and said goodbye. They retreated to the thin shade of a clump of stranded pines as Cabel took his water and then set off in his wagon to the north, towards the distant rim of Wirrengren Plain and out into the empty lands beyond.

She had come running when he and Cabel were leaving, as they rode out amid the dust and with the sharp voice of his mother fading far behind. She ran through their dust, her skirts bunched up in her hand and the other stretched out to him and pleading, as Cabel's wagon gathered speed, and it looked for one stumbling moment that she might be left behind. She ran barefoot beside them and in some danger from the wheels, squealing for help and a good legup, as they rolled through the netting gate, and out towards the drifts. He seized her hand and he and Cabel helped her up in an awkward tumble of bodies and grasping arms and wheeling legs, and then she threw her arm tight about the boy's shoulders to steady herself on the narrow rocking seat, pressed herself close to him, and together they kept on towards the open country towards the north and west.

Together they moved slowly northward by the route that led towards Windmill Tank, the route which led up through the sand drifts that marked the far edge of the Ridge, and on through low belts of dense mallee scrub, along a track that was at times a narrow rift cut many years before, invaded now by sandpaper tufts of saltbush, by spikes of lignum and spindles of dwarf eucalypt. They moved beyond into the open country with its low cover of dry yellow grass that moved in soft waves and all around them in the breeze. They sat alongside Cabel Singh and they passed their time in teasing and calling to the dog which played in and out between the wheels, urged on in laughter by Cabel Singh, as they rolled slowly northward across the open country that lay between them and Windmill Tank. Cabel let the horses run upon a long loose rein because they knew simply to follow the narrow track that wound out through the soft grey sand, that marked the trail for them through the waving grass.

As they rode he felt her press upon him, felt each motion of her body as she clung to him, breathless as she clambered into the cart and breathless and panting still in the vast expanse of freedom that opened as they moved out upon the plain, as excited as the boy at the open land before them and at the passing beneath their feet of the dry waving grasses of the plain, excited at the twisted shapes of stranded broken pines they passed here and there in sorry and bedraggled clumps. Eileen pressed always against him, the sweat of her body seeping through his clothing and upon his skin, the smell of her perspiration and her excitement mingled with the horses and the dust, the time moving slowly with the creaking of the wheels, but still and as always too quickly for the boy in this familiar exultation of movement from the Ridge, with its windmill and tall palms soon disappearing far behind them, soon masked by high sand drifts that they crossed as they followed the track towards the lands of Cabel's fables to the north.

At Windmill Tank Cabel stopped, but only for a moment, and he topped up his tank of water for the horses and encouraged his horses and his dog to take a drink, for it was beyond Windmill Tank that the tracks would begin to thin and run out beyond the plain and into the deeper sand drifts and the forests of mallee scrub. And after a time Cabel waved goodbye and left, the familiar sight of Cabel's wagon rolling on beyond Windmill Tank and out into the sand drifts and the ridges which led out into the sea of greygreen mallee scrub that lay beyond.

Together they passed the heat of the day in the patch of timber that lay about Windmill Tank. They waited, as the boy had always waited, until the cool of the early evening before returning home. They lay in the dust and soft bed of needles beneath the pines in the patch of timber, amid the fallen trunks and tangle of branches and the loose dirt and sheep and cattle dung that lay about the open concrete tank with its steady dripping pipe and long and filthy cattle trough and greenish crusted waters. They lay beneath the trees and talked, and they drank from the salty overflow and then they showered in it, letting the water fall upon their clothes and letting the drying of it cool them in the shade.

Eileen was quickly restless and began to climb the trees, and the iron ladder that led up to the rim of the tank, to peer out across the plain to see if she could still see Cabel or the tall palms of the Ridge. She decided to take a swim, to pass the time of the high heat of the day, and despite the boy's protests, she began to pull at her clothes, unbuttoning her dress and hauling it over her head, with the boy watching from the shade, pulling his hat lower so that he would not be seen to see, but watching all the same as she stripped off her underwear and stood in seconds naked and gleaming in the midday sun, her clothing spread in a puddle about her feet, stretching herself in the sunlight and running her fingers through her hair.

She called to him to join her, calling to him not to be so scared, that way out here it really didn't matter, that there was no-one for miles who could see them, and that just about everything they were wearing, both of them, was other people's old rubbish anyway. She stood at the foot of the iron ladder that ran up the side of the tank, coaxing and teasing and taunting him to come up and swim with her in the tank, standing naked and her clothing and sandals lying piled up in the dust.

She asked him if he was perhaps afraid to be seen naked with a girl, and he said that it was nothing to him, but that he just did not want to, and that the water in the tank would be filthy anyway. She laughed at his excuses and began to climb the ladder, squealing and leaping at the sharp heat of the iron rungs, and begging still for him to swim with her.

'Come, come! You can't just stand back all your life.'

'I don't need to swim.'

'Come on! You can't just always watch, watch others. You can't just be a watcher all your life.

'All I ever see you do,' she teased, 'is watch!'

But he sat deep in the shade, protected by his heavy hat, and still he watched her body as she moved up on the ladder, and still he watched her as she arrived at the top, as she stretched herself in the joy of standing high above the plain, stretched out from the ladder and raised her face to the sun, letting her long hair fall free in the air as she leaned back from the ladder. She gripped the top of the tank with one hand and waved the other above her in a graceful greeting to the light which fell upon her white skin and her small breasts drawn tight to her body as she arched up to the sun, her bare legs dimpled and marked in red by the twigs and burrs she had been sitting upon.

She placed her free arm behind her head and turned into the sunlight as she reached the top of the tank, letting her body drink in the heat and light, letting her whole body smart with the bright heat of the sun, combing out her thick hair with her fingers so that it fell more freely and still calling to the boy, teasing the boy and calling to him to strip his clothes off too, and join her in the tank.

'You know,' she cried, still turning and stretching herself to the white fire of the sun, 'if I had my way, we'd all live like this. Just about all the time. Except when it's cold.'

And when the boy just stayed in the shade and watched her and said nothing, just shrank into his heavy clothes and deeper amid the dung and dust below the shadow of the fallen pine, she swung back to the tank and moved cautiously to get in. He watched the falling pattern of her auburn hair as it swept across her back and the soft curve of her body as she stepped over the rim of the tank, the bright aura of her body as it crossed between him and the sun. He watched her plunging for a moment with delighted shouts and splashing, and then hauling herself up and back onto the rim, clinging to the top of the ladder, the rough rim of the tank biting against the soft flesh of her buttocks, her feet splashing noisily in the water and her hair falling about her shoulders in sodden tails, all the while calling to him to join her in the tank.

'Your dog goes for me, I shoot it.'

He stepped out from one of the flapping iron shacks, holding a gun, an old muzzle loader shotgun, to the boy's head. The boy rubbed his eyes. The white light behind him was too bright for him to see anything clearly for a time. The man stood back a bit, and then stepped around, so that the sun was not behind him, and the boy could at last see him, dressed in tattered clothes that were held together here and there by bits of rope and fencing wire. His hair and beard were long and filthy, and matted in strange flat shapes at angles to his head, as though set hard when he was asleep.

He had ridden north for days or so it seemed, and their travels had taken them out beyond the last of the Closer Settlement Tanks and out beyond the soaks into the gypsum country, across wide flat beds of open and untimbered hard white mud and scattered saltbush, and on across the gypsum plains that drew the heat and shone like hot ice in the sun. From the top of a low mound of piled gypsum he had seen the iron town gleaming like silver in the distance, only seeing as they came closer that the town was abandoned and no more than a short and battered row of broken wooden frames and flapping corrugated iron, set at the foot of a high mound of gleaming gypsum and surrounded by rusting hoppers and broken and abandoned machines.

The boy's voice rasped like shattered glass. He cleared his throat as best he could.

'We're looking,' he said, 'for Cabel Singh. That's all we're looking for. We don't want nothing else. He told us about this place.'

The man then turned the gun away from them and told the boy that Cabel Singh had come through that way some days before, but had not stopped as he usually did. He told them that the best way of finding Cabel Singh was to do just what he did, and stay still in one place. That Cabel Singh always came back again. That if you set off after him, like the boy was doing, you might follow him for years, just a few miles behind him. He said that the boy maybe ought to be careful in following anyone who moved as much as Cabel Singh, and

that maybe he ought to know a bit about where he was running from.

'You got any water?'

'There's two tanks left, without holes in 'em. I can give you
enough to get you on your way again. You can't stay here,
though. Nobody stays here.'

The boy looked around him at the sagging corrugated iron,
the street that was no street, the rusted tanks and car bodies,
the piles of drifting sand.

'Can't see as how I'd want to.'

The old man didn't seem to hear it.

'Where you from, son?'

'Down south.'

'That aren't much of an answer.'

'What kind of answer do you want? Anyway, I aren't goin'
back.'

'Don't hear nobody round here says you should,' the old
man replied.

'How old are you, kid?'

'Seventeen.'

'My arse, you are. You're never seventeen. My bloody arse!'

The old man shook his head ruefully, as though this
traipsing of lying kids through the desert was some sign of
the times. He asked if the boy had eaten lately and the boy
said he hadn't, and that they had all come up from the south
and over the salt, and that the horse needed feed and the
pup as well.

The old man told him that they should come with him and
maybe he would find something for them. The boy picked up
his few things, and together they fetched the animals and
walked out of the iron town and along a winding track that

led towards what once were loading bins, where the rusting shapes of cranes and hoppers made from old rails and the buckled walls of corrugated iron stood out against the empty blue, where iron cogs and buckled chutes and a scatter of sheds and engine rooms gave off the dull reek of dustcrusted grease and ancestor sweat and aging engine oil.

He led the boy into one of the sheds up near the snow mountain, the site of the engine marked by broken bolts thrust up from concrete islands, the corrugated roof shot through with dusty shafts of light. The shed, which was open to the south, was furnished from the wreckage of the town. To the northern side there was an iron bed with filthy covers and old newspapers upon it, and near the centre, on the edge of a vast hole, there stood a table and a couple of wooden chairs. There were odd drums scattered around the shed bearing tools and bottles and bits of clothing, and in one corner lay a vast pile of old clothing and illustrated maga- zines. In the opposite corner the man had placed his shotgun, and next to it leaned an old single shot, with a few packets of bullets and cartridges scattered on a nearby drum. One or two magazine covers with pictures of women on them had been nailed to the joists. Here and there, articles of clothing, coats and striped shirts hung on nails or sat in little piles.

The old man was a collector. Along one wall, lined up neatly amid the grease and the sand and salt that had drifted into the shed, the glow picked up a set of skulls, mostly of animals, but with human skulls among them; skulls of sheep, of dogs, foxes, kangaroos, and carrion pickers and birds of prey, eagles, crows and hawks.

'Ever seen one of them things before, son?'

He pushed a human skull into the hands of the boy, who was forced to take it.

'Last visitor I had, yer see.'

The boy said nothing, and it didn't matter as the old man chuckled enough for two.

'Don't you worry about it, young fella,' he laughed, hawking and hooting and slapping his knee. 'Don't you worry about it. There's a pile of 'em out here, to the north. Old abbo burial ground. Can get yer legs, arms, teeth, anything you want. Anything you want, I can get yer.'

The boy put the skull on the concrete floor.

'You got anything for the horse?'

'I can git yer a bit of chaff,' the old man said. 'Point is, what you got for me?'

'Don't reckon I got anythin' much at all. Nothing I don't need myself, that is.'

'I see you got a nice rifle there.'

'Can't give you the rifle. I need it to eat.'

'Well, I tell you what, son. When you catch up with this yer Cabel Singh, you just give him somethin' to give me when he passes by this way again. An' tell him not to go through again without stoppin' over.'

And the boy agreed that this was what he would do. The old man then offered the boy some crusted bread that had been baked in ashes, together with a few boiled potatoes, and he gave him water in a metal mug from a kerosene tin that was lowered on a rope swung from a beam into the concrete sarcophagus that opened down into the darkness at the centre of the shed in the form of what might have been the sump to some vast engine, or the pit where a flywheel had once spun. Then they gave water to the horse and the dog.

'You see, you can keep just about everthink in this hole,' he grunted proudly, and lowered the tin of water back down into the darkness again. The boy peered into the pit. He clung to the buckled rail that still lined one end of the huge sump, with its ropes dangling down into the dark, and leant over to search deeper into the oily blackness, hanging out over the dusty odours of very old grease and crusted dirt, and just a whiff of urine. Somewhere beyond the fall of the light was the oily bottom of the pit and whatever garbage the old man had toppled down there over the years. Just a few feet down, the light vanished into floating dust shot through with spears of light running down from above, from the holes in the corrugated iron.

'In fact,' the old man went on, 'it's not much deeper than what you can see. It just looks that way.

'Kind of makes you think, though, don't it!'

The old man cackled long at the idea of these thoughts that went nowhere, and sat himself down in a broken armchair, with the hot white light of the outside set behind him. The boy sipped the water and enjoyed the coolness and even the oily aftertaste, and he peered out into the glare, over the darkened face and the lights that touched and whitened the edges of the old man's hair and beard, and they waited and sipped in silence through the long heat of the day.

In the late part of the day the old man began to talk, saying that he supposed the boy was interested to know what he was doing there, and what had happened to the railroad that had come out to that place, and why it was rooted up almost on the day that it was finished.

The boy said nothing because he knew the old man would tell him anyway, but looked down into his empty pannikin, and from time to time out into the fading light.

'I came before there was anyone here,' he told the boy. 'I came long before the place got started. Before the gypsum, and before the rail. And then I came back again after everyone left, after the last of the wagons had set off down the line and they had pulled up the turntable and the last of the rails.'

'Does anyone ever come here any more?'

'Just about no-one. Now and then one of them hawkers comes through, and he gives me some of the things I need: powder for the gun, and flour, and things like that. I give him fox scalps and rabbit skins, and he cashes those in when he passes a town. Or so he tells me anyway.'

'Ever worry that you might just die out here, on your own?'

'Better'n dyin' surrounded by lots of nosey people as yer don't know.'

The old man went on to tell of his life in the abandoned town, and of the times before anyone else had lived there. He told of how he had lived in that place for many years, long before there had been any talk of a railway. He had lived out in the wilderness on his own, with water begged from stray travellers and from the soaks that lay hidden here and there amid the drifts. One day a cart had come out of the nowhere to the west, right up to his shack which was not too much more than a big rabbit burrow at the time, and in that same place that was now covered with the vast pile of white gypsum. Two city men in waistcoats and watches and white hands and a smell like soap had told him that he had no business to be there. Their company had a lease to mine in the area, but they wouldn't mind too much if he wanted to stay on there and work on the mine, and that if he liked, they would be prepared to put in a word for him to their boss when they went back to the south.

He told the boy of how he had put the dog onto them and onto their carthorses, and of how they went back along that track in a bigger cloud of dust than they made when they came in.

A few weeks later another group of men had come in motor trucks. These ones smelt of sweat and beer, and they shot the dog and pulled his shack over with the trucks, and began to rip up the country and pile it up in heaps to make it easier for the wind to blow it all away. He had carted away the wreckage of his shack on his back in the dead of night, had built it up again out in the scrub, and lived on rabbits and wild honey. Sometimes he came back to the miners' camp in the nights to steal water and flour, and soon he came to be known as 'the Bandicoot', and he told of how they had hunted him for something to do on Sundays, for a time. After a while one of them, a solicitor bloke who had a streak of kindness and about whom he would speak more in a moment, would put out water and food and sometimes even bullets for him. In time he had come to know the miners, and even led a couple of them to his camp and showed them his bones.

He told the boy of how, not long after this, another kind of truck had driven up to his camp with other fellows from the city who told him they were from the Development and Migration Commission and that his shack would now be shifted to allow a railway line to go through, that there was going to be a railway through the area because thousands of settlers were going to come and turn the wastelands into wheatfields. He had laughed at the city blokes and asked them just to look at the country if their eyes could take the glare of it and then tell him how anyone ever thought they were going to farm it unless they also were out of the city or just out from Blighty with the green mould still upon them and had never seen an axe or a shovel before. He told them that he knew better than anyone the country to the west, and that if it looked dry and useless here, it only got worse as you travelled to the west, and that this line was going nowhere.

The city men told him then and there that it was none of their damn business who came or who didn't and that they only worked for the government and their business was just to build railroads wherever the government told them to. They said they would build railroads anywhere and to wherever the government was willing to pay for it, and that the shack would have to go, but that he could stay and help them build the railroad if he wanted to. They could put in a word for him if he liked.

The old man no longer had a dog to put onto them, but he did manage to point out to them a short cut back to the Ouyen road, which he told the boy must have taken them out and way beyond the range of their petrol and left them with a goodish stroll and a colossal thirst, and maybe they'd even left their bones out there somewhere amid the drifts for him to add one day to his collection which, he confessed to the boy, still strange to say had no white man's bones within it.

When the railway finally came near, they began to build a town where he had his shack, with a line of corrugated iron buildings which they brought in large pieces across the sand on the back of trucks and put together in a day. The town was laid out in neat squares, even though the few buildings they brought with them were no more than shacks of weatherboard and iron, and it even had a spot laid out for a park and a war memorial and school. Then they brought in beer, and soon the gangers off the line would be trucked out to the new town at night, and they would drink beer and play cards and pick fights with the men who worked the gypsum. When the line finally arrived, some months later, a turntable was built just outside the town, so that anyone who came out along that line could turn around and get back again, once they realised where the line was leading.

That was exactly what happened when the line was first opened, some years back, when a whole vanload of important people from down south came up along the line, with a politician with a watch and a high collar, to open the line. They came with beer and chicken and speeches and even women in big hats to protect them from the sun. When the politician—the Minister of Lands it was, a fat fellow with a watch chain, name of MacPherson, and another little fellow in a suit to hold his papers and things—saw where the line had led to, though, they sent another truckload of people up from the south to take a closer look. The new truckload sent back word that the line was going to somewhere where no-one in his right mind would ever want to go and where no-one in his wrong mind should ever be allowed to go. Immediately and after vast expense, the line was closed and the rails ripped up and the gangers and the miners told to pack their kit and leave; and the only trains that ever used the Nowingi line were the one that carried the Minister out to open and to close the line in the same day, and the ones that carted the workers and all their things and then the turntable and finally the rails themselves back across the desert and shipped them off to some other place, where there was little doubt the same thing happened again.

He told of some who had in anger tried to take the whole town with them when they went, pulling the shacks over with the help of trucks and tractors and ropes and pushing the war memorial off its stand. There were also some who had come to like the sandflies and the heat and the daily march out across the sand drifts, who had got used to the beer and the cards and the fights and the steady westward creep of the new railway line, who decided that the shanties that had sprung up amid the gypsum were all they knew as home, who could still see nothing further out but green fields and bulging oatstacks and fat cattle, and who claimed that the dream was real and that all the soil needed was just a little rain.

He told of one man who got the horrors on the night when they turned the last engine around that was ever to be turned around on those shining new rails, on that last night when they had to finish the beer, who had raged and wept and fought and beaten upon an iron drum far into the night so that no-one could sleep—a man with education, the old man recalled, the same who had once been a solicitor, the same who had given him bullets and water, who had come from the city himself and who had told his stories in sobs and hard blows night after night amid the shacks and who boasted he had not only charted out the rail but had sunk more spikes than any other man. In the dying heat of that last night he had risen at last from his howling and the beating of the drum and had stripped himself naked and soaked his clothing and bedding in oil, and wrapped this around sticks, and set it alight.

He had rubbed himself in axlegrease or perhaps even taken a swim in one of the flywheel sumps like this one, for there were many at that time, and rolled himself up and down the hills of gypsum, and then raged from shack to shack like some reluctant and unburied corpse throughout the night, beating upon the iron walls and shouting oaths and trying to set the whole town alight, and there being no water to spare to save it. If the town had not been mostly made of iron, the whole thing might have blown away in smoke upon that very night, with nothing to remember it by but a few blown boilers and concrete footings and the skeletons of machines. He told of how the men, most of whom were drunk on the last of the beer, came out of the burning shacks and stood in what was to be the park at the foot of the broken war memorial, and watched the flames waving and burning far up there on the mountain of snow. No-one laughed, or even said that it was only the drunken solicitor with the horrors, because all seemed to feel somewhere deep down that what he did was maybe the one thing left to do.

The old man had taken up a pickhandle and stalked the naked solicitor, the same who had left out bullets and water for him in the early days, under cover of the shadows and the night. He had followed him up the slopes of the vast white mound of shifting gypsum that was piled up to the north of the town, where the solicitor leapt into the air and waved his torches in wild signals to the moon and to the distant rim of white sand drifts. He spoke in strange tongues and called down a string of curses upon the railroad, the company, the iron town that was now in flames, the city men and the new turntable that would take them all back the way they had come. He was worried that the solicitor would take off into the desert and be lost out there somewhere, and so he tried to talk to him, but the solicitor had made some pact with the moon and the glowing gypsum, and could not be talked to like a normal man.

He had crept up behind him, slipping and plunging in the gypsum, and had wanted to talk to him, to tell him that he knew about the pain, and to tell him that he would still be there when they had all gone, that he would look after the town and go on living there. But the solicitor had kept on raving and waving with his torches, and the old man had finally felled him with a blow to the back of the neck that might have killed him but only kept him quiet and at peace until they could get him tied and the sun came up and the fires died. The gangers then took their cards and their kit and anything that they could rescue from the smoking shacks, their engines and their elevators and their graders and anything that could be used or carried and filed onto tumbrel-carts drawn by the last of the engines that drew them to the east and over the sand drifts and back down the gleaming rails and towards some further execution of spectacular and useless effort, leaving everything about them to the ants and the lizards.

The old man had himself led the horse that turned the turntable for the last time, and then unharnessed it and pushed it up into the last of the wagons, where amid the dung and blowing chaff, still coated in blood and grease and matted gypsum, sprawled the sobbing body of the naked solicitor. He lay together with the last of his clothing and his books and his seals and his certificates all piled together into his drum, still struggling with the horrors and the pickhandle demons of the night before, still cursing the iron and the gypsum and the drifting sand and the company that had sent him out to cross it, and now choking in the smoke and grit that blew back from the fleeing locomotive up ahead which was running them all back across the saltpans and through the drifts, and fighting in his mind each clack and rattle of the bogies underneath him which erased, with each sleeper passed, the Nowingi railroad from the territorial maps.

When morning broke, he rode out through the last of the iron town and along the banks and cuttings and lines of new-grown scrub that marked the path of the old railway. He rode past earthworks and clearings and scattered dog spikes and buckled tanks and rusted trolleys and broken sleepers, until they came to the edge of the first of the great saltpans. The boy then drew his hat down further over his eyes, against the hot white light that blew in off the salt, and he pushed the horse and dog out onto the pans, across the thin saltbush beaches and out onto the floating plateaus of silver and unstable light that lapped and eddied and shrank into the filmy distances that lay ahead.

He forced the horse to cross the thin clay beaches, the rings of salt and banded mud and coarsewebbed grass that edged the shining pans. He goaded and kicked with his heels, and the horse shied and reared and twisted back towards the soft but certain soil of the plain, until the boy had to dismount and lead his animals out onto the silver frozen waters, the white unfeatured plaques of crystal that ran out before them across unmeasurable distances towards the inconstant fringe of waving timber that marked the far side of the pans.

They set out slowly across the low fretted waves of gleaming salt that crested and broke like tiny ocean waves and ran away before them in low burning ridges that fanned out towards the eastern shore and traced in wide and brittle arcs the sweep of ancient winds. They tested with each step the silver surface, the dog sliding without a mark upon the saltcrust, but each footstep of the boy and of the horse breaking through the brittle saltglaze, so that as they moved they left an arc of brackish footprints trailing out behind. Each step they took released a deep ooze of mud and black-ened salt to dry and harden in the sun, to collect in time its own low rim of blown salt and form new webs across the salt like the ceaseless wandering webs they crossed, the frosted nomad marks of kangaroos and coursing emus and the meandering salt trails of wild and thirsting cattle that had drifted across the pans.

The boy looked back along the long arc of muddy steps that now pursued them across the salt, and he recalled a tale that Cabel Singh had once told him and Hannah in the nights, when they were still small, of a vast lake that lay to the east, and of strange salt men who lived among the islands and made their home in the dead forests, creatures without voices who swam freely in the mirage waters and who lived on those travellers who dared to cross, who stole children away with them to live in their crystal kingdoms that lay just below the crust. He thought also of something that Cabel had told him when he was older, of the great saltlake that lay much further to the east. He told of how when you moved towards the centre of the great saltlake, all that you had been and done dissolved behind you in mists and moving waters, and all before you and all your thoughts of things to come slipped into shifting air and liquid light. That in such places all thoughts of pleasures grew to pleasures of a kind you never knew elsewhere, and the pain of thought there grew upon itself in greater pain. Cabel had warned him that it was perhaps dangerous in that place to think even upon the best that you knew, and especially the worst, with nothing but the shining of the air about you to tempt you into thinking that your own feeling was all there ever was, in that place of strange infecting emptiness where there was no familiar sight about you to tell that you were still amid the living, and within a moment's walking of the firm familiar earth.

When the boy thought that they were near the centre of the largest of the pans, they stopped and took a drink from his waterbag, and he chased the pup in wild hooting muddy circles on the salt. Together they looked at the circles they had made, and back towards the lost shore to the west and on into the mirage waters that floated to the east. Then he led his animals on a vast and coiling route that traced his own name in deep black letters upon the salt. When it was finished they stopped again and sat for a time at the end of the long and flat and unreadable scratches running back across the pan, and he saw that it had no more meaning to him than it did to the dog or the horse. He wondered, too, whether they needed to make any more sense of moving through this dry and invisible moving ocean than he did, and he watched the horse as it waited patiently, and the dog pranced about with its ears pricked and tongue lolling, waiting for more sport. He lay back upon the salt and spread his arms and waited as they waited, and he let all coming and going and east and west and all thought and even the route of the hawker and the finding of Eileen shift and melt and eddy and run for a time into the silent and shifting rhythms of the heat and rising air.

Joe took him in the morning, carting stumps. It was in the early morning, the day after they came back from Windmill Tank. Joe had woken him at first light and bundled him straight into the truck, as he had done so many times before. This was, Joe always told him, 'getting off to a good start', and 'getting in ahead of the day', as though if it were left until later, the stumps might run away. But the boy could see, as soon as they were in the truck, that Joe had slept badly and was deeply ill at ease, rubbing his mouth with the back of his hand in the way he had when he was unhappy, beating through the gears as though in anger at the truck, plunging into the deep furrows and drifts of loose soil and taking each of the narrow gates at a reckless swerving speed.

Now and then, when they came across a patch of exposed stumps, Joe would pull the truck to a stop. The boy would then slip across into the driver's seat, to take the truck at low speed between the dark knots of broken roots, and Joe would trot alongside, clawing at the stumps and heaving them into the back, now and then shouting something above the revving of the engine, some direction about the stumps, or about the paddock to follow.

Together they had worked this way many times before. The boy had watched Joe often as he flung the stumps with a loud thump in the back, sometimes tossing the stumps in quick succession with both hands, taking satisfaction in the fast rhythm of the work, running out from the truck and wrestling with the stubborn ones, cursing and levering and breaking when they clung to the soil, too deeply buried to be pulled away.

This time, though, Joe had moved more slowly, working closer to the truck. This time Joe had other things in mind, some deep unease that he could not express, or only in his cursing at the dogs and in cruel punishment to the truck and to the grating gears, as he made his way from one paddock to the next. Each time as they moved slowly past the stumps, Joe found a voice, half hidden by his work, his questions half disguised by the swearing and the heaving at the stumps, the revving of the engine and the dull thump of the stumps as they fell into the tray.

'Long walk, yesterday?'

The boy agreed that it had been a long walk.

'Just the two of yer.'

The boy just said again that it had been a long walk back. He said that what they had told his mother was the truth, and that they had just rested in the shade.

'She tell yer much, then? Did she have much to say? About things at home, and all?'

'Not much. Nothing much.'

'Don't suppose she talked about me?'

'Nah. Nothing.'

And this at least was true.

'She don't talk about you, Joe. Never.'

The boy then realising that this was perhaps not what Joe was wanting, that Joe did not share the secret shame about him and Eileen, about the nights out past the dogyard, that he wanted to hear from him just something Eileen had said, and even if it told of things the boy ought not to know. He could tell from Joe's working so close to the truck, from his rough and awkward questions, that he was wanting something more, Joe straining for some talk of Cabel Singh.

He wondered if he should think of something that Eileen might have said, if he should tell Joe something of himself and Eileen, about what had happened at Windmill Tank, the long afternoon and the falling water, and the shade of the Murray pines, and the lonely rim of drifts. He wondered if there was anything in all that happened that he could tell to Joe, some tale of the tank, and the mud and the long hot track, perhaps even some sniggering tale of Eileen's open dress which would satisfy Joe, which they could laugh about together, and then get back to the stumps.

He cast about for some kind of story like the stories he had heard Joe tell his mates, which would keep Joe clear of asking him more of what he knew, and of what Eileen had said to him as they walked back to the Ridge. These were things which could not be told to Joe, things which he could not explain even to himself, but which even now, as he lay alone upon the saltpans, in this haze of floating light, lay watching the dog and the horse as they roamed the shining salt, still played obscurely about his thinking, like shifting shadows in the wind.

He was led by a light that flashed and faded and then flashed again, and they followed it for a time along a set of winding tracks that wound backwards and forwards across the old Nowingi line. The light which came and went burned brighter as they moved eastward, and led them in the high

heat of the day to leave the cartwheel furrows and all the
fading spider tracks that crossed the Raak expanse. He was
led by the light to pull away from the cart tracks and the low
cobweb grid of dustworn stockpaths and the broken
sleepers and mounds of earth that marked the railway line,
and take instead a path of their own that ran towards the
light, a path that led them out beyond the last stray clumps
of twisted pine and buloke and shreds of binding grass, out
across the plains of lignum and cattlebush and onto the
clayflats that ran out to the north and to the east.

As he rode and the day drew on, the light that winked and
laughed and beckoned to them across the silver yellow
spaces shone more brightly, and towards the late part of the
day it led them beyond the clayflats and back into the saltpan country and into the salt graveyard of ancient forests, the
grey terrain of cracked and broken timbers, of fallen logs
banked up in blown salt amid shattered trunks and the splinters of sandstripped and blasted trees, still pointing upward
with cracked and ragged fingers, their green lights long
extinguished amid the thirsting salt and unbroken rasping
winds.

They picked their way through the dead forests, through
the bright pools of rippled salt and crosshacked beds of
tablet clay and the grey detritus of logs and fallen branches
rotting amid the salt. They passed by sandy banks blown up
against toppled trees, and tufts of windsown saltbush that
hosted hordes of insects that blew up in clouds and sang and
circled as they passed. From time to time they would cross
another track, the mark of some wanderer riding to the west
or north, leaving wagon tracks marked out in the soft crust
of the salt, or deeper in the soft parts of the clay; and

although the boy was tempted always to follow the tracks that led off to the east, they held to the glow before them, which still caught at the light of the descending sun.

As they came closer, the boy saw at last that it was a shattered windshield that had beckoned, the light of the sun falling upon the broken glass of an automobile that lay stranded and still quivering in a deep bank of sand that ran along the northern edge of the salt forest, the coughing sound of the running engine drifting in waves towards them as they wound through the last of the trees. It was an aging Buick, its rear seat and running boards packed with oddments, tanks, tyres and boxes, the sound of nothing all around growing stranger with this knocking and choking of the car, beating against the thick silences of the sand. As they edged in closer they saw that the car was skirt about by scattered baggage, by signs of some great sweating effort, with blankets and a couple of wheatbags and a shovel and a helpless mound of twigs and saltbush gathered together around the rear wheels, which had just dug deeper into the sand.

'Hey! Hey, you! Mister! Anyone?'

The boy drew out the pearifle, holding it down low and crossways so as not to look like danger, but checking that it was loaded all the same. He scanned the horizon, scoured the near sand drifts and clumps of timber and the saltpans and dead forests shining in the distance for any sign of an owner, for the sight of someone resting in the shade. They waited, even the pup, a hundred yards back from the steaming car, and for a while they watched it without moving, the car bucketing and coughing in the heat, a haze of air waving upwards from the crackling engine and the steaming radiator, the knock knock knock of a halfopened door beating heavily against the rocking coachwork and the only other sounds the uneven chug of the dying engine and the gentle hiss of an escape of steam into the coarse heat of the sky.

It was then that they saw a naked foot, the shoe and sock removed and lying in the sand alongside, a red and broken blister upon the ball of the foot perhaps the reason for the nakedness. The rest was pallid white and tufted with reddish whiskers, the toes sadly twisted and moulded into one another, the victims of a lifetime's sweat and leather, the big toe horned and yellow and waving to the south. Then they saw a hand, the back of a reddish and freckled hand, the knuckles skinned some time ago but now protected with an aging, darkened scab, the thick fingers spread apart and bent and pulsing in the sand. Then, moving around the choking car, they saw the whole body, propped up against the wheel, openeyed and clearly dead and set about by flies, yet still moving with the rocking of the overheated engine. The flies that crawled about the lips, the nostrils, the staring and untroubled eyes moved also with the shaking movement of the dying car, rising in dark clouds with each deeper cough, but settling quickly again within the moist recesses of nostrils, eyes and open mouth.

The boy rested on the horse, leaning low over the withers, still nursing the rifle on his lap. He called to the pup to settle down. Through the mask of black bushflies he recognised the mottled face and hands, the heavy jowls and reddish hair gone sandy, the snaggle of teeth and protruding eyes of the Debt Adjuster, who only weeks before had given him and Hannah a lift back from the siding at Speed, and who, the boy had been told, had just had a tussle with the sussos just out of Boinka Town. The boy peered down at the shaking body, heavily rocked now and then by a breathy misfire, looking through the swarm of flies at the expression on the Debt Adjuster's face, his bulging eyes open and staring out between the flies at something beyond the abandoned rail banks, across the dead forest, and over the flats of baked salt that lay between him and the distant trees and settled lands to the south. The eyes said little, the boy could see when he clambered down from the pony and waved the flies away with his hat. There was no dread, nor discomfort at the heavy chuff of the struggling engine, nor even surprise at whatever it was that rose against him from the saltwastes.

Never had the Debt Adjuster seemed so much at ease, not even with him and Hannah when he gave them a lift that day, talking to them all the way out along the Baring road as no-one had ever heard a Debt Adjuster talk, the boy knowing that he talked that way because week after week he spoke to no-one. Now he was letting himself go a bit with two bare-foot kids picked up along the track, tipping his hat to Hannah and running around to help her up and bowing as though she were a real lady, with an odd cracked giggle at his own jokes, and saying finally that no-one, not even the Inspector from the Closer Settlement Board, had the right to expect a man to carry upon his back all that a Debt Adjuster bore, and none of them, not the boy nor Hannah nor even the Debt Adjuster himself, quite knowing that it was their own place that the Adjuster was on his way to at the time, that the really bad news which stood between the Adjuster and all those cups of tea he might have had was this time to be their news, with the Debt Adjuster's face finally darkening with the knowledge of where they were all heading together and the giggles and the jokes and the pats to Hannah's knee now fading, and finally all of them driving on in silence over the bumps and through the lifting dust.

The boy could see no mark on the body, other than that of the red blister, a broken fingernail and a badly jammed finger with its own cake of flies, sand and congealed blackish blood that had welled out from under the nail. He saw the dried rivulets of sweat that had run through the dust that lay upon his face and arms, the dark moist circles that marked the underarms of his shirt and loosened waistcoat. He saw moisture that had seeped through the front of his shirt, through the thick redgrey hair that rose to his throat and merged into the stubble upon his heavy neck and loosened jowls. The flies, too, coming in joyous hordes from the depths of the saltwastes, explored the drying sweat, the cool of the nostrils and the open mouth, and played upon the sour dry pool of urine that had flowed, perhaps only minutes before, around the Debt Adjuster's loins. The open dried lips showed his bared and yellow teeth, the tongue withdrawn and drying and darkening with each moment passing. The boy drew back, away from the shaking Debt Adjuster, away from the heat and bleeding steam of the breaking engine, away from the raised batwing covers of the engine which quivered and flapped like the spread wings of some bleak demon blown in out of the dead forest, a dark and rusting angel sweeping in upon them both.

The horse soon wandered off, down to a patch of shade by the edge of the saltpan, and the boy and the pup continued to explore up by the car, adding to the scatter of objects and emptying the Debt Adjuster's things onto the track. He went back to the front of the car, to look again at the Debt Adjuster, now even more heavily set upon by swarms of black bushflies. He prodded the body. It was a bad place to die. It was a bad time to be travelling. The eyes, when he waved the flies away, were glazing over, the mouth drying, the raw odour of urine rising, with some new and darker smell. It didn't seem fair, even for a Debt Adjuster, to be left out there for the flies to crawl around and all over his eyes and for the circling wedgies to close in, for the body to get blacker and drier in this place, no better than a dead sheep left out in a back paddock, going black and swollen and stinking and blowing out, with not a soul to hear, in an explosion of foul air.

The engine stopped. There were two or three coughs and shudders, pitching the body forward, then back again against the wheel, sending a swarm of flies outward and then back, and then a deep silence, penetrated only by the soft hiss of steam, the cracking of heated iron, and the sound of sandflies piping around him in the still hot air. The pup broke into wild whoops of barking and yelping, circling the stranded automobile and barking and snarling at the Debt Adjuster, at the bogged rear wheels, at the waving panels, at the hiss of steam, at the bags and the branches and saltbush tussocks and at all the signs of useless scraping and digging and shouldering spread out across the sand.

The boy climbed into the back of the car and rummaged in the battered cardboard suitcase that held the dead man's clothes and toiletries, tooth powder and shaving soap. The Debt Adjuster had a family. The boy found photographs, yellowing pictures that had known too much heat and travel, of a shapeless woman in a blurred floral dress, and in one picture holding before her two restless children, squinting into the sun. Behind them was a low hedge and a picket gate, and behind that a singlefronted cottage with its weatherboard neighbour crowding in upon it from the left. The girl, who might have been ten years old, looked a little like the Debt Adjuster, with tightdrawn plaits, thicknecked and heavy jowled for a child. The photograph was perhaps taken by the Debt Adjuster himself, and the younger child, tie aligned and dutiful in socks drawn up to varied levels, moving in a blur of freckled happiness before the sun, the father, the camera. When he had given the boy and Hannah a lift, he had told jokes and stories about kids and patted Hannah on the knee and made funny popping sounds for her with one finger thrust into his ruddy cheek. They had all then tried it, on the road.

But the Debt Adjuster also carried with him hessian bags and cardboard cartons and leather cases filled with files and folders, heavy marbled books and coloured papers of many kinds arranged in bundles, in cardboard concertinas, in stiff card boxes and on clipboards, with many signed on behalf of the Inspector in a signature the boy could not read; there were contracts and liens, loan agreements and guarantees, documents of land and stock transfer, lists of assets and bills of sale, and certificates, insurance documents, powers of attorney and assignment notices, some of them sunbaked and yellowed into stiffness and bound up in ancient string, and many simply lying about in piles upon the rear floor below the seats, long lists of labour and debt and lies and sweat and hanging on, marked and torn by the footprints of others like himself who had clambered about amid the boxes and the files.

He flung the Debt Adjuster's suitcase from the car, and it fell open upon the sand. The boy saw among the clutter of clothes a packet in yellow newspaper that he had not seen before, and he jumped down and tore it open to find an old and heavy revolver, and a dozen bullets, thick snubnosed bullets that the boy knew were fortyfives. The gun was heavy and oily in his hands, and he sighted it at the tyres, at the body of the Debt Adjuster, and at the pup, who knew about guns and had begun circling and yelping again. They set up the Debt Adjuster's suitcase on a rise of sand. The boy loaded the chambers with six of the bullets and aimed it at the brown square of the case, holding the heavy pistol with two hands to keep it steady, uncertain how to aim it or even to hold it, for he had never fired a real pistol before.

When he tried to pull the trigger, the hammer lifted slowly, the boy drawing upon all the strength of two fingers to raise it. Then he stopped, and lay the revolver across his leg, and with all the strength of his hands pulled the hammer back and cocked it. And this time when he raised it, he had scarcely even meant to touch the trigger when the gun fired and bucked and bellowed in his hands, and the stray shot just whined off across the dead forest, with the pup starting and barking and hurtling out onto the salt to find and bring back whatever it was that had been shot. Then the boy pulled the hammer back again and shot at the suitcase and missed, the bullet kicking up a lick of sand a yard to the left. And then he shot the flapping door of the Debt Adjuster's car. He shot one of the rear tyres so that it hissed its way flat into the sand. He fired a shot at a hawk that was circling above the car, and he put a last shot into the Debt Adjuster's radiator, but all the steam was gone.

He rolled the revolver back in its tattered newspaper, and put it in his canvas sack, and put the rest of the bullets in his pocket. Then he stood upon the back seat of the Debt Adjuster's car and looked out to the low horizon all around, to the rim of distant ridges and the fringe of distant forests, and felt the play upon him of a strong and tempting breeze. He took in armfuls the notes and photos, the letters, documents and contents of all the Debt Adjuster's careful files. He took the Closer Settlement materials, the lists of debts adjusted or called in, and filed them off in handfuls to the wind. He emptied cartons, file boxes and the concertinas, and set handfuls of torn pages, the mortgages, stock lists and the deeds of title and loan and contract and set all their terms and conditions and provisos blowing off towards the south, releasing them in pink and green and yellow tinted flashes to a wind which drew them off towards the saltpans and the whiteblown forests beyond, the dog yelping and circling and snapping at the papers and letting one blow on again to chase another, some catching on the saltbush tussocks at the fringe and others skidding out across the baked glass and rippled frosting of the lake, with quick gusts and random willywillies circling the lighter papers up, around and round and up into the hot evening air, joining with the eagles on their unseen coils of wind.

The Debt Adjuster, the boy had been told, was not a bad sort of a bloke, who was, after all, only doing his job and word was that if he could let you through, he would sometimes do so, and that often when folks thought they were fooling the Debt Adjuster, it was really just that he was choosing not to see, and using what chance he had to keep the battlers on their feet. If there was anything he could do, overlook a bit of horse trading on the side, ignore the sight of a few bags of seed peeking out from under a tarp, round out the figures a bit either up or down, he would always do it. It was a lonely and a thankless task to be doing the rounds of the scattered farms and when you finally arrived there was only a curse and desperate lies to greet you and the sight of drawn faces from the shadow of lifted blinds and kids like your own kids kept back as though you were the very devil, and then the eyes following your dust off the place like you were some worse kind of snake or insect come to add to the heat and the dry and the sand.

No-one ever got to be very friendly with the Debt Adjuster, who would never accept so much as a cup of tea even from the most outlying places, because, he once told someone who got to wondering why their tea wasn't good enough for him, you could never tell when you might have to be the one to bring in the really bad news. The Inspector had told them when they were first taken on that debt adjusters could not afford to be in debt to anyone, not even and perhaps especially not to the tune of a cup of tea. For all that, everyone seemed to know that this one wasn't as tough as other adjusters, and that people who thought they could pull the wool over his eyes by moving dead stock from one place to another and shifting sheds and fiddling with the boundary fences should know that this one always saw a lot more than he pretended to see, and that he was big enough a man to put up with being thought stupid for the sake of being kind. He was just about as decent as anyone could expect a debt adjuster to be. And after one time when word got around that he and his car had been taken apart by that pack of angry sussos, the Debt Adjuster even drew a bit of sympathy as he drank alone at the end of the bar in the pubs and shanties and slept out in a tarp beneath his car even in bad weather. The rest of those in the camp got together and made them give the Debt Adjuster his wheels back, made them bring the wheels back from out in the mulga and help him jack up the car and let him go, though none of them rightly knew whether they did it as a kindness or in the hope of some new start or just out of fear that the next Debt Adjuster might be worse.

The boy then took the top of one of the sets of pyjamas and with it covered the gaping clouded eyes, the mottled jowls and yawning mouth of the Debt Adjuster, and pushed the ends in between the body and the mudguard, against the breeze. He covered the Debt Adjuster with his frayed tartan blankets and piled all his scattered clothes onto the mound. He untied one of the jerrycans of petrol from its bracket on the running board and poured it all over the car, over the tattered upholstery, over the bits of clothing and paper that were left, over the tarps and boxes in the back, the tinder fittings and the wooden floor, the motor spares, the engine, the hoses, the paintwork and especially the tyres. He piled all the branches the Debt Adjuster had collected and the tufts of saltbush around the muffled body. Then he poured the rest of the petrol over it all so that it ran deep into the blankets and the piled clothing and the saltbush, seeping down into the warm darkness and to the body of the Debt Adjuster, protected now from the flies and the circling wedgies, from the wild dogs and the foxes that would come on with the night, and the ants that had already begun to filter across the sands.

He lit safety matches, taken from the Debt Adjuster's glovebox, throwing them into the back of the car, onto the seats, and then onto the mound of blankets that covered the Debt Adjuster, the flames rising and the black smoke starting to billow, the boy flicking matches until he was beaten back by the heat and rising flames, which joined the heat of the air, the air above the car moving and shimmering and giving way to the clouds of darkness that rose from the burning car. The boy ran in and out, throwing more lit matches until beaten back by the rush of oily flames, the roar of the fire catching kapok and hessian, the cracking of metal and burning wood and the shuddering of the batwing covers in the rising heat, with the pup barking and starting and running round and round the car in ever wilder circles.

It was not until they were half a mile or so down the track that they finally mounted a ridge that had blown up as though for that purpose around a struggling clump of trees, and they looked back to where the fire burned high, the long folds of black smoke still rising from a low red glow, the smoke coiling and mounting thickly from the oil and blankets and clothes and kapok and petrol and somewhere in the midst of it all the last of the Debt Adjuster rising to meet the still warm air and the coming darkness, the last of his papers rising high above the fire and the heat and joining the scattered clouds that had sprung up with the red of the falling sun.

He set out to catch the last of the light, to put the ridges between them and the fire that lay behind them, now moving onto the last of the leaderless tracks left by the feet of stray and abandoned sheep that filed their way out into the wilderness in search of feed and water. He turned away even from those tracks which perhaps led only to another kind of dry death and a cage of bones amid the sand, and they picked their way over the drifts and the saltpans and the new-laid sand brought in by recent winds, making their way to the east and navigating only by the smoke that still rose in the west behind them, moving steadily across the plain towards Hattah on the Ouyen to Mildura road. Then they turned from the top of the sand drift and slipped away from those cart tracks which had led the Debt Adjuster to his ending. The boy wondered as they rode what the Debt Adjuster had seen in those last moments on the road. He wondered what it was that had led the Debt Adjuster to come to this place, so far to the north, where there were no farms to visit or debts to be adjusted, and he thought again of those moments with Hannah and the Debt Adjuster in the car as they ground their way along the Baring road, the Debt Adjuster's eyes red in the dust and taking on that strained and distant look and he wiping his mouth in a worried way with the back of his hand and not really looking at them any more, the boy shushing Hannah when she asked how long it was going to be, and all of them knowing that the going was better than what was to come, driving on with the Closer Settlement Board Inspector somehow there behind all of them, with the darkness beginning to come on ahead.

'**Y**ou watch them, don't you, Auntie Argie?' she would say as she ran her gentle hands about my neck and shoulders, knowing that she was giving pleasure, although I did no more than raise my hand to stroke the hand that brought to me this kindness.

'I've watched you,' the girl would tease, looking deep into my eyes, as though she might make me meet her gaze, might just one time have my eyes meet and hold and speak into the deep brown of her own, 'and I know how it is.'

Sometimes I wondered if I might speak to the girl, if I might try again the shape of words, trying the shapes at first in silence, and then letting them run upon the air, letting the words float into the spaces that shape the silences that rule within this house. They call me silent, as though they speak in those few harsh words that crease the air, but it is in the silences between us that the knowledge passes, and I live amid the silences because I know the shapes of silence best. It is in my quietness that they know me, and to it that they speak sometimes, in broken words and awkward whispers, and now I fear, and even with the girl, that if I end my silence, even the whispering will cease.

I too was a speaker when first he came to the house, the house of my father far to the south and in a greener place. He passed by the house and leaned across the picket fence and he began to talk to me, the first man to place his hand upon my hand, and together we learned with a speed of knowledge which was our bodies' knowing, out in the darkness and deep amid the trees and sheds that lay beyond the square house with its pickets and boxed rooms and curtains drawn.

Soon he came to me in the night, calling to me from the scrub like a lone mopoke in the trees long after all had gone to sleep. I would creep out to meet him where he would be waiting for me beyond the sheds and far from the dogs. We would lie together in the cool air with only the dark fringe of the distant trees to mark the shape of the earth and he would draw my clothing from me and pass his hands across my body. Together we would lie, our bodies answering deep to the white light of the moon, with only the warm sounds of animals restless in the night to mark the time, and the sound of turkeys carrying across the darkness to mark the distance, and sometimes the howling of a dog. There we left behind in the silences of the night all the words we knew could only tell us things that could not be, that what we did was wrong, we knowing in our secret world of night and silence and one another's arms that this could not be so.

When the words broke upon us and the house became my prison, we went off together. I had tried to speak to the room of angry voices and tell them in new words what it was that we had done together, but they told me then that it was not the words but all the knowledge of my body that was wrong. We went then to the city together, and then he died and no-one ever knew. All thought that he left me for another because I never spoke to any of them again, and they drew words of their own from their cage of words, that he was a lousy waster who led me astray. Then the baby died and has since been dead to everyone in the silences which followed, none knowing that there ever was a baby but knowing only that I was found as the words had taught them to expect, years later, hungry and ill and long secured in silence. My uncle brought me home and in the unknowing righteousness of true affection took me out of time and flung me into old age in my youth. In all the quietness of reluctant gratitude I have watched and moved within the silent and unspoken lives of others since that time, choosing my world of silences because I cannot tell a lie. In not speaking I cannot speak untruths, and live still for that time which was my own time, knowing it again and again through the sun and rain upon my face or the movement of an insect upon my skin or then, upon my shoulders, the fond caressing hands of the girl they called Eileen.

I was passed from one household to another as a broken sign of the truth of all the words they used, passed from one house to another with my silence as a lesson to new generations, until my niece brought me to this dry ridge, and now I watch the struggle of others to fit the cage of words. Except sometimes the girl they called Eileen, this girl who touched my body always with her hands with all the ease as though it were her own, as we had come to touch each other all those years ago, and the strange boy who was for me my child, who sometimes sat and talked to me as he talked to no-one, who talked to me of things that live beyond the cage. He told me of the strength and movement of Joe Spencer which he wished would be his, and the thoughts of Cabel Singh which he wished to be his. He told me of how, when he had the strength of Joe Spencer and the thought of Cabel Singh, then he would know Eileen. I sat not showing that I knew or heard or understood, because if I had, I knew he would not speak again, wishing always that he would not stop, this awkward boy lost in his borrowed clothing, lost in the flesh of others not his flesh, who leans yet again across the pickets and into the fears and wishes and the secret thoughts that run within the minds of others.

The girl had gone off alone for some days for the first time since she blew in on that windy day. Our world had shrunk when Eileen went off even for a few days, when she went off with Joe Spencer in the gig to town and then by train from over at Speed to some aunt or to some cousin in the south: as likely a story, my niece had railed, as any other thing she ever told us. Days after she was expected to return, Mary, the littlest of them all, had come running from the gate to say that there was a big cart coming over the lake, and that Old Tollie had said that it was probably Cabel Singh, and that he had, for the first time that Old Tollie had ever seen, someone sitting by his side.

The children ran down and watched as Cabel Singh's cart, drawn by two horses with a third tethered at the side, rumbled and clattered over the humps at the gate. It toppled and rolled as it pitched across the furrowed ground, sailing like a galleon across the dry lakebed, piled high in hessians and tarpaulin, bound up in places with rusted fencingwire and with twists of bindertwine, with all its jangling shopwares, lanterns, forks and spades. She sat alongside

Cabel Singh, gleaming in an aura of sunlit dust like a new bride, this time in hat and shoes and a broad smile and laughter to the children running out to meet the cart and trotting alongside, arriving in such style among a symphony of kettles and casseroles and bowered by the high hessian canopy and bolts of calico and galatea, the shirts and holland pinafores and other drapery piled high in the tarpaulin reaches of the cart behind her. Beside her Cabel Singh sat straight and tall, his face softened in the lifting dust and his dark clothes and white stock coated in blown soil, smiling and laughing as always as the children ran out to the cart and skipped alongside and were hauled up one by one to sit beside them, the boy clinging like a monkey to the tailgate. They made their way in laughter and procession and a joy of dust and squeals and barking up along that same track that she had trod almost in nakedness less than a year before.

I saw the Indian sitting tall and straight upon the seat before his wares, hearing his voice amid the greeting children, he knowing all their names and taking Mary up onto the seat between them, and Eileen waving grandly to all those who had for one more time stopped their work to watch her make her way up along the track, to watch Cabel Singh as he edged the horses off the track that led up to the house and over to the place where he would set up camp and show his wares. I remember the look within my niece's eye as the wagon made its way slowly up the rise towards the house and towards Cabel Singh's usual camping place in the sandy flat between the biggest pepper tree and the machinery shed. She watched the girl leaping down from the cart in a swirl of smiles and thank you and bare brown legs and a blowing skirt, jumping down from the cart like a young deer and embracing the other girls and squeezing them to her breast and moving in a high state of excitation with her skirt licking about her legs and a bare arm upraised to protect the broad straw hat from a thin willy-willy that had brought them in and played and teased about the yard sending dust and grass seeds like insects biting through the air.

She moved towards the house and I felt my niece fret and stiffen beside me and her knuckles whiten as they bit upon the edge of the layabout, my niece waiting perhaps in a kind of dread for some kind of information or explanation or perhaps even an announcement of some kind, waiting in an alarm drawn from the girl's happiness which even she could see, and a new and shining lustre in her eyes. The girl merely laughed at the dust which flew from her clothing and took off her broad straw hat and threw it on the layabout as she came up on the verandah, saying to us only that she had been overtaken by Cabel Singh upon the road just out of Patchewollock, and what a chance it was, after what had almost happened the last time she had made her way on foot from town. Reaching for the waterbag, she told of how they had talked without stopping all the way out to the Ridge, and of how her throat was full of dust. And my niece watched again the wet sack rise as she had watched it that time before, and caught at the bag as if the girl were about to make to shower in it again before the boy and the other children, and grumbled that they had expected her some days before and the rest of them with better things to do than wander all over the country wasting the time of others.

She came to me and kissed me and laid her hand on the back of my hand, and stroked my shoulders in friendliness. She sat and took off one sandal and shook from it a twig that had lodged there and smiled at the boy who had followed her as always like a small dog, as she sat on the wicker settee vacated in anger by my niece, with her left foot resting across her right knee, massaging her dusty toes and watching in some distant amusement the mother quelling the excitement of the children and then staring the men back to their work. Then we heard the sound of a hammer falling upon the anvil as they slipped back into labour again, and with only the boy still watching, the boy again clinging to the edge of the verandah and watching Eileen as she leaned forward on the layabout to knead and to caress her dusty toes.

Still he watched her, as he watched her in the nights when we went to the fire of Cabel Singh, who spoke always to me too as I sat quietly beyond the light, as though he knew I knew, and there the young girl Hannah watched Eileen, as they all watched Eileen as she listened to the voice of Cabel Singh. The one they called Joe Spencer sat at the edge of the light of the fire, breaking sticks into small pieces and building little squares and fences upon the ground and counting always the time that passed as he counted the trees he broke as he counted the times he so roughly took the girl they call Eileen, her cries coming up to me on the verandah in the nights. And all the while as they sat about the fire he sits there among them and in each of them my man as he was smiles at me and I smile at him, and I find him yet each day in the smell of the burning cowpats and the music of the insects upon my flesh. I think again of the time we had together which died not in that time but lives again always in the singing of my flesh and in the dreams of the awkward boy and the caresses of the girl who is now called Eileen and in the desire of the girl they now call Eileen and the smile of the man they now call Cabel Singh.

They followed the wide road to the south, taking the dirt track that ran alongside the gravel to save the horse's feet, working slowly down towards Hattah and towards the river which the boy knew from Cabel's stories he must strike somewhere to the east. The day was hot and the dust from their feet hovered long in the air behind them. There was little traffic on the road. Now and then a cart would pass them on its way to the south, the shimmer of phantom waters that ran across the road ahead dispersed for some moments by the clouds of floating dust. They saw a load of hay heading northwards on a lumbering wagon and a farmer and three kids in ragged clothing perched upon the load, their faces blank and shaded under broadbrimmed hats, neither speaking to him nor to each other as they passed. Further along, a truck piled high with mallee stumps oiled past them on its way towards the railhead in the south, passing in clouds of dust and flying gravel and with a broad red wink from the sweating driver, struggling with a buggered steering to keep it on the track. The boy led the horse slowly to keep it fresh for the longer stretches that lay ahead, and they often stopped and rested in the shade.

They saw the shanty at Hattah from half a mile or so away, the redrust of the petrol bowser standing out against the grey and yellow of the track, the whole ramshackle humpy and its tanks and sheds moving in the mirage waters flowing deep across the road. On coming closer they saw the owner, sitting in an old flannel singlet in the shade of his broom verandah, scratching his elbows and brushing at the flies drawn by the shade. He was around fifty years of age, with receding reddish hair that was thick and matted around his ears, and he looked away from the boy as he arrived at the shanty and began to tether his horse to one of the stakes that supported the verandah. He looked away and said nothing, as though there were nothing upon the road that day but one hot and dusty kid after another.

'Mind yer bleedin' horse don't go silly,' he mumbled finally, still looking out ahead of him and into the scrub on the other side of the track rather than at the boy.

'Had a bloke's horse as went silly once. Tied to that same damn post. Took most of the place with it half the bleedin' way down to Ouyen. Bastard had t'spend half the day puttin' the place back together again.'

The boy said nothing. He untied the horse and let it wander. There was a canvas deckchair empty next to the owner and he flopped into it, fanning himself with his hat, and the two of them sat for a time and looked out into the scrub which was the same scrub that the boy had walked alongside for hours and the same scrub that the owner had sat there looking at for months and maybe years. After a time, the boy finally spoke in a voice that was not his, so dry was it with the dust of the road.

'You got a tank? Could do with a bit of water.'

'Man don't get rich handin' out water t'every loose bastard as wanders up and down the road.'

They sat again in silence. The horse found a trough below a rickety tankstand to the side of the shanty and the owner showed no sign of stopping either it or the pup from taking a drink.

'You hungry, young feller?'

'I reckon I am.'

'You got any money?'

'Nope.'

'Didn't reckon yer had.

'Well,' he grunted, 'don't reckon I can have yer dying' on me, out here in front of everybody. Wait a bit an' I'll fix yer summat. Not feedin' yer nag.'

The man struggled from his canvas chair and went off and came back with a shank of lamb and some cold potatoes and some raw and stringy carrots that he pulled from a small garden behind the tankstand and washed off in the trough. He brought the food to the boy and they sat in their chairs in silence again, with a fine view of the empty road and the blank scrub to the front.

'Where you from, kid?'

'Down south.'

'Your folks know you're up this way? On yer paddy?'

'Aren't got no people,' the boy mumbled, gnawing at his bone. 'Big bushfire, just before harvest. Wiped them all out, whole family, the home place and all. Me and this horse and this dog is all that was left. Maybe you read about it some-where.'

The owner ran his eyes over the boy and his bone.

'Well, no, I just don't quite seem to recall that. Just don't seem to recall anythin' of that nature happenin' hereabouts at all.'

He shook his head and scratched his elbows, as if this were the tenth boy that day to come through with some cock and bull yarn to tell.

'You want to find someone to keep an eye on yer, kid. At your age. Give yer a belting or a feed or whatever.'

The boy then told the man as little as he could that was true in order to find the truth of whether a hawker called Cabel Singh had passed that way and whether he had a girl with him. All the man could say was that maybe a dozen hawkers had been through but they wouldn't stop at his place because what business would a hawker have with a storekeeper anyway, and that the only kind of blackfellow he'd seen lately was a halfstarved character with a blunt axe you could scarcely lay open a paddymelon with and the sandy blight in his eyes and a tablecloth around his head and not even a waterbag, who stopped in and nearly drank the horse trough dry, who told him he was a shootcutter looking for work and who also asked him if Cabel Singh had passed. He told him that this fellow had finished his drink and tried to set off back in the same direction from which he had come, and the owner had to take after him and turn him around and point him to the south.

The owner then laughed and told the boy that it wasn't too difficult to find Cabel Singh because in point of fact he generally managed to find him every month or two just by sitting where he was and looking up and down the road, but that if he wanted to find him sooner he should take the track that led off to the east, towards the river and Kulkyne.

When he finished his meal the boy took whatever food the

man would give him and filled his waterbags and hauled the last of his chaff upon his back, and they set off towards the red dirt track that led off into the scrub to the east.

He saw that the owner had had enough of talk and was already staring back into the scrub, but he thanked him for the food and water anyway.

He lay upon his bed and listened to the sounds of movement, the last sounds of the day. On the night before she left, he had gone to bed when all the others went, to lie awake below the waving hessian, listening to the noises of the house. He heard his mother moving in the kitchen, the sounds of cupboards slamming, and then the sound of sighing in his parents' sleepout, and the lowering of the lamps in all the rooms, except for Eileen's. By turning in his bed, he could see part way into the house, along the corridor that ran between the darkened rooms. He could see from his stretcher in the sleepout a shaft of yellow light from Eileen's room, which banded the passage wall. Outside, he could hear the sound of turkeys, and for a time the howling of a cat under the house, and soon a bitter snarling fight, and then no sounds at all.

That night she had played her cards, her game of patience below the etched glass mirror, with the younger children already gone to bed and fast asleep. His parents were each absorbed in a book, and Eileen played on her own, and all in silence as though peace had been restored, the boy wondering if perhaps all might be as before, if he and Joe and Eileen might just go on as before.

'What are you playing?' was all that he had asked. She had

ruffled his hair, with his mother glancing over for just one moment, and then back to her book. His thoughts of Eileen at the tank, of their walking back together in the night, were fading quietly with the familiar days of heat and work, of fencing with his father and with Joe collecting stumps, all thought of other things made unreal by the slow routines of the house, the sight of Eileen looking to the younger children and the needs of the house, and no more talk from his mother of how Eileen must leave.

He sat with her, soon joined there by Hannah who had tired of her book, the three of them under the Colman's light, with Eileen dealing out a hand to each for a game of memories. They played as always, excitedly together, but with voices hushed for his parents' reading, and for Auntie Argie who dozed quietly in her chair.

As they played, the boy still probed for Eileen's gaze, looking into Eileen's eyes at every opportunity, trying still to see some shade of what had passed. Hannah had not forgotten their return from Windmill Tank and she too watched Eileen as they played, watching for some sign to the boy, seeking always for some secret knowledge of the kind Eileen used to give her, some knowledge now, of Eileen and the boy. But Eileen played just as always, laughing softly at the wrong choices they made, and snatching up the cards to deal again. Eileen's memory was quick and precise, and she could deftly win each game, but she played with them again as children, ruffling their hair and teasing them, and ensuring that, from time to time, each one might win a hand.

He lay upon his bed and waited, hoping that all would be as before. On many a night he had listened for the sound of Eileen leaving for the dogyard, late in the night when all the others were asleep, lying awake and dressed upon the bare mattress below the hessian, and knowing that Eileen would soon go down to meet Joe in the darkness beyond the restless dogs. He had listened to the sounds of Eileen moving late about the rooms, to the rustle of her clothing and the removal of each garment as she made to prepare for bed, humming a tune as she arranged her things and creaking about the loose boards of the house until one of his parents would call to her to be still. She would move back to her room, and the boy would lie still and watch the soft yellow glow of Eileen's lamp still burning long after the other lights had gone out.

On that last night he had listened, too, from his place upon the stretcher, watching the yellow band of light, waiting in the silence in the hope of sounds of movement, for the light of Eileen's lamp to soften and go out, and for the rustle of Eileen's clothing and then the creaking of the boards, waiting in the hope that all things would be as they were before, and that all that he learned at Windmill Tank would fade back into familiar things, like new sand upon the drifts.

He took the track that led towards the east and into the heavier timber that lay in the direction of the river, and the scrub around them creaked and sang in the afternoon heat, and the paper fronds of loosened bark waved to the lightest gust that filtered through the trees. At around midafternoon and still far from the sight of water, he stopped and tethered the horse to a parting shaft of mallee, and it stood about twitching its tail and shaking and winking the flies from its eyes as he sat on a bank of sand and took out a meat and pickle sandwich that the man at Hattah had given him to eat upon the way. He laid it out on its scrap of newspaper to secure it from the redblack bull ants and the sand that lifted now and then in the afternoon breeze. He gave the dog a drink from the crown of his hat and, knowing that he was moving towards the river and to water, showered himself lightly from the waterbag. The dog worried itself a neat sandy cubicle in a mound of rabbit burrows that had recently been ripped, and lay with its nose resting on its forepaws, ears intent and eyes lined down along the red stretches of road and the tunnel of arching branches that marked out the track to come, and they waited, the boy, the horse and the dog, for the last of the heat of the day to pass.

Then the dog pricked up its ears to a tinkling and rattling that sounded in the distance, a little like an approaching cart. Within minutes they saw that it was a bicycle upon the track, an aging frame of rusting iron that bucked and toppled as it hit the waves of loose sand that lay across the track. The boy could see the rider straining, rising high and straight-legged from the saddle, pushing heavily at each bank of sand, weaving where possible to avoid the softest parts and wobbling fearfully in the deeper banks, reaching out a steadying foot here and there where the frame began to topple.

The rider was a man no longer young, perhaps the age of the boy's father, in dungarees and broad cloth braces over a sweatringed and dustcaked flannel singlet, with brown work-mottled arms and patched and repatched plunging knees, striving from a seat dropped far too low on the bicycle to keep the frame erect and running forward. They watched in silent awe as the contraption rattled and foundered and toppled towards them through the sand. The rider wore a cloth cap in greasy tweed and thick spectacles that now and then caught the flash of sun. His thought was all in his legs, in his heaving knees and straining calves, in the next drift of resistance on the road, and in a grunting ballad of some sort that he swore and heaved his way through as he made his way towards them.

He seemed not to see them until he came almost to the place where they were resting by the side of the road. And when he did see them, he was startled and the bike wobbled and almost brought him down with it, as he wobbled to a shaky halt. Neither said anything for a time. The rider mopped his brow, grinned awkwardly and set his cap back a bit on his head, leaving his hair plastered in a band of sweat across his forehead. He was sandy haired, the hair receding but brushed forward in front, the rest too long, the grime and sweat recording the soggy arc of the shape of his cap. His spectacles were heavy, thicker than the boy had ever seen before. His nose was sharp and marked in reddish layers, a skin which should have stayed indoors, much damaged by the sun. Through those moving pools of glass, his eyes were blue and active, inquiring despite the silence, and the boy sought deeper safety within his hat. The man said nothing though, but just fanned himself with his disgusting cap, and after a time took up again the tune of his ballad, as though the boy nor the horse nor the pup were there at all.

'Bad stretch,' he finally offered, and drew his bicycle over towards the side of the track, as though away from the passing traffic.

The boy offered him the waterbag, which he accepted without a word. He propped the bike up on a stump of mallee and set himself down on a rise of clay next to the boy.

He sat with knees splayed apart and his head thrust forward, his cap now in his hand, shaking drops of sweat into the dust. Then he rolled and lit a cigarette, which he held between deeply stained fingers.

After some time the boy picked up the waterbag and took a swig. He passed it to the man again and shook it in front of him.

'Drink?'

'So. Kid's got a tongue.'

He laughed, and the boy felt the blue eyes swim about him.

'Only when I got something to say.'

The blue eyes enjoyed that. He repeated what the boy had said over and over to himself and chuckled and waggled his head. Then he lay back in the sand with his arms folded behind his head, and he began to talk and to ask questions, but not questions like the ones that others asked.

'Where are you going, kid?'

'I'm looking for Cabel Singh.'

'If that's the case then you'd be better off just standing still. I know your Cabel Singh. Everybody knows that Cabel Singh travels in a circle.

'You trying to pick up the end of one of his yarns, eh?'

'Could be.'

'What are you going to do when you catch up with Cabel Singh?'

There was too much in that for the boy to answer. He would find him, and then think about what he would do.

'Cabel always travels on his own. Not even his mate Mullah travels with him much.'

'Not sayin' I'm going to travel with him. Just going to find him, that's all.'

The man smiled kindly at that, and stopped his questions, and the two of them looked out across the red soil of the track and at the scrub to come. After a time he spoke again, without looking at the boy or waiting for an answer. He spoke to the scrub, to some invisible listener out amid the dry leaves and flaking bark.

'Your mate Cabel and I talk. Like he talks to few people, I reckon. Or maybe to you? He and I sometimes camped together. Down towards the river. We've talked all night sometimes, until the sun came up, and we had to go our separate ways. Even then we had to promise each other that we'd catch up on the rest of it, the next time our paths crossed.'

The boy thought again of his time on O'Sullivan's Lookout, drifting off to sleep while Cabel smoked his bubble pipe and looked out into the night. He thought again of the wind moving his hair and the sweet smell of the smoke, the deep glowing of the embers and the white slash of his smile in the weak light of the moon.

'He doesn't seem to need to sleep like the rest of us,' the man went on. 'Or maybe he sleeps in his cart in the day, and just stays up all night and does his thinking.'

He winked at the boy.

'He's a bit of a poet, our Cabel Singh. Did you know that?'

The boy said nothing.

'A poet, that's what he is. But there's not an awful lot to say about this place, young fella, because there's not a lot of people here, and not a lot happens. That's what Cabel says. That's why I came back. I'll tell you about that in a moment, why I came back. What Cabel says is that these are good spaces for launching dreams in because there's no tall trees to clog up the sky and there aren't many people around to trample through them. And those that are tend to mind their own business. About the place itself, you can't say much. But if you are going to say anything, Cabel says, you've got to say it long and slow and in lots of scattered bits and pieces, because that's about the only way things happen here. Nothing fits up with anything else, except just now and then, and when you least expect it to, like when Cabel and I meet down by the river. Or you have to pick some bit of a thing that everybody else has forgotten about or never gave two hoots about anyway, and show that this little thing, like that red berry over there on that bush—if you look around you, kid, you'll see that it's about the only spot of colour any-where—you've got to show that one little thing is the centre of all of it, and the thing that pulls it all together. You know what I mean?'

The boy didn't, and there was no red berry or a spot of colour anywhere that he could see, other than in the pale blue eyes that swam about him, but he nodded thoughtfully, because he felt that it might one day have a meaning for him.

The rider said that he was a bagsewer, on his way to sew a stack of seed on a farm off to the east and south of the river. The boy asked him how he felt about spending his time sewing bags out in the open in this kind of heat, and the man told him that he couldn't see very much—that something bad had got in his eyes when he was in the war—but that he could still sew bags because bags were a matter of feeling your way and not seeing, and that because he could see nothing much, he could think about just about anything he chose while he worked along the open stacks.

He was, he said, just like the boy when he was the boy's

age, a traveller and a wanderer. It was before the war and long before the Closer Settlement Board started to chop up the place and run fences and tracks across it and hand it out in useless bundles for folks to break their backs on. He had travelled the country on his own, just like the boy was doing, and that was before there were any houses or shops at all and no fences and very few tracks and he had almost died, once or twice, when he had wandered too far in the heat without water. He was drawn by the emptiness and the flatness and the sameness of it all, and often he would leave his parents' block without a word to them, and walk for mile after mile through the scrub and into the night, just wanting to see something that was new and different. As he walked he would paint scenes about him from the books that he had read, and he would plot out on the sand drifts and amid the seas of scrub the stories he had read and the things he had dreamed. He told of how the place had never answered back and the stories as he grew older only bounced back off the scrub and the empty skies, and somehow life and all the stories about life that he had ever read, and all the things that anyone ever said about it, seemed to be going on somewhere else, and that all the things he couldn't see when he was able to see just got in the way of his thinking.

The boy began to feel as the bagsewer spoke about the sky and to the scrub that here was someone who might understand if he told him something about Eileen and the fires that led the way to the sustenance camp and the fleeing surveyor and his family and the Debt Adjuster staring out into the dead forest. But the bagsewer seemed to have got into a way of talking and wasn't about to stop. He had decided, he said, that it was important that he should tell the boy a story, and he could make of it what he would. So the boy just took another drink from the waterbag and sat back and listened.

'When the war began,' he went on, 'I was one of the first from hereabouts to join up, because I wanted to see the world. What others suffered I almost enjoyed, and in some ways even the worst of it, which was a hell on earth—though not much worse in the mud over there than what I've known in the heat around this place. Your mate Cabel, he's seen worse. And when the war was ended and everybody was sent home, I managed to stay on for a bit, my head still full of death and ruins and needing somehow to clean it all out before I came back.'

The bagsewer took another drink, and wiped his mouth with the back of his hand.

'Life in Paris was very difficult at that time. The streets were full of others like myself, leftovers from the war, most of us still only part believing we were still alive and whole, and with just about nothing to go back to in the places that we came from, all mucked about inside by what we'd seen, but somehow all of us still looking for something good that would match up with the worst of it, something that would help us know that what we'd seen was strange and bad. After a time of it—of watching ordinary blokes on ordinary looking days getting themselves blown apart—after a time of it, you began to wonder about what's ordinary and what's not ordinary, and when the worst that you can ever imagine starts getting ordinary, you begin to get the feeling that nothing will ever seem extraordinary enough to be worth thinking about.

'I looked for work in Paris. There wasn't much that I could do. I couldn't see a lot and didn't have much of the language and was just one among thousands of the living dead at that time, moving hungry through the streets. Eventually, after nearly starving, I managed to pull together enough of the language to be able to get work of sorts, sometimes loading boxes, sometimes building and after a time, in a bar.

'I lived in a large apartment building in the Old Quarter, a crumbling old palace that had become a rabbit warren of rooms and plywood partitions and staircases that ran around both inside and outside the building, and dunnies slapped on the sides, way up in the air, with the whole place a hive of movement with people above and people below and some of them as mean as you could ever imagine and some of them kind and helping to keep the others alive, with butchers and bricklayers and piano teachers and women taking in laundry and even a few stray thinkers like myself.'

'I've heard about Paris. That's where they eat cats and horses.'

'Eat just about anything that moves. An' make it taste good too. Place is about as different from this place,' he waved his hand out towards the seas of thick scrub that ran towards the river, 'as you're ever going to find. Only bare earth you'd ever see is what you dug out from under your fingernails. The rest was stone, tar, concrete, gravel and iron. And people, people, people, all on top of one another, like you could hardly imagine, swarming up and down the buildings like trench rats, and all shoving their hands into one another's pockets and tearing the food from the mouths of one another's children and getting their hands on one another's bodies and even slitting one another's throats when given half a chance.

'An old palace, it was. They say that Mozart himself once

lived there. Do you know who Mozart was, young fella?'

The boy did not.

'Wrote tunes for the piano, Mozart did. Famous tunes. Hundreds of years ago and all. Well, in that place I took a room for a time with two sisters, twins they were, who were just about identical, or so I thought when they took me in. They were strangers in the city too. They came up to Paris from the country, and didn't know anybody and were working like me in the oldest part of Paris. One worked in a bakery, and worked through the night, and the other in a shop that sold lace and underwear, during the day. They took me in because they were looking for someone to help with the bills.

'I say you probably can't imagine how people live on top of each other in those places with family upon family in the same building and people piled in huge numbers into single rooms, and crowds of friends and strangers alike moving up and down the stairs outside and beating on the doors. Day and night hardly seemed to make a difference in that place, as the days grew shorter and nearly vanished anyway, as the winter came on and the cold came down upon us, but with the lights of the city burning all around us through the night, and the little apartment lit almost as brightly through the windows after you turned the lamps off. The girls took the only room, which had its own narrow iron bed which they shared, though mostly one after the other, and I had a folding bed—just an old army stretcher—in the tiny hall, so small that you could hardly open the door when the stretcher was set out. Apart from that, there was a tiny kitchen and a stinking hole they called a *cabinet turc* on the ground floor at the rear of the building, and a heavy pump and basin set into the wall of the landing, from which water could be fetched.

'The girls would talk to me for hours, early in the morning for Adrienne, back from a night's work at the *boulangerie*, and late at night for Adelaïde, after she returned from the shop where she worked such long hours, and while she waited for Adrienne to wake so that she could take the bed. Sometimes, on Sundays and other times when they were free, Adelaïde and Adrienne would either share the same bed, or one of them would unfold my bed and lie on it through the day. Sometimes I would come home to find a halfnaked girl slumbering in my bed, and more than once I fell alseep across the table in one of the old wicker chairs that made up the rest of the furniture in the room.

'Hour after hour I spent sitting on the side of my own bed, listening to the yarns of one or the other, and sometimes sharing with them stories of where I had come from, of the birds and animals and empty spaces of home, and the mud and the rotting flesh and blasted soil and toppled walls which was just about all I knew of the France that lay outside Paris. And after a time they began to tell me more about themselves, and why they had come to Paris, why they had left behind their parents and a large and comfortable house, they told me, down in Blois, to live with a stranger in this rabbit warren.

'The girls were, I guessed, around twenty years old, and were identical twins, both greeneyed, tall and slim, with long, thin noses and fine, light olive skin, and light brown hair that always caught what light there was to catch. I was told that Adrienne had a gold flash in her left eye, that Adelaïde was the one with the deep pockmark on her left temple, but that wasn't much use to me because of the gas that had got into my eyes, and after a time I simply decided that if it was daylight, then I was speaking to Adrienne, and that if it was night, then it was probably Adelaïde. And after not too much time had passed, I felt I knew which one I spoke to by the things she chose to talk about, and the way she chose to speak of them.

'Things all worked pretty well for a time, despite the odd dispute over the bills and my bed sometimes being left out in everyone's way, and the daily tangle of sodden bread and unwashed dishes and drying underclothes. It worked, too, despite a sadness that I soon saw in each of the girls, and particularly in Adrienne, and despite an anger that I felt in Adelaïde. I would catch her sometimes glaring at the yellow long unpainted walls as though she felt imprisoned in that tiny place. The girls seemed to appreciate the way, though, in which I never seemed to mistake which one was which. They even seemed to like the fact that I was so ugly—*tellement laid* they said I was—the fact that I was not, to them, a man at all because of my rough ways and my bad eyes, because of the fact that I spoke so little French, and because I once told them that I wanted to be a poet; and after a time they both began to touch me when we talked, and caress me as a brother, or put their arms in mine when we went for walks, just over to the Jardin du Luxembourg, or out to the Bois de Boulogne, the three of us walking arm in arm in the weak heat of the Sunday sun, and I felt that suddenly I was really in the very thick of life—for years, you see, we had lived closer to the dead than to the living—enjoying the sun and the pleasure boats on the water and the pallid apartment children laughing with happiness at a freedom they hardly knew, and Adrienne and Adelaïde tugging and chirruping on my arms.

'These were my happiest times, and I knew for once that I was with the living again, that life was real and true and happening all around me in a way that it never came to be out here where there was nothing, never a hill, or a stream, or anything like what you read about in books, to break the endless stretch of scrub. Nor was it ever real to me out there in the trenches, with all the soil turned over and nothing looking like anything that sane men ever saw, and you as likely to be telling your yarns and fears in the night to someone who, when the sun came up and you looked into the blankness of his eyes, turned out to have been through the worst and out the other side. But here, on those days in the Bois de Boulogne, with Adrienne and Adelaïde at my side, it seemed as though what I'd read and what I'd dreamed and what I now was had at last come together. I can't explain it more than that.'

It was explanation enough for the boy, whose eyes were shining. He passed the water over to the bagsewer, who took it without looking, and went on.

'I soon became like a pet within that tiny apartment. The girls were more and more at ease with me, throwing off their things as though they were alone with each other, and bathing themselves as though I were not there, and they were often to be found when I came home, the one or the other, curled up on my stretcher half clad or even less, because they knew that I couldn't see much with my bung eyes, that I could only see the broad shapes of things, and things that moved; and sometimes I would squat on the floor for hours and admire whichever sleeping girl it was, the white glow of her *chemise de nuit* and the soft olive tones of her bare skin and the smells of soap or sweat or sleep upon her and the glint from the lamp in her tousled hair. The closeness grew upon us quickly in this way, and soon caused me nearly as much pain as pleasure, I can tell you, not knowing where my desire ran or to which girl, or whether it was just a sort of rambling passion that had as much to do with the city and the crowded and crumbling palace and the four walls of the apartment, as it had to do with either of the girls.

'You know why they were there, in Paris, in that tiny apartment? Well, it turned out there was a story—a "past", as Adelaïde explained to me one wintry evening when we were alone together and her sister was at work, a dark and secret reason why they had left to come to Paris. She curled up next to me on the bed and placed her arm about me in a way that she never had before, and she hid her face against my shoulder, as though she was deeply ashamed of what she had to tell.

'Two years before, she told me, the girls had moved with their parents to the city of Blois. They had already, in the village called Chatelguyon, been trained as teachers and were well educated in this way to work at Blois. Unfortunately, chances for teachers in that place were scarce, and finally it was only Adrienne who could find a post. She began to work as an *institutrice* at the local primary school. It was a bad chance for Adelaïde, who was left at home, and this led, in time, to a deepening of her sadness and her anger. Nor were her parents at all helpful, praising Adrienne daily, and contrasting her fine efforts in finding a place for herself with the unwillingness of Adelaïde even to stir from the house. Few knew that Adrienne even had a sister, and those who saw Adelaïde when she went onto the streets of Blois thought that it was Adrienne they were seeing, and they would greet her, and Adelaïde would stare through them coldly, and word soon passed around that Mademoiselle Adrienne was oddly *versatile*, and cruel in the way she treated others.

'Finally, one day—maybe six months after Adrienne had begun work at the school—she fell ill, and for more than three weeks she was laid up in bed with a fever, and eventually someone from the school came around and outlined the fragile terms of Adrienne's position, and told the family that if she could not soon return to school, she would have to be replaced, that with so many young men returning from the war, positions like that of Adrienne's were in high demand.

'It was then that the deception began. On the next Monday morning it was not Adrienne who went down to the school, but instead, with careful instructions from Adrienne on every detail of every pupil and every room and every other teacher, it was Adelaïde, armed with Adrienne's books and Adrienne's clothes, who went down to the school to teach. And if the whole business had only lasted those few days, and Adrienne had become well again, all would have been fine.

'But there was something that Adrienne had not been able to bring herself to tell Adelaïde, something that had happened at the school that she had tried to tell to Adelaïde a number of times but had never quite got around to it, perhaps hoping that there would be no need, and that she would soon be well. Perhaps she was too unwell to talk about anything as complicated as the business with Monsieur Darphin, who was the director of the school and—in short—the attentions he had been paying to her during the last few months of her work at the school, and—perhaps more importantly—her response to that attention.'

The blue eyes swam back to the boy, testing his attention. He smiled at the bagsewer and encouraged him to run on.

'There was perhaps, she told me, nothing indecent in the attention shown to Adrienne by Monsieur Darphin, though he would not have wanted those attentions widely known. His wife had died during the influenza, more than a year earlier, and maybe he was just looking for a mother for his young children. He was tall, still in his thirties, Adelaïde said, and with a fine military air. Nor was Adrienne too unhappy about those attentions, because she was—and here, Adelaïde hid her face deeper in her tangle of long brown hair, and began to weep against my shoulder—sometimes strangely free with men, and somehow weak in the face of men's flattery and altogether *un peu trop légère* was how she put it, in ways that had already been the cause of their leaving Chatelguyon in the first place, though that was another story which, she begged me, for poor Adrienne's sake, she would prefer not to have to tell. But Adelaïde soon found herself one evening after classes, with Monsieur Darphin's eager hands upon her body and fumbling in her underwear and then angry words upon his lips about what had happened to their "little understanding". It soon emerged, as she backed away and rearranged her clothing, that Adelaïde was not Adrienne, and in the embarrassment to follow, the post as *institutrice* quickly vanished and the two girls found themselves on the train to Paris, with tearful promises yet again from Adrienne and a determination to put the mistakes of Chatelguyon and Blois behind her.

'And the reason why she was now telling me this was because she had noticed in recent weeks a sad but familiar change in the behaviour of Adrienne, and felt that I should know that Adrienne had told her just two nights before that she thought she was in love with me. She told her, she claimed, to avoid another awkward situation as at Blois, and she said that she had become used to the heavy spectacles and the awful French and to my rough ways around the house. But Adelaïde had been through this before and not just once, and she felt, though it pained her to speak of it, that I should be aware of the weakness, this strange *faiblesse* of her sister, and be careful to give her no encouragement. I thanked her for the warning and reassured her and stroked her hair and told her that I would mind what she had said and think carefully about what I must do.

'But through the days and nights to follow I found that what she had said had played upon me, and I found that suddenly Adrienne was in my thoughts and in my dreams. I longed each morning for her return from the *boulangerie* with the smell of flour and bread upon her, and I would sit and talk to her for hours after Adelaïde left for work. I noted a new warmth in her manner and, I thought, a special brightness in her eyes and a new friendliness in the things she spoke of that was not there before. I noticed, too, that while Adelaïde seemed more careless and even bold when I was there, with her undressing and her moving almost naked about the room, Adrienne seemed more modest, far more cautious, perhaps blushing if I could only see, and I felt that this too bore out the truth of what Adelaïde had said. And in no time the whole tiny apartment was seething with another kind of life, with Adrienne's care and Adelaïde's carelessness each taunting in their different ways, and when Adrienne moved about the room I followed every movement of her body. I hung upon every word that she spoke, and in the nights when she went off to work I would brush past her undergarments in rich spasms of desire, hardly daring to touch them or even move them aside in the usual way, and I knew that all that I had ever read of, all that my books had told me, was happening within that tiny place, for I had never known and indeed had scarcely spoken to a woman in my life before, and never to a woman with such experience of life, a woman *un peu trop légère* like Adrienne.

'Eventually, and like the damned fool I was in getting myself over to that country in the first place, I made to let her know. It was in the late morning and Adrienne was lying on the bed, still smelling of the night's flour and new baked bread but with her outer things thrown off and her body flung in limp exhaustion across the bed. Cold it was, outside, but the apartment was closely heated and the curtains drawn, with the room lit only by the soft light of the lamps. I sat by the bed and watched her until she woke and smiled at me. Then I reached over and touched her face, and she still smiled at me and asked in drowsy kindness why it was that I was not at work, and I explained that I had sat for hours watching her. I placed my hand upon her breast, because I did not know what else I should do. I tried to kiss her on the mouth and press her down into the pillows, and suddenly her body squirmed and her arms pushed against me and her legs shot up into the air. She struggled against my weight upon her upper body and she broke free and came at me with shrieks and nails and useless slaps which caused no pain but made it clear enough that I had made a mistake, and that my time in the palace and that tiny apartment was at an end.

'And when she was calm enough to speak and when my foolish apologies were at an end, it came out that Adelaïde had spoken the truth in almost all she said, but that it was Adelaïde and not Adrienne who had forced them to leave Chatelguyon, and that it was Adelaïde who had taken the position of *institutrice* at Blois. It was Adelaïde that had encouraged the approaches of Monsieur Darphin and, indeed, who had taken on a fever just so that Adrienne would go down to the school and be set upon by him, and that a doctor had told her parents that it was not so much that Adelaïde was *un peu trop légère* but that deep inside she was confused in some way about whose life was which and which mind—this was what the doctor said—belonged to which body, and that such things were not unknown, but not much understood.'

The bagsewer was silent for a time. His eyes roamed about the boy, who had never heard such things, who cast around, struggling to find pictures in his mind to fit the things he had been told, wondering how he was supposed to know what the story meant, wondering if the bagsewer told such stories to everyone he met upon the road, or only those who spoke of Cabel Singh. They watched for a time the pup, nosing about some rabbit burrows, and at length the bagsewer spoke again.

'After that I went for a long walk through the frozen streets, too troubled to go to work and knowing that I would lose my place, but turning over and over what it was that Adrienne said, wondering if that meant that it was perhaps Adelaïde in her own strange way who was in love with me after all, and even in one crazy moment whether being in love was something that I could now shift across from one person to the other, and what the hell did it matter when I was never quite sure which one was which at the very best of times.

'But in the end, when I went back to the Old Quarter, I found all my things in a pile in the yard and the sounds of a mighty row going on upstairs. Every now and then while I stood below and shivered in the courtyard, a window would open and another thing of mine would be flung down at me, to smash upon the cobblestones or take its place upon the pile. And finally, the girl who came to the window with another shoe or a book or bundle of papers to hurl down, paused there in silence, the soft light of the lamps behind her and her hair moving about her face in the wintry breeze, looking down at me as I stood with my arms clutched about me for warmth, in the light of the courtyard lamp. But I could not read the expression on her face, whether it was sorrow or anger, and I could not even tell, for that matter, whether it was Adelaïde or Adrienne who waited in silence at the open window and perhaps waiting, I have always wondered since, in case I might say something, in case I might have words that would nurse us all back to happiness. But the cold wind and the shocks of the day had taken all my poor stock of French away, and I just took a few small things—a very few, for I left most of my life to that point in the pile in the court-yard—and I left whichever girl it was with her hair blowing in the wind in the upstairs window, and walked off into the night.

'I walked down to the river that moved through the city, with all its solid walls of stone and all its tales and toil and teeming life. I sat through the freezing night by the banks of the river, wrapped up in all I had brought from the apartment. As the night grew colder I sat back to back with a stranger—another soldier I imagine it was—with the two of us silent and probably not even able to speak the same language, but sitting against each other, with the chill of the stone rising through our bodies, sitting back to back by the edge of the river and watching the rubbish move in brown circles in the water. When the light began to rise, the two of us simply rose in all the stiffness of the early morning and walked away from each other, never speaking and not wanting, when the light of the morning came, to look into one another's eyes, not wanting to know the worst that the other knew, and each of us perhaps wondering the next lonely night and the next if the other were back there on the stone bank of the river, watching all that we knew and all that we could ever dream move like night mists about the moving water and fade away in the morning light like the last of the smoke off burning stubble, and suddenly thinking only of home, and vacant roads and the lure of empty spaces.'

The boy came upon the water in the late part of the afternoon, as the bagsewer had said he would, when the shadows were longer and the worst of the heat had gone from the sun. The insects teemed about him as he made his way through the thin green grass and over the broken bark and down to the water's edge. He saw for the first time an expanse of water that was not bounded by low rims of mud and hard dry banks. He saw vast fields of water flowing from a place that lay beyond his sight to the east and rolled past him and on to pass a bend that lay miles to the north and to the west.

He saw for the first time the vast white gums with their deep floodbands and stretching limbs that lined the steep and dusty shores and stepped out into the waters of the river, and he saw their shrieking burden of hundreds of white sulphurcrested cockatoos. He saw for the first time the flow and ripple of a rolling current and the eddies and the whirlpools that moved around the snags that jutted from the waters and reached out from the shore, the milling waterbirds and the turning logs and branches that moved with the toiling muddy green of the waters, and the patches of thin grass and the damp mudpans that ran off here and there from the water's edge, the swamps and billabongs that stood off from the flow.

For hours there had been no relief in the low flaking scrub and loose red sandy soil beneath their feet. There was no sign as they moved along the tracks of a change in the greygreen bushland that lined the route, no smell in the hot afternoon air of water and no sign of restlessness on the part of the horse. The bagsewer had told him that the horse would know when the water was near, and that the dog would surely find it first. But they came upon the water unexpectedly as they moved over a bank of loose soil. They saw it spread out in front of them, winding off for miles into the far distance and through the stands of tall drinking gums and smaller waterlogged eucalypts that stood thin but straight from the water's edge. Here and there along the banks they saw the green and stooping forms of willows, the dense leaves drinking and wafting in the currents that ran and eddied about the water's edge.

The horse stepped down to the edge to drink and the dog quickly plunged in and swam around and around in expanding circles from the bank. The boy began to throw sticks out to the dog, as he had done in the tanks that they had passed in the wastelands, but here the dog was now struggling with something that was new, the movement of the water which drew him off to the north, with the dog swimming hard against the current and snapping at the stick, and swimming back to shore sometimes far downstream, barking and racing back with the stick to begin again. He sat for a time in the dust and the crumbling sheets of bark beneath the gums and watched, and listened to the swirling noises of the cockatoos as they settled and then resettled themselves in the trees above him, flying in shrieking and indignant arcs from branch to branch. He thought again of the bagsewer sitting on his banks of stone, so far away and long ago, his back against the back of a stranger, and high above them, the noises of a teeming city echoing through the night.

He tried for a time to measure the distances across the water, and looked about him at the waterbirds and listened for a time to the sounds of the other birds in the trees, the Major Mitchells and the galahs and the jays and the magpies, and he watched the wild ducks and the ibis and a stalking crane and the many bobbing divers feeding on the river. He watched, too, in a drowning fascination, the slow twists and eddies of the thick brown water as it rolled up from unknown places to the south and far past where he sat, and on and around the folds and sandbars to the north.

Later, when he had rested, he took his rifle and walked off through the trees, and within a short time he had shot some rabbits for himself and for the dog. He gutted the rabbits in the rough way that he had learned from Joe Spencer, tearing

a long split in the thin skin of the stomach with his thumb-
nail and spinning the carcass around and around and then
flicking it hard so that the gizzards flew out and through the
air. He kept two young rabbits for the pup and set the other
two aside for skinning and for cooking when the darkness
fell.

When he returned to the river, the horse was standing in
the cool of the water on a sandbar that led out in shallows
from the shore, and the dog was playing in the water around
it, hurtling out onto the sandbar and splashing back in again.
The boy plunged in with them, stripping his filthy clothing
off piece by piece, wringing out the dirty water and the
sweat and flinging them to the shore. The three of them
played in the shallows, the boy splashing the horse and the
horse rearing in play and the dog barking and splashing
backwards and forwards across the sandbar as the sun fell
and the shadows of the gums ran out across the water, and
the mosquitoes came in thick hordes to sing about them as
they played.

All the time as they played, the people from the tall trees
watched in silence, emerging one by one from behind the
trees as they splashed and barked and laughed, first shy
naked children set about with flies and looking as though
they wanted to join in, and then two women in faded frocks
and bare feet, and then a group of grown men who had been
summoned. These last of the bush people watched the three
strangers playing in their stretch of river, the pallid skinny
figure of the boy slapping at the insects and caking himself
with mud, the old pony rearing and protesting, yet never
moving away, and the crazed pup whose noise had set the
whole forest and the waterbirds and the vast unsettled

waves of cockatoos in a state of grave alarm. They stood silently in the shadow of the trees, in their baggy clothing and barefoot in the dust, and simply watched them play.

In time the boy saw them and hurtled from the water, running up the bank and grabbing at his sodden clothes and holding them about him, holding them over the mud and sand that clung to his bare body. They continued to watch him and his animals without a word, continued to watch him as he struggled to get dressed, hopping about from one foot to the other and getting his legs trapped within his wet and tangled trousers, simply watching the white and naked boy alone with an old horse and a dog, playing together in the heart of the last of the unbroken land, playing at the heart of the last of the wild country, in the long belts of uncleared and unwanted scrub and deep river forest that was all that was theirs when the last of the maps were laid out.

When he was dressed, they asked him to come with them. They led him along the river for a hour or so along a dusty path and back towards a camp on the bank, where there were another dozen or so resting under humpies of bark and hessian and kerosene tins and sheets of corrugated iron, or sitting in the dust before small open fires, all clad in castoff rags and living amid the wreckage, the cans and bags and clothing they had fished out of the river, living on what the river sent them. They welcomed him and his dog, who snarled and sniffed around and quarrelled for a time with the camp dogs. The boy then skinned his rabbits and spitted them over one of their fires, and shared them with whoever wished to take a piece.

They asked him in the way that others did about where he had come from, and the boy told them everything, about the girl who had gone missing and the Nowingi railway and about Cabel Singh. They told him that Cabel Singh always passed this way, and that sometimes he would stop and give them bangles and marbles for the children, though they had seen him pass just days before and this time he had not stopped. They had hoped for his advice on a problem that they had, about which Cabel had long known, and about which and perhaps later, the boy could help them. They talked to the boy of the country, and the last stretch of river forest that was theirs, and the boy began to talk as he had never spoken before, mixing his own stories with the stories that Cabel told, and the bush people nodded because they had heard these strange things before, and now knew that they must be true. And they told the boy of other travellers like himself, others who came through these parts which people now call Kulkyne, where there were no real roads and no talk of clearing, and how they had been told that they could perhaps stay there always, even though it was not the land the old people knew, living off what they could trap and fish along the river.

As it grew late they spoke to the boy of another visitor and they watched the boy carefully as they spoke of a white man who had been through, on his own like the boy, and who had also stayed. They spoke of a white man who was still among them, and said that the boy should sleep, and that in the morning they would take him to meet the other white man who slept out in the trees, and at a distance from the camp.

In the morning the boy awoke to the movement of the

camp and the smell of the fires, and the men came to him and took him then to show him what they had. They led him up from the riverbed, and out a hundred yards or so through the dry twigs and dust towards a platform of branches, raised beyond the height of a tall man above the ground. Beside the platform there was a log that had been rolled into place so that someone could climb up and inspect the platform. This they motioned to the boy that he should do, and they stood back respectfully as he clambered up the log to see what they kept amid the trees.

The white visitor was dead, as the boy knew he must be. The body lay spread out upon the branches, in red and white striped flannel pyjamas. The red dye was still bright, a strange flash of colour in the wilderness of grey and yellow and dusty green, though the white had taken on a yellow muddy colour, and the cloth was fraying and was torn in parts. The pyjama trousers were held in place by a wide cotton drawstring which was neatly knotted around the waist by a double bow. The jacket was neatly buttoned up with six white bone buttons, the last leaving the neck comfortably open, the wide lapels and collar of the pyjamas neatly lined with a red cording. And although the pyjamas were torn in places and had been troubled by the wind and rain and birds, they had been arranged neatly in place that morning and perhaps each morning by some caring hand.

The body was that of a man of around forty years of age, the boy guessed, though he may have been younger. The length of the summer and the drying by the sun and the ravages of birds upon the face had pocked and dried and tanned the skin and had drawn it back upon the bones so that the corpse, which had perhaps once been fat, was now shrunken back to bone and dried muscle. In its dried state, the body did not look distressed, and the only sign of anguish lay in the arms, which bent upwards at the elbows, each forearm then standing identically erect with the wrists turned inwards and the palms buckled and the fingers spread like claws and seeming to quiver in the hot morning air. The clawed fingers pointed back towards the abdomen, as though grasping at some indistinct idea, as though struggling at some rich conclusion there above the flowing water, amid the shading trees and floating bark. He noted that the hands were not hands like those of Joe or his father, were not the hands of someone who toiled in the heat for a living, and he noted that the pyjamas were not like the old singlets of Joe either, and that the man's nails were not long or broken and his hair, not long before his death, had been neatly cut.

There was no outline of a mind at all, no idea etched upon the birdpicked features, the pillaged sockets and the withdrawn mummy lips, nothing the boy could know of the man that this had been, but only the white grin of exposed teeth and wisps of redyellow hair that fell away in thick tufts from the temples. The boy could see no signs of violence upon the body other than those wrought by time and the sun and the hawks and the crows: no deep creases or sharp lines to break the finely drawn skin in its fragile hold upon the bones; and the boy thought then of some story Cabel had started to tell on his last visit, about a clown who lived and laughed and spent his whole life in a tree by the river, and he knew that Cabel had passed through this place.

He clambered down from the tree. There was a dry odour that was not at first strong but which then had crept upon him as he had looked over the corpse, an odour that was not like a decaying sheep or horse, but thick, older, drier and obscene.

He looked at the men in disbelief.

They told him that they had put the body there, to protect it from the dogs. That they had talked of burying it in secret, but were worried that one day someone would come looking for the man, and that the secret might be discovered, and that this would bring trouble to them all.

The boy spat, and hawked and spat again, but could not get rid of the dull raw odour that had somehow taken hold of his clothing, his thoughts, the inside of his mouth.

'But how long has it been here like this? Aren't you told anybody?'

The men looked at one another and shuffled about. They said that they did not know anyone that they could tell, and were worried that someone might think that perhaps they had pushed him in.

They told him how they had found the corpse. One after-noon, a few months before, a couple of them were fishing in the river when they saw the body coming down, washed along by the current. It was some time before they realised what it was, with the earthy waters of the river disguising it, and there was just a quick rolling flash of red now and then to show that this was something more than the usual snags and cruising logs and camp wreckage that flowed along the banks. They ignored it for a time, but finally it was caught up on a snag a little further down the river, and then one of the children swam out and saw the clawed hands and the barred red and white of the pyjamas. They had all talked about what they should do for a time, and in the morning, because it was still there, the men went out and dragged it in. It didn't look too bad at that point, they told the boy, swollen and bloated white but still with eyes and all, as though it had just gone into the river a day or two before.

There had been an argument about what to do with the body, which had lasted for a day or two, with some wanting to take it into town and others just wanting to set it on its way down the river again. Finally, they decided to set it up in the trees, away from the dogs and the foxes, and simply wait. There were those among them who did not want to stay, because of the body in the tree. But most felt that they had to stay, because if they went and someone came to claim the ground or came to fish, they would soon find the body because of the red pyjamas and the smells which sprang up in the hot winds that filtered through the gums, and then they would think that they had left simply because of some guilt about the body, and someone would come after them. So they had stayed on, some wanting to go but most feeling that they now needed to stay. They simply waited, which was something which to that time they had never done, stayed waiting with the body, trying to keep the birds away and wondering what was to become of them, with the food that they could catch along that stretch of river now shrinking by the day and the proper time to be gone long past. They were haunted for the first month or so by the stinks that rolled in off the body on the afternoon breezes, and now they waited each day for punishment of some kind to come down upon them, on the river which had provided all they needed and now cursed them in this way.

The oldest among them then asked the boy what he thought they could do, and the boy finally told them that he would take the white visitor from them and give it to someone in a town, and that he would make sure that he was the last person seen with the body, and that he would just tell whoever asked him that he had found it lying by the river, so that they could pack up their camp and move further along the forest in their usual way. The men spoke among themselves for a time in a language that the boy did not understand, and then came back to him and told him that they agreed that he should take the body to the nearest town, which was Annuello, far to the south of the river, and that they would help him to arrange things so that it would not slow him down.

They took the body down from the trees, and they pulled down the platform too, and bound it together more strongly with fencing wire so that it formed a kind of sled, and they bound a long thin sapling to each side of it in the form of shafts. They dragged it over to the horse, which had been broken to a cart and which stood about patiently while they adjusted a rope wrapped in a sugarbag around its neck as a collar. Then they said goodbye to the boy and his animals as he set off back down along the river towards the southeast and Wemen, where he would meet the track, they told him, that would take him down to Annuello and Manangatang.

They waved goodbye to him and the children followed him for a time until they slipped away without a word and disappeared among the trees. The three of them trudged on through the river forest and along the soft soil that ran down to the water, in the hope of finding their way back to the track that they had left, dragging behind them their sled with its mute and bouncing load in its red pyjamas, and with its stinks now rolling over them in a light breeze that had sprung up behind and its upraised hands still clawing at the sky.

When they were two or three miles down the river, and long after the children had faded into the scrub, the boy untied the sled and dragged it further out into the scrub and far away from the water's edge, as he had known that he would do. He dragged it far from the water's edge because the current was running to the north and back towards the direction from which he had come, and would take the body with it and back up to the camp. He piled the soft earth and then dead logs and heavy branches upon it in a place where he felt no-one would ever find it, where it would be safe from wild dogs.

When he had finished his work, he sat upon the mound he had created and tried to think the sorts of thoughts that he knew he ought when someone was being buried. Nothing came to him, and he looked out into the scrub and back towards the river, and even to the dog and the horse for some kind of guidance. He wondered for a time what his father or his mother might have said at such a time, or what the priest might have said if he had been there, and whether it was some kind of sin to say nothing, and to leave the man in pyjamas hidden out in the bush without a word to anyone, because it felt like the sort of thing that might well be a sin. It felt like a sin, too, not to say some holy word over the body, and the boy wondered if even a holy word could have any kind of meaning when it was spoken to no-one, just out into the trees or only to the horse and to the pup, and that if it was the thought that mattered, then he could say to anyone who happened to ask that he felt genuinely sorry for the man in the pyjamas, and for his family, and that he had said so to himself, and that God knew what he was thinking anyway. He wondered if the words needed to be said at the time or soon after when someone died, and that this man had now been dead so long that there was only a husk left behind, of no more moment than a shed snakeskin or the dried skin of a sheep, and that the fate of his soul had long been decided. And he wondered, too, for a moment whether the word of someone who was breaking a promise at that very moment, breaking a promise in carrying out that burial and even in speaking that very word over the dead, would not lay a further curse upon the man in red pyjamas, and add to the restless burden of his death.

At Wemen he left the slow green reaches of the river and they rode off to the south, out of the shade of the river forest and the tall white gums and back into the low scrubland and out onto a gravel road that led towards the south. After a time the road wound beyond the scrubland and out into the cleared country, out into tracks that ran between bare ploughed acres and open yellow wheatstubble, with the sun blazing off the stripped fields on either side and the earth about them lifting in the hot and wandering winds that blew up as they left the fringe of the last of the scrublands, and they moved out onto the unfeatured flatland that led off to the south.

By the late part of the morning they had moved beyond the fringe of scrubland and into a new kind of desert with trim netting fences and yellow toppled stubble and iron sheds that shone in the sun from many miles away. They crossed the bare flats of cleared and loose and shifting soil where even the spaces that lay to the sides of the tracks had been cleared and burned, the country shaved and broken and submitted to the square, a map of neat white gravel roads and thin and filleted lines of timber and sometimes laden trucks that rolled up from the distance at a mighty sliding speed and sprayed them with flying sand and gravel as they passed.

They moved beneath the bowing wire that ran from post to post along the tops of the fences, the telephone wire that linked the north to the south and which quivered and sang in the heat above them as they passed the lignum flats of Wemen channel and onto the main road. The kids from over at Tempe had once told him that if you put your ear to the wire you could hear the voices moving along it. He edged the horse over to the wire and stood upon its back, and he heard along the wire only the sounds of distant singing, soft pining lamentation that ran across the country and rode up and down with the swaying of the wire to the movement of the wind.

They felt again the bushflies come up with the heat of the day and the earth and the insects begin to sing again in the heat which rose up in white sheets at them from the glowing of the gravel, on the road that ran down through Annuello and Manangatang and on through Chinkapook and Chillingollah and Waitchie to the south. The boy moved the horse off the gravel and onto the soft earth of the sidetrack which wound through the shreds of timber that ran by the side of the road, so that its feet would not be injured by the stones.

It was in the late part of the morning that they came across a clump of uncleared timber that lay about a schoolhouse, with a group of children, no more than eight or nine of them, running out into the yard. The schoolhouse was a small wooden box of a building with a low verandah, which had been placed amid a clump of pepper trees to try to give it a little protection from the sun. A girls' and boys' outhouse stood at the far end of a yard of worn red soil and straggling trees, and there was, to one side, a corrugated iron shelter shed beneath a pepper tree. A solitary telephone wire, fragile and stooping in the heat, ran to the schoolhouse from the road. By the side of the school there stood a rainwater tank, and the boy opened the school gate and led his horse over towards the tank, the children running to gather about him as he walked, laughing at the split and curling hooves of the horse and the sole of one of the boy's boots which had worked loose along the roads and flapped at them as he walked.

She emerged from the schoolhouse, a young woman with blonde hair, with round spectacles and a worried look in her blue eyes, eyes that were a little clouded by the spectacles, that looked at him and then out at the open road. The boy saw a large bicycle leaning against the school tankstand, and decided that it must be hers. She was not too much older, it seemed to him, than Eileen was, and she sheltered her eyes with her hand as she looked at him leading the squad of curious children over towards the tank, squinting as though trying to see his face underneath his enormous hat, her other hand set firmly on her hip.

He raised his army slouch to her, so that they could see each other.

'Miss.'

'What are you doing out on the roads? In a heat like this?'

'Need a bit of water. I got water for me. I need water for the horse.'

She judged his age, and her voice took on authority.

'Shouldn't you be at school?'

'Too old for school. I'm older'n I look.'

'Well, you can take what you can carry. Make sure the tap doesn't stay dripping.'

Word had already passed in whispers among the children that he stank something awful, and they began to screw up their faces and hold their noses and some of them giggled, and the teacher told them to be quiet. The boy could still taste in his mouth the odours of the corpse, and knew it must be this that they could smell.

'It's just the blinky dog, Miss,' he explained to the young woman on the verandah.

'He went for a roll in a dead sheep. Always does it. Can't stop him when he gets goin'. Stinks like a polecat.'

He saw her nostrils narrow with the reek of it, and she made a gesture as though to wave away a fly.

'Where have you come from?'

'Down south. Just took a mob of sheep up to Hattah, an' now I'm goin' home.'

'Well, you just shouldn't be out on the roads in this heat. No-one should. And mind you don't leave that tap running.'

And she turned and spread her arms out to shepherd the children back into the school, as though protecting them from the deathliness that clung about this young and filthy traveller.

The children went in, and she stood at the door for a time, watching him as he filled his waterbags and prepared to set off back to the gate and out towards the road. He wondered if she were watching him to see that he did not steal anything, though there was nothing to take but her own bicycle, and what would he do with that? Or did she watch him out of some concern that he was so young and out upon the roads, and that the filth and the bad smell that hung about him meant that he needed to be looked after still, or that perhaps she had even heard some tale about a boy like him, out on his own and wandering upon the roads. He looked again at the flimsy telephone wire that ran through the low trees and over to the schoolhouse.

He set off again along the road, now empty in the middle heat of the day, and he watched the high wire that ran above the fence beside them, thinking now of all the voices that ran upon the wire, the voices on the wire now moving with him from place to place, with news perhaps of a boy upon an ancient horse, and of the Debt Adjuster still smoking by his car out in the desert, voices that might charge him with leaving against his word the body by the river, the voices singing up and down as the wires waved in the breeze, even telling tales perhaps of Eileen, and what had happened to Eileen. He looked up at the wires and wondered if the teacher's voice was now sounding along those wires, telephoning to the towns ahead about a boy and a bad smell and a dog and a foundering horse, and wondering too if Eileen's voice had run along the wire, if Eileen had already telephoned the Ridge to say, Yes, I am well and gone off upon the roads with Cabel Singh. I am not hurt and the blood was only the blood of my release, the blood of my release as I stripped the dress from my body so that I might be born again along the roads with my friend Cabel Singh.

She called to him to help, to help her clear the rubbish from the top. He watched her as she splashed into the tank and vanished from his view, and finally he stripped off his shirt and boots and as an afterthought his hat, but did not remove his trousers. He climbed the ladder after her. The tank was

full of water from the bore, clear enough below but with a
greenish scum clotted with leaves and grass on the surface
which she had already begun to clear, clinging to the side of
the tank with one hand and skimming the surface with the
other, lifting handfuls of the scum and tipping it over the
side. The boy plunged in beside her and the two of them
busied themselves for a time in pushing the dirt and blown
leaves and feathers and the green slime over the rim.

They moved back for a time into the shade of the clump of
pines, Eileen refusing to put on her clothes, but lying in the
dirt instead and drawing the dust and pine needles over her
body and letting the dirt dry in thick cakes within her hair.
She rolled in the dirt like a horse taking a dust bath, writhing
naked in the dust and shrieking with the fun of it, becoming
filthier than the boy had ever seen a human being before,
caking herself all over with the mud that lay about the overflow, decorating her hair in grand and careful style with the
long strands of green weed that drooped from the sides of
the tank.

He sat with her with his shirt off and his white skin
exposed sore and gleaming and his trousers rolled up as far
as they would roll, wishing that he too could take a further
step and throw off the rest of his clothes and play with her
in the dirt, wondering why his sex need be so violent and
absurd against the smooth and easy forms of the girl, whose
body seemed so like the circle of the sun and the movements
of the track and the soft leeward arc of the sand drifts; so he
kept his nakedness hidden but was grateful still to know she
knew of his own excitation. He joined in the fun as far as he
dared, letting her cover his body with the thick black mud
and trace within it circles with her fingers, letting her paint

his face and his chest and stomach, letting her cake the mud upon his head and in his hair in a high pinnacle decorated with bits of stick, tracing warpaint over him in great bands of mud, the two of them shrieking and running about in circles like the savages they had seen at the pictures in Patchewollock, shrieking at the distant drifts and hallooing back in challenge to the Ridge.

He rested upon the jagged concrete edge while she thrashed about awkwardly in the water, kicking herself from one side of the tank to the other, and soon she almost drowned herself because the water was deep and she could not swim, almost drowned herself when once she let go of the rim and failed to kick herself across to the other side and began to sink and thrash and swallow water just an arm's reach from the rim. He scuttled around the edge, risking a cut from the rust of the iron lining, and reached out his hand and grabbed her by the hair as she plunged and choked and sank. She managed to grab his hand and came up gasping with her hair caked in slime from the far edge of the tank. He hauled her back to the edge, and she pulled herself up on the rim, gasping and choking, all ungracious coughing and spitting out of water and her legs up and over the edge and the boy helping her where he could and she still spitting water and green slime and laughing and coughing at the same time.

She sat on the edge alongside him and steadied herself against him, twisting and combing the water and filth from her hair, combing its length with her fingers and sitting bare and white beside him, and her skin again catching the white heat of the sun and all the waving yellow light of Wirrengren Plain, her skin cool and taut against him when she rose up from the water, cool and beaded in water and strings of green, her nipples erect and her breasts pressing against his skin as she twisted her hair in a long dank plait. She wiped the water from her shoulders and her breasts and joked with him, but not in mockery as he might have dreaded when she saw the movement in his baggy trousers and his erection pushing contrary to all his wishes against the wetness of his heavy trousers. She knew that his body seethed, but was not now teasing or taunting, but simply letting the laughter run with the freedom of it, with the flow of the water and the tracery of green slime, with being naked out there on the impossible edge of the wilderness with no-one but the admiring and excited boy raised against the empty sky, their bodies both moving with a motion of their own to the nakedness and the water and the heat and the gleaming of the sun.

They perched on the edge of the tank above the vast dry plain with its mournful little clumps of pine and its hot and blasted grass, with the Ridge far off and over the high drifts to the south and Cabel Singh gone off and all his dust faded from the air and now far out of sight. They sat upon the rim and raised their bodies to the sun, and he felt within him a movement from the darkness of silence and shame and embarrassment, a release from the cage of his thin arms and hollow chest and baggy betraying trousers, not thinking now of the foolishness of his body in the place where Joe's should be, not measuring now his thin arms and bony shoulders against the deep moving thickness of Joe Spencer; and soon he began to shout and laugh like Eileen, hearing his own laughter ring out across Wirrengren Plain as loud, and for the first time, as the laughter of Eileen.

Then they began a game, of moving around and around

inside the tank, pulling themselves hand over hand around the rim, and faster so that soon they became giddy with the spinning, with the water splashing about them and flowing over the edge and taking the last of the green scum with it. And as they moved, faster and faster, it was the whole Wirrengren Plain and the sky above them that began to reel and spin, the sun itself now darting in bright starts and wheeling circles about the sky, their bare and turning bodies the centre of a moving world, with the open sand drifts to the north and the rim of Murray pines that lined the ridges to the east and all the dark forests to the west and the flat and waving grasslands shifting places with each other, the faded colours of the drifts and the grasses of the plain and the grey soil of the distant pine country moving into one another, below a sun that had lost all grace and stately rhythm and bowed and yawed to their wild motion, wheeling crazily in absurd starts and circles for them as it rocked about the sky, the two of them shrieking with the joy of this power they had discovered from the depths of Windmill Tank, where they had set the whole resisting world upon their fingers and run it off its base, where all that they knew and all familiar shape and pace and outline had wound out into cir-cles and simply spun away.

He entered the town in the depth of the night, the boy leading the horse through the furrowed track of clay and gravel that served as a main street, which ran between the half dozen shops and sheds that made up the centre of town, and the wheat and oatstacks and iron sheds over by the railway line that ran up from the south. The town lay at the edge of a wide belt of uncleared timber and here and there in the scrub that lay to the west of the main street, the boy could see the light of the moon shining upon further iron roofs, and the tanks of further houses scattered through the scrub. The town slept in darkness as they moved along the street, the only sounds the yelping of dogs disturbed by their movement, and the barking of the pup in return.

They passed in silence the weatherboard shops with their high painted and peeling facades announcing the sale of drapery and wire and pollard and chaff, and he thought for a time that he might lead the animals through the town and out the other side, and then steal back to break into one of the stores and take whatever it was that they needed, for it was more than a day since they had eaten. But he saw that there were people living at the back of each of the stores, that each store had its curtained windows and garden to the rear.

He searched the buildings for signs of a light and of someone stirring in the night, for his waterbags were empty and his animals were restless. He felt a weakness in his knees and an aching in his stomach, and he knew he must not wait until the morning light before finding something for them. He led them along the street and past the houses and the silent shops, and over into the station yard, between clumps of giant cactus and through patches of uncleared timber, and they came to the shelter of the oatstacks. The boy took the blanket from the horse and laid it out for the night, letting the horse graze on a long loose lead around the edges of the stacks, upon the grain that had fallen there and upon the tufts of faded grass and raw saltbush that poked up amid the trees. He unrolled from its newspaper the stinking bone that a woman on a farm south of Manangatang had given him, and gave it to the dog. As it settled down to gnaw at the bone he was left to sit on his blanket and think, and to know the emptiness of his belly and the dryness of his throat.

He climbed to the top of the stack, which on the side that was near to the town had been built up in easy steps, and he looked out over the dim shapes of the town. He climbed further, running up further stairways left by the stackers, until he reached the top and looked out over the shacks and sheds and houses that fell back from the main street and into the belt of timber that lay beyond the main street. He recalled a tale that Cabel had told them, about a town that went to sleep and never awoke. You could pass through it daytime or night and find everyone asleep, whether in the street or in their beds, and you could pass through it a year later and find that it was the same, with the cobwebs building upon the slumbering bodies in their chairs and in their beds and even out on their verandahs, rocking gently in the shade. If you went into any one of those houses, where everyone slept their lives away, the sleep would come upon you too.

Standing high above the town, he cupped his hands together and made low and husky mopoke calls, sounds that Joe Spencer had once taught him how to make, sounds that sounded so like a real mopoke that he had helped Joe once to coax an owl up to the house from miles away in the depth of the scrub. Somewhere in the distance, among the darkness of the belt of low timber, a dog howled in response to the call, and then settled again.

Nearer to where he stood, he saw a faint sign of light from the window of a house, a large house which he had not been able to see from the level ground. He sat and watched, and listened in the darkness, and soon his ear caught faint strains of music coming from the house. He climbed down the stack again, and tethered the horse and the pup, and crept over to the town, over towards where the light shone in the window. He crept towards the house and found that he was hearing the sound of a gramophone, of the same faint music playing, and winding down and being wound up and then playing again.

The house with the light was a banker's house, part bank and part living space, larger and in better order than most of those around it. The bank itself had a square wooden facade and bold lettering, and was clad in a form of timberwork that might at first be taken for solid stone, painted in a light cream shade which gleamed as the moonlight fell upon it. The window with the light was in the house behind the bank, facing out towards the scrub, and the boy crept to the rear of the house, over a low picket fence and through a clutter of rich vegetation, an old glory vine that spilled over a creaking trellis and a vast overspill of purple flowered Morning Glory, rich and funereal in the night. Through this he felt his way, expecting at each moment to be disturbed by a rage of barking and the raising of lights within the house. Instead, the house was silent apart from the low strains of music and the sounds of crickets and the pup yelping over at the stacks, and he moved around the house and past the rickety mixture of leantos and sleepouts that ran along the back.

He crept up to the window and looked inside. The window looked into a living room, a large room lit only by the light of a kerosene lamp turned low, a room with heavy varnished furniture and large etched glass mirrors on either side that caught the yellow flame of the lamp in the half darkness and reflected the moving form of a woman who danced alone in the room, who turned and swayed to the music which played upon a large gramophone that stood in one of the darkened corners of the room, playing a popular song that the boy had not heard before, *When I pretend I'm gay*, over and over the same words, *When I hold back a tear*, dancing until the voice dragged and yawned out into the night, *I'm only painting the clouds with sunshine,* and stopped and then began again.

She danced slowly to herself, holding her arms about her in a close caress but with one hand free, one hand held up closer to her face with the palm facing upwards and the fingers drooping back, her hand holding a cigarette which she moved loosely in the air as she swayed in time to the music, the smoke hanging in thin threads in the air and tracing the outline of her movements long after the movement passed. The boy watched as she danced, her face always away from him and looking towards the gramophone as she moved her hips slowly to the music, dancing while scarcely moving her feet, dancing to the music as it played, stooping to replace the arm of the gramophone at the beginning, and dancing again until the gramophone ran down.

She wore a long nightdress of a silky fabric, cut to leave her back and shoulders bare and, as she moved, the nightdress caught like a mirror the light of the lamp and the reflections of the light of the lamp as well, and the boy watched the lamplight and its reflection soften and vanish in the folds of the garment and upon the contours of her breast and shoulders, and in the faint light he could hardly see her face at all even when she turned back from the gramophone, for she had long hair which, like Eileen sometimes, she had tied in a long loose plait which moved about her shoulders and caressed her naked back as she moved about the room, long hair which fell across her face as she stooped to the gramophone, or to light another cigarette. Sometimes she would turn in his direction, to blow smoke at the ceiling or towards the open window, and then she would wrap her arms about herself again as she moved with the slow rhythms of the music, embracing herself or so it seemed to the boy against the vacant lengths of the night and the silence of the town, and he felt that she would move in this listless and slow rhythmic way even if she knew that he was there, and that he must not breach the deep absorption of her dance. He watched her dance through many playings of the same record as it wound down time and time again, the singer's lilting tenor dragging low and mournful in the night until she lifted the arm and set it moving once again.

The rear door was a warped and flyscreened frame which creaked loudly as he touched it, and clamoured with each inch he drew it back. He held it open with a stump of wood and crept inside. The first room was a cluttered hallway with boots, coats and hooks and gardening tools. Beyond this and to the left was the kitchen, with tall builtin cupboards and a fitted sink of a kind he had once seen in a magazine, and painted in a pale greenish hue that drew the moonlight in. At the far end of the room was a doorway leading out into a further passage and the room where he saw her dance. He fossicked in the darkness of the cupboards and the meatsafe and came at length upon a halfcarved leg of lamb, his fingers slipping in the cold and aromatic fat, and he bundled it up in his coat, together with a loaf of bread that was sitting on the sink, and then turned for the door.

But she had heard him, and she struck a match. She entered the kitchen without a sound and struck a match and put it to the wick of a large Colman lamp that hung above a table to the side. She slipped across the room and barred his way to the door, the boy scuttling awkwardly to the table, trying to hide himself below the table as the light rose in the room.

'Come out. This is foolish. Come on out and speak to me.'

And the boy stood up awkwardly, still holding half exposed the leg of lamb.

'Take off your hat, now that you are inside. We take our hats off inside. Let me look at you at least.'

He did as he was told. The woman looked him over. She gave no sign of anger or of fear at the intrusion. Then she smiled and drew a cigarette from a packet that was resting near the stove. She lit it with a shake of her head and a blowing of the smoke about him, and then she smiled again.

'You do not need to steal, you know. If you are hungry, you only need to ask.'

She was, he saw, some years older than Eileen but not as old as his mother. Even in the half light he could see that she had protected herself far more from the sun than his mother had done, or that Eileen would ever do, and that her hands were not worn in the way that his mother's or even as Eileen's hands were worn. She wore two rings upon her left hand, and the rings flashed in the glow of the Colman. He saw that she had large green eyes and a pretty face, though her face was pale and her eyes swam with light, as though she had been weeping. Her long brown plait licked about her shoulders as she tossed her head and blew the smoke about her, and her eyes seemed full of a kind of laughter in seeing him shrinking away with his handful of meat, damp and slippery in his hand.

She still wore only the nightdress, and the boy looked away awkwardly, took off his hat and looked about him and anywhere but at the woman, because of her undress.

'I'm sorry.'

He pushed the leg of lamb awkwardly onto the table.

'I'm not a thief. I'm travelling. With my horse. Everything is closed. I had to eat.'

The woman threw her head back and clasped her arms about her. She blew the smoke into the air, and laughed.

'And so you chose this house. The bank.'

Her voice had an odd metallic ring to it, and it rang in his ears for a second beyond each time she spoke. She spoke always more loudly than she needed to, as though she were speaking to some further listener, deep in the house, who was listening to them both.

'Well,' she said, placing the cigarette on a plate beside her, 'then you must eat. And then we can talk about what it is that I must do with you.'

She took the boy down to the table in the largest room, with the gramophone still playing. He saw now that she was the only person in the house, and she lowered the blinds and drew the curtains over so that they would not be seen. She prepared food—slabs of lamb cut from the stolen bone, and some tomatoes and bread and butter. The boy sat and ate, hungrily despite being trapped in this way, and the woman sat across the table from him and blew her smoke in slow coils which wound about him and her eyes laughed and played with him as he tore clumsily at the meat and bread.

'How long is it,' she asked when finally he looked up from his plate, 'since you have washed?'

'Don't need to wash,' he replied. 'There's just me an' the horse an' the pup. I don't see many people. On the road.'

He told her that he had left home, that his parents were dead, and that he was carrying with him everything that he owned, and that he was making his way towards the south where an uncle of his mother's had just left him a huge farm in his will, with a truck and horses and even a tractor. She told him that he seemed a little young to be moving around the country on his own, and he said that this was what happened to people when all their folks were dead. She spoke then of something that she had heard the day before in Manangatang, of a boy about his age wandering around the country and of food stolen and telephone wires cut, and the boy told her that everywhere he had been people had told him that the times were about as bad as they had ever been, and that he had seen many odd things on his way down to the south and it did not surprise him that there should be other wanderers loose upon the roads.

After he had finished eating, the woman said that she would talk to him, but that first he must wash. She led him to a room with a large white bath and running water, and drew the blinds and insisted that he get into the bath and clean himself, because he smelt more like a horse or a dog than a human being, and that if he did not wash soon he would be sick and be covered in sores, and he could not afford to become sick while he was travelling upon the road on his own. She added with more laughter in her eyes that he should not arrive at his uncle's house in the south in such a condition, and that boys who were about to be rich should also be clean. While he was bathing she brought him soft towels and a clean shirt and despite his protests took away his clothes and soaked and washed them, and strung them out to dry across the vines at the back of the house. When he was dry and sitting on the sofa swathed in towels, she came back and again despite all protests knelt beside him. She took his hair in her hands and combed it and cut it, so that, she told him, he might look like a young man again. As she did so it seemed to the boy that she caressed his face and his neck and shoulders, and he wondered as she moved about him, kneeling on the sofa but leaning over him as she moved about him to cut his hair, running her hands across his neck and shoulders as she did so, tracing the shape of his face with long caressing fingers, and letting him feel her body move upon him, whether she treated him as a child younger than he was, or as a man much older.

When the boy was dry, she brought him oversized pyjamas—faded red and white pyjamas—that had been, she said, her husband's, his second best pair, and she left while he dressed, and then returned to sit on the sofa beside him, her feet drawn up beneath her, sitting back a little from him so that she could smoke her cigarettes, but idly caressing his hair and face with her free hand as she spoke. She lowered the light of the lamp, and they sat at the fading edge of a circle of light in the same room where she had danced, and she began to chant a kind of story, not to the boy who sat alongside her but to the town and the silence and the night, speaking in a softer voice through the haze of intruding drowsiness and the coiling of her smoke. The boy felt about him the sweet odour of stale perfume and tobacco and perspiration from her body, her breasts and bare shoulders smelling, he thought, like the soft smell of bread soaked in warm milk. She told him then a little of herself, of a husband that had gone away from her some months ago, a husband that had been the banker, who had gone north on business for some days but had never come back again, a husband of whom there was no trace since and only an empty car parked by a river, and no letter, nothing to let anyone know of what had happened, or why he had gone off.

She told him of the husband who had gone, the husband much older than she, a man back from the war who moved always in a grave silence, who had been pleasing to her parents, that he and his mother would come to tea and he would sit with his saucer upon his knee and stare at her with his mouth hanging always slightly open and no word on his lips, and how her mother would soon begin to chatter like a crazed magpie to fill the silences and to cloud the scowls and lookings up and down of his mother. Somewhere in all this she found herself a married woman, alone with him and in a bed in a strange hotel miles from home, listening to the rain upon the iron roof and coming to know one another's bodies in the same time that they came to the knowledge that they would not know each other's minds, each discovering at last in those fumbling moments in the darkness what loneliness was, and thankful for the mercy of a beating rain. The boy sat without speaking, thinking sometimes of his animals but watching mostly the woman who spoke and blew her smoke about her, her eyes still shining amid the circling of the smoke.

She told of how they came to live in this barren place close to the saltlakes, and how he had begun to spend his time upon the lakes, and always on his own, though she did go with him once with a picnic packed, and they had sat amid the dry grass and thistles, with rocks to hold down the corners of the tablecloth that she spread upon the sand. She told of how they had sat in silence, she wishing that he would be gone so that she could enjoy that vast and whitened desolation as a real silence, and not just as a blankness, as some lack or hole that opened in the speech of the other.

Sometimes he would stay out at night, drawn back out to the saltlakes, and he would come back in the morning, sometimes after days away, covered in blown salt with his eyes salty red and his clothing filthy and his boots blackened with the thick dark mud that lies below the crust. He would tell her that he had roamed across the salt, backwards and forwards across those vast expanses in the moonlight, measuring with each step its length and breadth, plagued into sleeplessness by such vacancy, and planning always, in mingled rage and fascination, some mad assault upon its emptiness.

She told the boy that the only companion of his soul was a solicitor who would come over from Ouyen or perhaps from Wycheproof, and how sometimes they would sit under the vines and talk for hours into the night, and how they would drink beer and speak of things of which she never heard men speak, strange dreaming things of cities floating on the lake, and of inland seas, and some plan about a vast channel that would bring water across from the river, all the way through the dry country to flood the lake, so that the land around it would become green and fertile and grow strong crops every year. These talks would go on into the night, and sometimes in the morning she would find her husband had not gone to bed at all but had sat up right through the night, his lips dry and his voice hoarse and his eyes glowing, with the solicitor gone off at some point in the night and her husband left burning under the vines. By the end of the day the gleam would have passed and his eyes would no longer be shining and he would come back into the house grumpy and exhausted and sometimes even violent, looking at her as if she had come between him and his dreams, and sometimes then he would seize her and twist her hair about his arm and wrist, and love her with a pain and violence, and then collapse into a deep but troubled sleep.

She told the boy then that he might stay with her until her husband returned, as he must soon return, but he told her that he must make his way down to the south because those who looked after his uncle's property might think that he was dead and give the property to someone else, and that he had other relations there who would look out for him. He told her finally that he was looking for a man and that when he found that man and found out what he wanted to know, he might come back and see if she still wanted work. And finally, when she pressed him further, and put her hand upon his and asked him why he was really travelling—a boy so young, she whispered, and so hungry and filthier than she had ever known a boy could be, out upon the tracks all on his own, and half the country, to her certain knowledge, out and looking for him—it was then that he told her about Eileen, and Cabel Singh.

He felt the warmth of her hand on his, and it was the first time he had been touched since Eileen had painted his body in mud at Windmill Tank. He felt the touch of her hand and her laughing but ever kinder eyes drawing words from him, words that did not spring from thoughts he ever had, thoughts which came in feelings through the sight of her pale skin shining in the glow of the lamp and the fall of the satin that traced the slow curve of her breasts and her long loose plait falling in dark rhythm about her shoulders as she shook her head and blew the smoke away from her face. He began to speak as he had not spoken before, not even to Eileen at Windmill Tank, feeling as he spoke things that were not even thoughts taking the form of words and listening to his own mind move amid the smoke, feeling the tears moving in his eyes, which were perhaps the result of the smoke that blew about him, the stinging aromatic comfort that wafted through the air. He found that he wanted to talk to this woman as she placed her hand on his, to tell her that he was looking for Eileen and Cabel Singh upon the roads and that he would spend his life wandering the roads looking for Eileen and Cabel Singh if he needed to, because the more he travelled the more he understood but the more he seemed to need to know, and only Cabel Singh could help him to understand, only Cabel Singh could help him now to say what it was that he now needed to say, the magnificent obscure and incommunicable thing that rose out of the fire-light and ran him across the plains. He said that he would rather die out on the roads than go back to the place he had come from without the life that he would come to share with Eileen and Cabel Singh.

He found he wanted to tell her about the Debt Adjuster in the car on Raak Plain and the family in the storm and the woman watching the fires, and especially the body in the tree and the bloody dress in the stable, for these were the things that had broken all he knew into pieces and it was for this that he now needed Cabel Singh. He told her in tears that came from nothing but perhaps the stinging smoke and broke upon his eyes and made unreal the room and the woman who lay beside him, swathed in the thick brown hair that hung about her face. He told her of his moving through the deserts and along the creeks, even a little of Windmill Tank and what had happened there. It seemed that the smoke brought tears also to the eyes of the woman as she listened, and she kept her hand upon his hand as though she knew that he would stop if she no longer touched him, as the words seemed to move from body to body, not hanging in the air as most words do and waiting for the meanings to be given to them, but running from and living in that warmth.

They ran through the night and down along the thin cleared path that was the Chillingollah road, the boy wearing only his damp and flapping shirt, the rest of his clothing tied wet on the back of the horse, the animals restless and wide eyed at being woken in the depth of the night and quickly watered and drawn out upon the roads again, and the boy clutching still the leg of lamb between slipping fingers, running hard against the latter wisps of night.

They ran through the last of the night and down along the narrow track that led off to the south, the boy clinging to the horse's halter and the horse snorting alongside and breaking wind as they broke through the whips of straying mallee and through the drifts of sand. They ran through the last of the night with the light of the moon still flickering through the trees, and the boy clutched about him and in his bags all the food that he had managed to take as he crept from the house, thinking again as he ran of the young woman asleep on the sofa beside him, of how he had taken from her sleeping fingers the last of her cigarettes as it burned towards her skin, of how he placed his hands on her shoulders and eased her back upon the sofa, of how she woke for just a moment with a drowsy smile. He had lowered the lamp yet further and knelt beside her for a time as she slept upon the sofa in the low pool of yellow light, holding her hand still as she lay and not wanting to let go of the warmth that had drawn from him the words and the feelings and the tears, not wanting to leave, but knowing that what he knew, the wisdom given him upon the roads, rode too harshly across her dreams. In a sudden start he saw that he must now be out on the roads again, before the wanting and the long deep sleep grew too far upon him.

Down towards the south along the Chillingollah road they ran, and as the light grew from the east, down into a country that he already knew from the tales of Cabel Singh who told him of the white lake to the west which was Lake Wahpool, which shone always like scattered mercury in the midday sun and stretched from Old Tyrrell Downs Station to the south. He told him of a smaller saltpan to the east that was Timboram, of how the dry creeks that led out from Timboram would take you south and down a line of timber and lignum channels that you could follow for many miles as it wound down to the south. You could travel along it with the last of the birds and the animals that still roamed down from the north, and you could pass by town after town and farm after farm, and yet never be seen by another living soul. The creek that ran south out of Timboram was a river of life that ran through the heart of the dead land, a river of tall box timber and dense scrub and soft mudpans and teeming life that no man would ever have need to own and so no man would ever feel the need to destroy, and you could travel along it through the cleared and blighted country for many miles until you came, in the end, to the southern country where it stood green almost all year around, with rivers that never went dry.

He stopped for a moment when they were far from the town and drew on his wet and heavy trousers and his boots. Then they began again to run, the wetness chafing sorely at his legs, the boy knowing of his cruelty in listening and not telling of what he knew, of his leaving her in the night with all her wounds wide open, knowing only that her dancing in the night grew from her doubt and dreams, that her dancing in the night was the only light that burned in that town where all were sleeping, and that if he destroyed the doubt, then the dance would end; and he knew now why it was that Cabel's stories never ended. He saw her again, spread in peace upon the sofa with one hand dangling with the cigarette, and the other curved upon her breast in the silky yellow light of the Colman. He now knew why it was that Cabel never entered houses, because they were too fragile for the knowledge that he carried on the roads, and he decided that he would now live always in the time of doubt and within the ready sway of dreams.

'A penny for your thoughts,' was all she said. Knowing that I had thoughts, when all others had an interest to forget or, like my children, simply never knew, and had grown to think the silence was the sum of all there was.

'A penny for your thoughts,' she chirped, moving about me like a sparrow as she took things from the table, with the children's mother long gone from the room.

'Why would I need thoughts?'

She smiled and told how she had listened as I spoke to Auntie Argie, that she and the boy together had once listened as I spoke to Auntie Argie in the evenings, when all had left the table and gone off into the other room.

'Why would you need to know my thoughts?'

I pushed my chair back from the table and made to leave the room. She spoke to me always in this way if we found ourselves alone, determined to ignore my silence, teasing as though she knew my need to speak, ignoring my silences and all rudeness and moving about me with her laughing questions, until I began to wonder if I should tell her all my lost and buried thoughts, if in her happy evening

198

chirruping, she might tell me her tales of the living, take up my stories of the dead, and make me live again. I wondered what it was she and the boy might have heard me tell old Argie, wondered what the two of them, this waif in from the wind and this awkward and resisting boy of mine, could make of what I told.

This place is worse than the Somme. I might have told her how, for years, they told us there was no place worse than the Somme, but then we came to know that pain and filth and terror is one kind of pain, and pain and filth and waiting is another, and that slow years of immeasurable useless toil is yet another, and with no relieving promise of a death amid the wire. Then we knew that the reward for the Somme was worse than the Somme, as we lie buried in a land that flows about us as deep as the underearth we first knew when we crossed over, when we crossed over that first time, thrusting at the screeching bundle of mud and rags and the sweet treacle smell of bodies long unwashed that came over the lip, scuffling and writhing in the mud, fighting like schoolboys over the same rifle and embracing close as the mud drew us in, and then looking at this thing that stuck from me, where it should not have done.

He put his foot against my chest as I sank deeper, and pulled upon the blade and the blood followed, bright and glorious red against the mud, and together we watched it rise and flow. He looked at me amid the shouting of the others, and I thought he would stick the blade in me again because I had no force to stop him, but only to shake my head and ask him not to do it, and in a stranger's voice. He paused as the blood ran out in pools across the mud, and then lifted his rifle and the blow fell. I could not tell through the mud and the terror in his eyes if he meant it as a kindness, but it was the wound from the blade that quickly healed, and the blow to the head that lives with me still and takes me far into the scrub at night. I walk through the pain that comes in the night, wondering still if this pain, like the green block of our return, was meant as a kindness, and wondering how much more such kindness I can bear, wondering if the pain is from the blow or from the thought, and the pain of the thought of it as a kindness is still with me, when all the anger and terror is gone.

When the pain and the knowledge comes to me in the nights, I walk along the tracks until the tracks run out, and then I walk along the lines of fences until the fences run out. Then I choose some distant ridge or the gleam of the moon upon a sand drift somewhere to the north and I walk through the scrub, beating against the pain, beating the whips of flaking scrubland and seeking with each step to run the pain into the earth, moving like the Indian, the Indian who knows as well the blade, but who has lived to walk above the earth, who walks above the earth against the pain. When the light begins to show I come back to the Ridge and begin work for the whole day's length, setting to work again in this place where you made the mistake like the man in the play who said too soon 'this is the worst', in this place which is worse than the Somme, the Somme where we turned green land into the country of the dead, where rotting limbs and longforgotten bones rode back to greet us with each upturning of the earth. And so we set again to work each day to turn the sea of woodlands into black and knotted roots, the dead stumps of the departed forest working back, rising like knotted fists and twisted fingers grasping for the light, working back year after year through the new turned soil and studding the dead and naked land yet one more time with its own impotent bones.

She agreed to marry me, or perhaps it was her parents who agreed that this last and skinny daughter, already at that time the creases running deep across what God had meant to be a pretty face, should go with this young man with hands that showed a good toiler. In the moving care that he showed for those scrawny and halfstarving horses that he limped down with him from the north, they saw a future for their daughter and he carrying a good Irish name and talking quietly, of a father with land and brothers, but brothers gone off to other parts, up north and to the goldfields in the west. So she married me and we took the blessing from the white hands of the priest and left them in the southern springtime in a decorated gig with horses fat and breaking clean wind and striding on ahead. Back with me she came because the rains had broken for a moment in the north, and as the gig moved northward her heart began to shrink.

I felt her hand tight on my arm as the water dried upon the tracks and the soil began to flow loose beneath our wheels. I felt her nails break my skin as the trees shrank back and writhed away from us and the tracks grew straighter. I felt the last smile die upon her face as the horizon dropped and fell away and she found herself soon with my father and the sisters of my father on the block they had taken up and cleared forty years before. This was her beginning and our end in the dry country, her beginning with the aunts who soon took away her books and crochet hook and tied a four bushel bag upon her back so that her

*failing knees could tell her what they were and what she
was not. She lived on there, and then further to the north in
the raw country, and the children came, and all that she
could not say to the children or the aunts she said to me,
waking me in the nights even in the days when the darkness
brought with it sleep, waking me and taking me through the
pain of the day and the injustice of the light upon her eyes
and an aching back and the closed heat of the house and all
the reproaches of the breaking land, pressing her rage upon
my body in the nights and holding her arms about me and
her nails deep within my skin in dread that I might sleep
and she be left alone in the darkness to contend with all the
anger that coiled around and around the house and beat
upon the walls and crackling roof, that railed against the
onset of the next day's blinding light.*

*At times I sat at the table with Auntie Argie in the half
light of the evening, the main lamp taken into the other
room, the pair of us alone together as I tasted the blisters
and the broken skin of the day, with Auntie Argie sitting
perhaps only because the girl had not yet come to put her
hand on her shoulder, to lead her from the room.
Sometimes I would speak to her, in a voice I thought the
others could not hear, would sometimes tell her of things
that I knew I wished but dared not tell the girl, the words
as lost in Auntie Argie as in the earth and sand and the dark
sky in the nights, but with me perhaps hoping that in
explaining to Auntie Argie, I might find words to tell the
girl.*

*After a time the girl would come in and place her hands
upon her shoulders. I saw old Auntie Argie smile and soften
to the touch, her withered body gently move and bow to*

meet the fingers of the girl that ran about her neck and shoulders, her mottled hand raised to stroke the hands of Eileen. Eileen would look at me, her dark eyes measuring my silence as she caressed the old woman, as all the while I too longed for the caress of a kind hand like her hand, the feel of the hand of another on my shoulders, but with the memory living still of the deep caress of the blade, of a foot upon my chest and the eyes of terror in a filthy face and the drowning of dreams of life and green growth in dying forests and creeping salt and seas of barren soil.

She would stand before the low glow of the lamp that filtered from the other room, standing with her hands upon the old woman and her eyes upon my silence, and I found I wanted to tell her yet one further story, of a time when the fighting was over, when I went off to wander among a city of the living with but the dead before their eyes, there living like a candleflame, a life as fragile as a candleflame amid all the flames that burned up and down the streets of Paris, sitting on the stone walls of the river and weak with hunger and watching the muddy waters swirl and circle, and thinking to slip in amid the oil and moving papers.

Beside the river I sat with another of the living dead, in whose eyes I knew the pain. We did not need to look again into one another's eyes, but back to back we sat upon the stone banks of the river, and never speaking, he who may even have been a German for all that I knew and even in all that confusion the same boy who struck but would not kill me, the two of us just weeping through the night in all the silences of stone. We let the chill of the stone creep up in the mercy of unfeeling through our bodies as we sat, and back to back to avoid each other's eyes, watching the brown *waters that coiled and ran about the surface of the river, the eddying papers and the currents that ran about the banks and jutting quays and high casements of stone, and it was in those moments that all those thoughts she wanted, and all my hopes and dreams, were lost down into the deep, all my thinking sunk down amid the darker streams that ran unseen below.*

He came in the late part of the morning to the edge of a vast swampland, where the trees grew taller and white gums replaced the box and mallee and the twisted trees and thorny bushes that marked the dry creek's passage from the north. He rode across wide and open mudflats that were carpeted with crumpled bark and rotting logs, and he saw in the distance silver mirror sheets of water that lay off into the darkly shaded marsh that lay beyond. Together they walked out of the dry country and waded at length into the still and listless waters, sometimes stagnant in stranded pools banked by deep drifts of mud and leaves, and sometimes reaching out in channels that ran about the base of the gigantic whitened gums which rose from the detritus of the forest, the channels running around them and off towards the wide waters to the east. In parts they waded deeply in the darkened waters and the soft sucking mud below, and the boy pulled off his clothes and set them on the back of the horse.

He led the horse, with the pup swimming cheerfully alongside, and they made their way from one mudbank to the next, moving always onwards and towards the south and east, stopping now and then on a mound of branches or on a fallen log, before moving on again, through the dense tangle of toppled logs and banks of mud and stranded drinking trees. They sat for a time on a mudbank under the shade of a toppled gum, a gum that seemed to have grown longways across the water and not up and down as the others did, and there they ate the last of the food that the boy had taken from the house at Chinkapook, the lamb and the tins of food, and the horse fed upon the green shoots that lined the edge of the swamp.

Sometimes the forest seemed to close over and they moved in a cool shade of semidarkness, even in the middle heat of the day, and then the forest would suddenly open again to show ahead of them long stretches of open water studded only with grey skeletons of stranded longdead trees, the waters broken now and then with the brightness of a brilliant gum that cut the waters like a shrieking spirit, or with the dark and rotting spine of some sunken log. All the while they looked about them in the dim and filtered light, at the flights of jays that hurled screeching past, and at the swimming snakes and the waterbirds that flew on ahead, or that swam in veering paths that parted the still waters ahead of them, and led out between the trees. As they moved, the boy watched for the things of which Cabel Singh had spoken, for the birds that looked more like sticks than birds, and the banded snakes that ran across the top of the water. He saw other and even stranger things, the dark crusty nodes that billowed from the smooth naked whiteness of the gums, where branches had fallen or been broken off, and the dried husks of insects, large husks complete in every way and crouched like living insects about to take their flight, but empty and transparent to the light, waiting in an eternal vacant patience upon the rotting logs.

Towards the late part of the day they came across a fire, and the sound of voices. Through the grey whitish slats of drinking gums, the boy saw coils of smoke rising in the distance and the top top top of woodchopping coming to him across the waters, the echoes sounding far around the lake, its rhythms broken by the indignant shriek of jays which winged in black and white fans out across the mirror water each time the chopping broke. They approached the fire across the green fringes of the swamp, the eddies of crusted lapfoam and soggy grass that moved gently at the edge of the open swampwaters, and as they came closer they heard from near the fire the soft rhythms of a long litanic cursing, or so it seemed, though it was in a language that the boy had never heard before. It was the voice of a man, he saw as they approached, trying to fit an axehead to a resisting shaft.

On a spit he saw the withered carcass of a rabbit, half eaten, dried out and blackened by fire and by the sun. By the remains of a fire the man sat wrestling with the axe, his lips moving in a long stream of soft abuse as the head refused to slip over the handle, a stream of what must have been curses, but so smooth and liquid and flowing in sound that it might perhaps have been a song. The boy stepped forward, crumpling the bark noisily beneath his feet so as not to take the man by surprise.

'Can I eat?'

The chopping stopped, and the man who had been wielding the axe some distance away now kicked his way back through the rotten limbs and crumpled bark towards the camp, and the others by the fire. He was tall and tanned half black by the sun, with dark black hair that was thick like wire. He wore an old flannel singlet on which new sweat bands under the arms leaked into the old and he carried his axe like a weapon. The boy had one eye on the axe, which was small and like a live thing in his hands. His other eye was on the carcass on the spit.

'Can I have something to eat?'

It was the man who crouched by the fire who finally spoke. He was of the same age as the axeman, around thirty years old. His face was creased and burned deep red by long exposure to the sun, and when he spoke, the boy knew that these men were unlike any he had met before, and he recalled his father speaking of Italian woodcutters who lived out in a swamp that lay far to the south and cut sleepers for the Ultima line, who minded their own business, and so no-one minded them.

'Where you from, kid?'

He pulled a leg from the rabbit and threw it to him. The boy missed it, but picked it up and wiped the dirt from it and began to chew. And he only spoke again when he had finished.

'Up north.'

'Where you mamma, eh? Where you people?'

'I aren't got nobody. Not any more.'

'You wanna watch out for snakes, kid. You know tiger snakes?'

'I reckon I do.'

'They not like other snakes. They'lla go for you. You gotta watch out.'

The one who had been chopping spoke in his own language to the other by the fire. Then he turned to the boy.

'Don't wanta no trouble with kids. Kids is trouble.'

'I aren't trouble. I'm going to see my uncle.'

The man pulled another section from the carcass and threw it to the boy, who chewed at it, stabbing at it with his teeth, his lips drawn back from the hardened black crust.

'Long time since you eat, kid?'

'A while.'

'Other people's kids is trouble. We don't want no trouble.'

The boy stopped and looked at the one with the axe, and hoped that he would go back to his work. Then he spoke more kindly.

'You need something else to eat, kid? Anythin' elsa you need?'

And without waiting for an answer, he walked back through the trees with the sound of his boots crunching through the fallen bark and rotten timbers, and left the boy to speak to the logcutter by the fire.

Their names were Joe and Alfio. In the night, they asked the boy why he was travelling, and he told them of Eileen and Cabel Singh. The logcutters told him that Cabel Singh had not passed by that way, or at least, he had not stopped to seek them out as he usually did, and that he must turn back to the north, because their camp was the most southern point of Cabel's round. They told him the way up to the north which was Cabel's route, and they named to him the towns that he would pass and the country that ran between them and the great saltlake which was always the last of Cabel's journey, which was not a circle as the boy had been told, but a great spiral which rolled around the country and which found its end at the very centre of the great salt-lake. Why it was that Cabel Singh always ended his journey at the centre of the lake, no-one ever understood, and the one they called Alfio said that if you asked Cabel Singh why he ended his travels there he would laugh at you and tell you that you were mistaken and that this was not where the journey ended but rather the place where it began; and if you asked him why it was that he chose such a place for the journey to begin, he would laugh at you and tell you that you were mistaken, and that this was where the journey ended. They both knew what it meant when a man answered a question with another question or sent his questioner around in circles rather than out along a line, and they would then laugh with him and the question would not be asked again. They said that they had told Cabel their own story many times, and he had told them many stories in return, but never one that told them much of a man called Cabel Singh.

The logcutters said that when they had first arrived in the country, it was difficult for them to find work, that they could speak little English, and that no-one trusted an Italian at that time, and so they had gradually drifted out of the towns, and up towards the north, where labour was short and people knew the value of a good pair of hands. They had worked their way north, living by their axes, shootcutting and splitting timber, until they reached the river and then began to look for work along the river and around the newly irrigated areas, in the country between Wentworth and Merbein. They picked grapes and other fruit on many of the small blocks along the river, and finally they had been approached one day by a local stock agent, who had told them of work on a nearby property, and how they would be 'put up' for as long as they liked to stay, and paid a reasonable wage.

The boss, the stock agent explained, was a woman who had lost her husband some time before, but who kept the property running, working it with the help of hired labour, and he explained to them that her place had long been the best and most profitable property in that part of the country, and people even said that, with its white fences and splendid gardens and red roof, it looked almost like a property to the south. He had also told them, too, in a low voice and in a confiding way which they hadn't taken too much notice of at the time, that although she seemed quite a good sort of boss to work for, she never seemed to keep her men on for too long, and he found that he was often asked to be on the lookout for workers, like themselves, who were passing through.

It was a beautiful place indeed, with a large garden set out in front of the house, bordered by a tall white fence, the house itself standing high and bright on a slight rise that looked out over orchards that were, even as they pulled into the long gravel drive, being watered in high spraying arcs from a pump down at the river. The house was cooled and shaded by well grown trees and dense shrubbery, and the logcutters could see that the fences and the orchards were all in good order, with the trees running in neat lines up towards the house, which was freshly painted and shone red and white in the sun at the end of the drive, which opened out from a ramp decorated with wagon wheels and ran between the orchard trees up to the gate.

When the truck arrived up at the house, the owner came out on the verandah, wiping her hands on a small towel. She was a large and capable looking woman, with her hair cut short and a firm set to her jaw; and behind her, in the shaded depths of the house, they saw two men moving, whom they found out later were her sons, large pearshaped boys with hair in spikes and pallid faces, who moved softly about the house and were never seen in the sun. A fine looking woman she was, in that place where most of the women seemed somehow beaten out of shape by the labour and the sun and the dry wind. She was a little like one of their own women, they told the boy, with her olive skin and dark hair and dark eyes and her full and rounded body, quite unlike the boxframed and withered women they had seen so far on most of the places they had worked. And they noticed in the months they worked there that she took good care of herself in the sun, with creams and oils to protect her skin, and always a large hat and sometimes a veil. She came down and looked over each of them with the eye of someone looking over stock for sale in a cattleyard, but shook their hands firmly, like a man. She took care to remain on the last of the steps so that she stood over them, and she spoke to the agent in words that they did not understand.

She pointed them down to their quarters, which was a shack located among the sheds at the far end of the yard, to the west of the house. It was a small weatherboard shanty with a verandah that looked back towards the house, and it had a corrugated iron leanto at the rear, with its own tank and taps and running water. The shack was freshly painted, too, in the same colours as the house, with a bright red roof. It was here, she told them with words and gestures, because their English was not good, that they would take their meals twice a day, brought over by the Girl—she never called her anything else—and it was here that she would meet with them and give them whatever instructions they needed. And she told them that they were not to come up to the house or into the garden that lay to the back and the far side of the house at any other time, unless she sent down for them. The Girl, she told them, came over from a nearby farm most days of the week, and she would also bring them out their lunch, if they were working away from the house, and she would look after their clothes and other things.

For some time, all things went well. The work was not difficult, and they lived in a comfort, in their gaily painted shack, which they had never known before or since. The owner made it clear that she expected them to do what was needed without being told, to see that the fruit was produced and picked, that the animals were fed and the pump fuelled and the sprays cleaned and moved, and the fences kept in good order. They knew the business of fruit properties well enough, and how to tend the trees and prune and water. They rose with the sparrows and ate well and sang heartily as they went about their work, until the sun went down. And after the first few days they began to take their lunch—usually cold mutton and pickle sandwiches with a little tomato—out in the orchards, where it was brought to them by the Girl, who was also pretty and lots of fun, and she would sit with them on the ground and teach them words in English, and laugh at their attempts to speak it back.

The Girl, they told him, was called Gladness, though at first she had laughed at them when they called her that. She was about fifteen years old, and had left school the year before to help on her own family's fruit block, a mile or so down the track towards Wentworth, but had come over to help the

Lady, as she always called her, and to earn some money to send the other children, her brothers and sisters, to school. Gladness was hessianhaired and sunnyfreckled and did not have much fun at home, and loved to laugh and be teased. The logcutters were not so much older than she was at the time, and not so beaten by the sun and the work that they could not enjoy the laughter and the flirting, and Gladness soon joyed in an attention she never had elsewhere. They sat on the grass between the trees in the orchards and Gladness would spread a blanket on the ground and they took their lunch together, joking and telling stories and playing songs on an accordion in the fitful winter sun; and sometimes when they laughed together one or the other of them would see the tall figure of the woman who owned the property, moving between the fruit trees, watching them as they talked together, watching them in silence from the shade.

It was one day such as this, when they were talking and teasing with Gladness in this way, resting in the shade of the apricots and rolling about lazily in the grass, that the Lady suddenly approached them from the depths of the orchard and broke in upon the laughter, though with smiles rather than with reproach, and motioned to the logcutters to come with her back to the house. They went through the white gate and up through the garden and crossed the verandah for the very first time. They entered behind the woman into the shaded rooms that lay beyond, the long, cool corridor that ran the length of the house, with its small tables and hall-stands, and the big frosted glass doors at the end. It was many years since either had been inside a house that was so large, so clean, so elaborately furnished, and they pulled off their hats and turned them around in their hands and kept themselves well away from the clean wallpapered walls and from the small and breakable things that lay to either side, following the owner cautiously down the darkened corridor and peering into the large and dim and heavily furnished rooms that lay to either side. They passed the large and pallid sons sitting silently in the half darkness of the living room, who did not say a word. Once within the cool and closed air of the house, they began to smell the odours of their bodies rising about them, and they began to feel the heaviness of their feet and the nails of their boots dragging and catching at the carpet that lay beneath their feet.

They lingered back, and when she reached the end of the corridor, she turned, and called, 'Come this way. Come with me.'

She smiled and placed her hand upon the arm of Joe, and bid them both to come with her through the garden and down to the yard at the rear of the house. There, amid a rich tangle of bougainvillea and passionfruit, she showed them the entrance to an old underground separator room, lying three quarters below the surface of the earth, a room that had been dug many years before to keep the milk cool through the day. The door, in heavy timber and strapped about with steel, was locked, and she sent Joe down to unlock it.

'What I will now show you,' she told them, 'is a secret. But I know now that I can trust you. And even the Girl must never know.'

They stepped down into the darkness of the separator room, and when their eyes adjusted to the light, which filtered in thinly through a high window overgrown with vines, and through holes in the corrugated iron roof and from the door, they saw in one corner the crouching figure of a man in chains. For a time, they held their breath, because the place stank with the dull odour of old human faeces and rotten bones, and the figure in the corner shuffled and cringed and pulled about him a blanket made up of opened wheatbags, to shield him from the light that streamed in through the open door.

'My husband,' she said. 'This is my husband.

'People think that he died years ago,' she explained. 'No-one knows that he is still alive, and kept down here. We had to tell people that he was dead. The banks would have taken the property at the time. This is what we had to do. You see, there was no choice.

'You see,' and she spoke quickly to them, as though they needed to know all, and everything all at once, so that they would not judge her too quickly, and too harshly, 'we had to act, in order to protect this place. The beauty of it. Nothing was going well. The work was not being done. He was a thinker, my husband was, and would too often be found down by the river, "just thinking" as he called it, while the birds played havoc with the fruit, which was rotting on the trees. I talked to a lawyer, a man who was wise in the ways of this part of the world, who knew what dreams are needed in this place. My husband was now ill, sleeping out upon the riverbank and talking to the waterbirds, with all the birds from miles around nesting and feeding on our trees.

'The lawyer came to me at night, and we went down to the river and had him sign the powers to me, which he did happily enough, and I told everyone that he was going to Melbourne, to a rest home. In fact, I put him here in the separator room. It was an easy lie to tell. It was even true, in the beginning. He was, for a time, in a rest home in the city. Then I brought him home, here. You will see that he is not unhappy. He has his time, now, for thinking, lots of time for thoughts.

'Your task will be to bring him food, each evening. At about sundown. Sometimes to wash him and to cut his hair. And to talk to him, if he wishes to talk. Normally, he does not talk. He will smile at you, and he may even tell you that he wants his freedom. But do not release his chains. There is a risk of violence. I tell you this for your protection. Nor does he always appreciate why it is that he is here. He does not always understand why it is that he must live this way.'

There were many things that Joe and Alfio wanted to know. They wanted to know how long it was that he had been there, in that reeking cellar, and how it was that no-one, not even Gladness, seemed to know that he was there. The woman answered a few of their questions, but just a few, and from that time they began to look after the chained man in the old separator room, and gave him his food, and always kept beyond the length of the chain, and never spoke to one another about the filthy man in chains. And soon they never spoke to one another about anything, except when they needed to for the work of the day. After a time it was only when Gladness brought their lunch that they ever spoke at all, speaking to one another only through what they said to Gladness, and Gladness young and laughing and happy to be teased, and never knowing that she was now their only language with each other and their only relief from the weight of silence that had come upon their lives. And yet, they were content for a time simply to have a place to live and good meals, and to work out in the open, and never to speak of the man in the cellar, of what had become their secret shame. The boy might find that strange, but he had to understand they were both young at the time, and she was a fine looking woman and their boss. They were a long way from their families, and nothing seemed very real to them in a new country where they could not even speak, and it felt that nothing that happened to them, no matter how strange, would ever leave a mark.

And there was Gladness. As the winter months passed and it was spring and warm, she would bring out their lunch, and sing and chirrup and laugh, and they would tease her as they used to, but now with unease at the monstrous things beyond the fine and gleaming house at the end of the orchard. In time Gladness finally began to notice the change, and would ask them what was wrong, but their heads were full of things they knew they could never tell her, of the filthy being in the underground separator room at the rear of the house, who would peer out at them from under his thatch of filth and knotted hair. He smiled kindly at them now as they came down into the darkness, and as the months drew on would rattle his chains at them, but gently, to ask them to cut him free.

Never would he speak, but only make signs that seemed to tell them things. Normally it was almost dark when they took his food down to the separator room, and they scarcely saw him, a figure huddled in the corner under a pile of stinking wheatbags, shuffling forward to the end of his chain to take his food, and slinking back into the corner of his room again. He never spoke and never complained. At times each of them tried to speak to him but with no answer and only a shuffling and a gurgling from behind that heap of sacks, and so they thought that perhaps the woman was right and that no other thing could be done.

It was with the lingering of the light, though, that this began to change. As the months drew on through September and October, it was still light when they took his food down in the evenings, and cleared away his tank, and filled his water, and they began to see his face, and not just in the dull glow of the hurricane lamp. He was a man perhaps in his fifties, though he might, with a wash and a shave, have been much younger. They chopped at his long and matted hair now and then, with a large and none too sharp machete that was kept near him but beyond the reach of his chain, in a corner of the room.

One night they both went down to feed him, and Joe took a pair of scissors, with Alfio standing by just in case he became violent. But instead he simply sat and chewed on a bone, smiling at the attention as they cut and hacked away at the filthy hair. So they then took a bucket and some soap and washed him, because he was still calm and smiling. Then they shaved him, and when they had finished they showed him his face in a mirror, and he wept and then he sang to them, though not in the words of any language that they knew, and then he wept again and beat his fist upon the floor.

It was with the lingering of the light that they began to talk to him, because by this time, through their lunches with Gladness, they had begun to know enough English to be able to make sentences, and to ask questions. They noticed, each of them as they tried to talk to him in that dim underground light, that though he would not speak, he smiled at them— his rotting teeth exposed in a broad grin—and that he seemed more than pleased to see them each night. He would beam with pleasure at the food they brought him, and would watch as they moved his tin and brought clean water. Finally, one evening, they stayed later, and Alfio played his little accordion to him, and Joe played the drum with spoons upon an upturned bucket, and the husband laughed and beat the machete in time to the music on the packed earth floor, moaning and howling exactly like one of the dogs in the dog-yard when it was Alfio and Joe's time to leave. The dogs outside took up the chorus and howled back as the log-cutters found their way back down to the shack.

After that, each night when they took the husband his food, they would sit about in the separator room for a time, and play and sing with him, and the man began to keep his room much cleaner than before. He would sing and tell them long poems which they never understood but which, they could tell, moved from great joy to sadness and then to joy again, with long passages that they could see, from the distant look that came upon him as he sang, told of worlds and times that ran far beyond the world of the separator room, with long softly spoken passages of a gentle passion that moved first the speaker, and then all of them, to tears. These were the poems and thoughts, they understood, that he had sung to the birds upon the river, and they would dry their eyes and clap when he had finished, and then they would all sing again.

Soon the woman from the house heard this, and said that it was 'starting again'. She heard the dogs taking up the singing and the sounds of happiness and the long chanting of the poems from the separator room, and she told them that if they insisted on staying down there in the nights and disturbing her husband, they would have to pack their bags and leave. She had, it seemed, made one of her rare visits to the separator room, and had seen the husband clipped and shaven and washed, and she stopped them on their way down to the shack, and was angry at them for making a fool of him, and mocking him by showing him what he was not.

It was at that time that they decided to release him, they told the boy, and to send him off along the river. It was after one of their lunches with Gladness, when they began to ask her questions about the house and the areas of the house and the garden where she was not allowed to go. She began to see some direction in the questioning and became upset and went back to the house in tears. It was then that they knew they must leave the place and the woman who kept it in such order, and the poor beast chained in the cellar room at the rear of the house. They decided to release him, even knowing that it would be the end of their time there, and the end of hot food and running water, and of talking to Gladness in the orchard.

That night they took a crowbar with them to the separator room, and levered his chains open, holding their noses against the new smells that rose from him, despite his washing of the week before. They gave the husband some of their own clothes, which they helped him to put on. Their idea was that he should make his escape from that place, and that they would leave him down along the river and he would live there by any means he could, perhaps even die there, somewhere down along the river, because even that would be better than what he had known in his dark hole in the ground. They gave him some extra food and a waterbag, and led him up, out of the separator room and into the dying light of the day. At the top, as he blinked and squinted in the fading light of the sun, they told him by signs and words to wait until everyone had gone to bed, and then to make his way off through the forest and meet them down the river. And the man grinned, and nodded as though it had all made sense to him. Still grinning, he stepped back down into the darkness again.

That night, the logcutters told the boy, they slept only until the middle of the night, knowing that their time at the splendid house was now over, with no idea of what would happen to them next, and only really caring for the fact that they would not see Gladness again. They gathered up those few things they could call their own, and left their gaily painted outhouse and ran down through the long lines of the orchard and out through the neat white gates and off through the night. They ran along the river in the direction that they had sent the husband, off into the dense forests of gum and box and belah that lay along its banks.

They found him sitting beneath a tree, waiting for them as they had bid, and for the rest of that night they ran together along the banks of the river, and they slept the next day in the soft soil by the water's edge. In the late afternoon, they ran again. All through the next night they ran, until they were many miles away. They ran along the river until they saw how easily their soft prints in the sand might be followed, and then they ran out along one of the dry creekbeds where the timber had not been cleared. They ran along the mudflats and the floodplains and through the lignum forests and over the saltpans, and still the husband kept beside them, running with them through the scrub. They passed through towns and hamlets and past silent farms and yelping dogs and protesting turkeys in the depth of night, and back into the swamplands and through the stagnant waters and over the teeming mudbanks, until they came upon the cleared country to the south.

Still the husband ran with them, and in the nights they would sometimes stop for a time and light a fire, and Alfio would play upon his accordion, and they would sing far into the nights together, in the depths of the scrub. He came with them all the way to the south, and then he stayed and lived with them, they told the boy, sometimes working with them and cutting redgum sleepers for the Ultima line, but mostly sitting out in the middle of the swamp and singing, and telling his thoughts to the trees and waterbirds.

From time to time as the years drew on, they wondered what the fine looking woman might be thinking, alone now in her shining house with her pallid and silent sons, with the separator room door gaping open and her husband gone and she not able to tell a soul either that he had been there or that he had gone, probably glad in some moments that she no longer had the burden on her hands, and no doubt terrified at others that she would one day find him living, and singing at her door again. And when the husband died, and that was some years after they had come to that place, they buried him on an island far out in the swamp and never told a soul. From that day to this, they told the boy, they had stayed and worked on the edge of the swamp, hauling redgum sleepers into town and taking their cheque, and living by themselves, with no more English between them now than that which the girl Gladness had taught them, many years before.

*

He rode off in the early light, taking what food the logcutters could give him, and he made his way around the southern edge of the swamplands and back towards the north, moving from the still waters and the forest of heavy gums, and out into the lignum country, the low flats and floodlands to the west which would take them to the path of Cabel Singh. He left the deep shade of the creekbeds and the soft footing of cracked and lifting mud to meet the narrow track that ran through belts of box and belah, and out into the cleared and open country that led off to the north.

For most of the day the track was deserted. They were passed at one time by an aging Ford, a battered saloon cut down to a tray with a load of melons and mallee stumps, making its way slowly to Culgoa and the north. The driver was a spotted youth in a cloth cap, not too much older than the boy. The dog chased the Ford for a time and the driver abused the dog, before trying with a lurch to the left to run it down. He accelerated off down the track in clouds of oily smoke.

After a time, when the air had settled, the boy called to the dog, which was wandering too far afield. He rubbed the pup's head when it returned, and held it between his hands in the way he had sometimes seen his father do with the bigger dogs, cradling its snout in his outstretched hands, caressing it and imprisoning it in a way the dogs seemed to like. He spoke aloud, because they had heard no voice all day.

'Dare say you're wonderin' what we're doin' out here, with nothing to eat, an' miles from anywhere. Walking around and around in circles. 'Cos you probably know, deep down in that dog head of yours, that we're now headin' right back up again towards the places we come from in the first place. Right?'

The dog broke away and pranced back, barking and snapping at the boy in merriment.

'Well, maybe it's because I'm just a bit crazy. Maybe it's because Cabel Singh is a bit crazy, and that's why he just keeps rollin' around and around in great big circles. Maybe we'll just end up back at our place again, with your mates back in the dogyard. Maybe we ought to have just stayed there in the first place to wait for Cabel Singh to come back again, like everybody says we ought.'

As they rested in the shade he saw a horse moving along the track towards them, moving so slowly that it seemed hardly to approach at all. The horse came slowly, raising little dust, and he saw that the one restless and shifting rider he had seen at first turned out to be three children, in a line, all with large hats and mounted on a large redbrown draught, their legs sticking out at the sides. Behind them they towed a large brown mass which dredged the dirt before it, the big draught making slow work of it, despite the goading of lines of small bony heels and some heavy work with a switch of mallee by the eldest, who was, the boy decided, no more than ten years old.

They came slowly towards him, their hats pulled low and their eyes hidden from view until they were close to where he sat. Their noses were oddly wrinkled and their nostrils pinched and their mouths half open, and now and then one of them would spit, off to the side. Their hats and clothing and faces were thick with flies. And as they drew closer and the boy stood up, he could see that they were towing behind them the carcass of a horse, the rotting carcass of another draught mare, tied with long ropes to the collar of the one they rode and part fixed on a sled, a wooden contraption which raised the front part of the carcass, but not enough, to help them drag it along.

The horse had been dead for some time, and now the reek blew over them and on towards the boy. The towing horse stopped as the boy walked out onto the track, familiar with the custom that they must stop and talk for a time before moving on. The boy stood beside the draught and squinted up at the children above, untroubled by the coarse gusts that blew up from behind.

'What you fellers goin' to do with that damn thing?'

The smaller ones looked to the eldest for an answer.

'It's our Uncle Ted's,' he said. 'We're takin' it home.'

'What the damn hell you goin' to do with a dead 'un. Specially one that's been dead this long.'

The smallest one spoke, but not to the boy.

'Is he the Debt Adjuster, Billy.'

'Don't be damn stupid. The Debt Adjuster's an old bloke. With a car an' a suit an' all. An' books an' everything.'

The little one wrinkled his nose at the invading stinks. The children all shuffled about on the horse, and agreed that it was pretty bad, and had got worse with the heat of the day.

'Our dad says we got to bring it home,' the big one said. ''Cos the Debt Adjuster's coming. Our dad's expectin' 'im any day. He'll pay us compo for it.'

The boy folded his arms and took a closer look at the dead horse, which had rolled half over, its legs erect and quivering in the air.

'Reckon you fellas'd be doin' the world a favour if you just got this damn thing off the road and out of sight. Surprising thing is you got it this far. Thing's ready to fall apart.'

The boys didn't want to discuss the dead horse. Their dad

had told them to bring it home and that was all. They sat in silence for a time. Then the littlest one spoke again.

'What's your name?'

The boy thought long and hard about that. He did have a name, though it was now many days since he had heard it spoken, and even before then it wasn't much in use. He had another name which the kids over at Patchey had given him, and that seemed to suit him better than the one his parents had given him, years before, before he was anything to name at all.

'They call me Splinter.'

'What's the pup's name?' the middle one asked.

'Just "pup", I reckon. How far is home?'

Home, it turned out, was just up the road a bit, and the boys were able to point to a distant windmill, to show him where they lived.

'Do you reckon your mum could give us somethin' to eat?'

'Aren't got no mum.'

'What about your dad?'

'Our dad don't like strangers comin' round.'

The silence threatened them again, and the big one looked to go.

'You fellers want to see something?'

It was a long time since the boy had been among other kids. He fumbled in his canvas bag and pulled out the roll of newspaper, unwrapping it before them so that the revolver and bullets fell out upon the sand. The boys on the horse strained over to see.

'Jeez. Is it real?'

'Reckon it is. You watch.'

He loaded it with two bullets, and brandished it about,

looking for a target that he could be sure to hit. The white insulators on the telephone wires shone invitingly in the sun but were too hard to hit.

'Just hang onto the horse.'

He pulled the hammer back and fired out into the trees. The big draught twitched and flicked its tail at the roar of the gun, but nothing more.

'Jeez. What do you reckon, Jim?'

The big one just curled his lip in deep disdain, knowing that firing shots into the scrub was just a damn fool thing to do, and he kicked the draughthorse on the flank so that it began again to strain at the collar. Slowly the dead load began to move again, leaving the boy and his animals beneath their tree, the littler ones turning to watch them as they drew away, the carcass grading a broad path through the sand, thickening the air with its stinks as the movement raised new gusts and new clouds of flies. For a time the pup pursued them down the track, barking and snapping at the carcass, until pelted sticks and cursing drove him back.

With Eileen he had waited in the shade, amid the dried dung and scattered needles and below the Murray pines, until it was cool enough for them to take the low and winding paths that led across Wirrengren Plain. They washed themselves in the trickle of tankwater that ran down from the spout, avoiding the murky green of the water that lay stagnant in the troughs, but their hair still sat out in spikes from the mud and drying water, and they set out barefoot and half clad across the burning sand, the boy laden down with his load of heavy clothing, and even his slouch hat crumpled in his arms. They walked, sometimes side by side and sometimes with the boy dragging back with his awkward load, and Eileen sang and whistled and shouted at the treetops, and hurled useless sticks at scuttling rabbits and the hawks that soared above.

Now and then she would turn upon him, teasingly.

'What are you thinking? What did you think of that? Today, and Windmill Tank?'

No-one had ever asked him about his thoughts before. No-one had ever thought he would need them, with the slow routines of the Ridge, and the long trudge down to Baring school, and the long hours spent with Joe who didn't waste much time in thinking things.

'Nothing. Nothing much.'

His thoughts were brimming, but not with things that he could say. All that he could do was to talk again about what had happened out at the tank, not talk in thoughts but only tell in whatever words he could find about the hard rim of the tank, and how the water felt and the sight of Eileen between him and the sun, their moving around the rim of the tank, and the giddiness and the fast movement of the earth. He tried some words out, in his mind, words of a kind that he might use one day if he had to explain what had happened at Windmill Tank, but they could not be used with Eileen, who had felt the rush of cool water herself, and the mud in her hair and the dirt between her toes.

'Nothing,' he said, and Eileen grinned, because she had nothing like thoughts either, though her mind was full as well. She touched his arm and helped him with his things.

They walked on through the late part of the day, mile upon mile across Wirrengren Plain and through the low pine forests, and up towards the last line of low hills and drifts that lay between them and the Ridge. They climbed up through the loose sand, and rested for a time beneath a tree at the top within sight of the Ridge, its tall palms and windmills able to be seen from a mile away, even with the falling of the sun.

And there she had begun to talk. Eileen grew more serious, upon the distant sight of the Ridge, and demanded that they wait for a time, that they stop and talk. She began to tell of her time out on the roads, and a little of the life that went before, and of what had happened on the day that she arrived, when she came alone and almost naked along the Baring track. She spoke to him of Cabel Singh, and how he had met her on the road just days before. The boy listened carefully as Eileen spoke, the two of them looking out towards the Ridge, the curl of smoke and the flying windmill, and as they spoke, all seemed to move away from them, to fade away into the distant falling darkness, as she told him all that she had to tell, of her time upon the road with Cabel Singh.

Through the darkness of the night he saw the fire, at first like a red coal glowing amid the dark ashes of the night, with the odours of boiling eucalyptus floating to them on the breeze. As he moved closer along the Berriwillock track, he began to see that the fire was not just the usual dying glow of piled and burning mallee, but a fire that was still being fed with branches, a fire around which bodies moved and voices called, a fire sending long and moving shadows out into the scrub. The fire burned amid a patch of uncleared mallee, and near to a large iron building, a shire hall or Mechanics

Institute, with the fire sending wild and long stretched shadows against the corrugated walls.

As the boy grew closer he could see bodies moving about between the glowing fire and the bare walls, their shadows flickering against the darkness of the scrub, and he heard hoots and laughter and the sound of breaking bottles and the sounds also of sobs and abuse drifting in waves to him and his companions through the soft air of the night. The pup pricked up its ears and tried to run on ahead, but the boy stepped down and took the horse by the halter and put a tether on the dog, and led them slowly through the timber and into the fall of shadows that ran out from the flame.

Two fires were burning brightly. Around the main fire, half a dozen young men played and drank and danced like pictureshow Indians around the fire, and shouted to each other, and boasted and called out in loud voices to the night which smelt of beer, and the flow of recent blood. The other fire was a high wall of yellow flame that still marked out the form of a hawker's cart, licking through the last of the hessian and canvas and running along the wooden frame and down the wagon's shafts in bright rivers of hot flame. As the canopy of the cart began to topple and the plywood buckled and began to fall away, the boy saw the outline of piledup goods, of clothes and sheets which caught the fire and sent it higher, the flames reaching far above the heads of the dancing men who coursed around it, far above the iron roof of the hall, the coils of smoke and glowing ash winding upwards and fading into the night. Before the cart, spread out in a pool of blood, lay the carcass of a horse, the blood still running freely through a huge wound in its head, the mark of a shotgun placed close.

Between the cart and the hall, he saw the figure of a man sitting, or rather lying, bound by twine to a sapling. He was slumped, resting in a halfkneeling, halflying position, with his head to one side, and the boy could see that it was the body of an Indian with his turban off, and his long hair pulled about him, the occasional flash of the fire, showing the brightness of red as the blood ran about his silver hair in thick clouts of deep red. As he crept a little closer, he could see that it was Old Sally, who had told him he would soon be moving south.

Among the dancing men, the boy saw he knew two or three, and then he saw Joe Spencer, dancing about the burning cart and over the carcass of the horse, stark naked and heavily painted in mud and horse's blood, bottle in one hand and a woman's hat in the other, hooting and laughing, and leaping over the horse. He recognised, too, Joe's mates from Patchewollock, some standing off to one side and chuckling in their beer. He recognised another, with a stupid smile, made hideous by the paint on his face and the strange shadows cast by the leaping flames, holding the shotgun that might have killed the horse, saying nothing but just caressing the gun and staring at the slumped and sobbing form of the old Indian.

The boy broke into the clearing, holding the Debt Adjuster's revolver high, trying to steady it in both hands. He screamed at the dancing men to stop, but his high thin shriek was drowned by the hooting and laughter. Then he pulled with all his strength at the trigger, and the revolver fired, loud and flaming in the night.

The dancing men immediately stopped. There was a startled silence with only the roar of the blaze of the burning wagon and the occasional groan from Old Sally to intrude upon it. In moments, Joe Spencer, in his crude warpaint of mud and horseblood, now wearing the woman's hat, saw that he knew the boy, and wandered over, ignoring the revolver which the boy now pointed at his head. Joe was stumbling drunk and having trouble fixing clearly upon the boy and his revolver in the moving light of the fire, but stumbled over to speak to him as though the pistol were not there, to take up his command of old.

'Where the damn hell have you been, kid? We been looking everywhere. Police and all.'

The boy stared at Joe, refusing to be coaxed. He began to snivel and the heavy gun now wavered in his hands, but he kept it pointed at Joe's head.

'You been lookin' for me, Joe? This what you call lookin' for me?'

He looked at Joe as though for the first time. Joe wavered on his feet and moved closer to him, ignoring the pistol at his head.

'There's things you don't know about, kid. Lots of things you just don't know about.'

No-one moved, and the boy and Joe simply stared at each other. Someone from over near the truck pitched a bottle at the boy and a couple of Joe's mates laughed and someone else mumbled something about giving the little bastard a good kick in the arse before somebody got hurt. Joe motioned to them in a drunken way to shut up, and they did so, and they waited while he argued with the boy.

'Come here,' he motioned to the boy, trying to lead him a little way from the fire, away from the hearing of the others who were chuckling again and opening more bottles over by the truck.

'Come away.'

The boy refused to move, keeping the wavering pistol still pointed at Joe's head.

'Aren't nothing you can tell me, Joe. Not any more. Not now.'

Joe looked around him, at the fire, burning lower now that the brittle plywood and hessian had gone. He looked at the dead horse in its spreading pool of blood, at the old man strapped to the sapling. Joe stopped in the silence, and it was as though he were seeing it still and stark for the first time. He wiped his mouth with the back of his hand.

'We aren't hurt him much. He'll be all right.'

'All right for what? Half a dozen of you? Why?'

Joe was confused, but the drunken courage didn't let him down. He tried to move closer, as if to lay hold of the boy's shoulder, or ruffle his hair, or cup a hand around the back of his head and send him twirling about as he used to do.

'It's for her. You know that. It's because of the girl.'

The boy surveyed again the scene of blood and fire and wreckage.

'Yeah, Joe. An' she'd thank you for it.'

'Anyway,' Joe fumbled for some excuse, some explanation that would satisfy the boy and get the revolver away from between them, 'it's the other bastard we're really after. This old bugger is just his mate. We was just wanting to know where his mate was.'

The boy said nothing, and felt a rush of hot, betraying tears. Joe saw this, and cajoled and coaxed, lowering his voice, trying to draw the boy out of his rage and panic and back into the old ways, taking the boy within the circle of his whispering, against the faces that circled them at the edge of the shifting light.

'Come on, fella. Come on, f'chrissakes. You can untie the old bugger as soon as we go. He'll be all right. Look—he tore into that bloke over there with the shotgun, an' we had to hit him. Better'n laying into him with the shotgun, eh? Then we tied him up and while we was doing it, some silly bastard shot the horse and put a match to the wagon.

'This is a bad time, kid. About as bad as it gets, I reckon. You want to go back home. They're all worried about you. The other kids and all. Your people. Even the police. Cooper's got some damn fool notions in his head, too. An' there's some yarn goin' about you been cuttin' fences. This is a bad time and there's been some bad things happening everywhere. Up north, and everywhere.'

'T'aren't his fault, Joe.'

Joe looked deeply into the boy's eyes and lowered his voice even further as he came in close.

'I'm not saying it is. Cooper's not saying he did anything. We just want to find him, that's all. We just want to find out a few things. We reckon he knows something. Or he'd have hung about a bit.'

The others over by the truck were getting restless now that they had dropped out of earshot, and a series of mutterings and oaths were starting to replace the hoots and shouts and laughter.

'Is this how you find out things, Joe? This what you got in mind for Cabel, too? 'Cause maybe he knows something about you? Maybe he knows something about you as you don't want him to know?

'Why did you hit her, Joe?'

And in that moment Joe shouted in anger and lunged at the pistol, and the boy stepped back, and held the revolver steady and screamed to his friend Joe to stop. And then he pulled the trigger.

He pulled the trigger but the trigger was heavy, raising only very slowly the hammer which he had forgotten again to cock, and it was in that moment, as the hammer rose against its spring, before it fell under the pressure of the boy's straining fingers, that Joe was able to duck his head away so that the shot grazed past his ear and off, whizzing out into the scrub.

For a moment they stood, both openmouthed, gaping at each other. And Joe, with his ears ringing and the flash of the charge still burning before his eyes, leapt upon the boy and punched him hard in the stomach and again across the ear, and wrestled the pistol from him, twisting his fingers with the force of it, and pitching it far out into the scrub.

'Jesus Christ!'

He stood over the squirming, winded body of the boy who floundered in the dust, clutching his stomach and gasping for air, and gasping for air himself.

'You'd bloody shoot me! Jesus Christ!'

Someone started the truck, and the others began to climb aboard.

'You'd bloody shoot me! Jesus Christ!'

Joe backed away from the boy. He backed over to the truck, where the others had now gone silent because they had seen what had happened, and even drunk as they were, they knew that Joe was near to being a dead man. They helped him climb into the back with them, mumbling some rough condolences and getting ready to go.

'Dangerous little bastard.'

'All the kids up your way as crazy as that one, Joe?'

Joe took no heed of them, and spoke only to the boy, still squirming in the sand. His voice was hoarse, almost tearful.

'Go home, kid. Just get back home. I'll let your people know I seen you, and that you're all right. That I'll do for you, all right?'

And when the boy had caught enough breath, he shouted after Joe, shouted over the coughing of the engine, a foolish whimpering voice that travelled nowhere against the revving of the truck.

'You get on home too, Joe. There's lots of things happened, like you say. An' you just need to get on home.'

'You leave it alone, kid. You don't understand.'

The driver wheeled the truck around sharply in a way that sent a wave of sand out over the boy, who knelt in the light of the fire, his arms folded over his injured stomach, bent over and still gasping for breath.

'You get on home,' Joe yelled over the roaring of the engine and the churning of the tyres. 'Your people's got enough problems without you goin' and gettin' yourself shot or lost or in jail or something.

'I'll be back there in a couple of days. I'll tell 'em I seen you, and that you're wandering about the country half starved an' filthy like a crazy person or some mad abbo, with a gun and all, scaring the daylights out of people.'

As the truck set off in another spray of sand, the boy made his way over to where Old Sally sat bound to the sapling, moaning softly as the boy drew his knife and slit the twine and helped him to sit up, so that he could staunch the flowing out of Sally's blood. And then he took a brand of burning cloth from out of Sally's wagon and limped out into the scrub to see if he could find the revolver.

*

He lay deep in the dark of the night and listened to the sighs of Old Sally, the sounds of Old Sally moaning beside the embers of his wagon, and the wind teasing the ribbons of bark that streamed from the trees about him, the long banners of paperbark that flapped in the moving air and ran off in the wind to the south. He lay in the warmth of the sand with his blanket drawn around him, his clothes dank on his body as he perspired in the close night air and his head still aching from Joe Spencer's blows. He thought of Joe gone off, Joe gone off drunk and violent with his mates, and he felt more alone than ever, in the darkness of the night. He felt again the heavy air of the night and the whole sky above with its burden of stars move about him. He looked up into the night from his bed in the sand and now found himself at the centre of all that he saw, the half light of the moon and the familiar welcome of the stars giving the night in friendship to him in ways that never came with the heat of the day and the rage of the beating sun.

He listened to the wind as it beat through the leaves of the trees above, to the humming of the wind as it rose and fell and teased the loose bark on the trees around him, and in the distance and far to the south, the sound of the engine of an electric generator on a farm that lay beyond a belt of uncleared scrub, beating in a soft and stable rhythm into the stillness of the night. He listened to the animals that moved in the night, the lizards or perhaps it was mice that fossicked and scuttled in the fallen branches and thick tangle of dead leaves and strings of paperbark and the rank grasses and roly-polies that lay about him, banked up against the stubs of trees. He listened in the quiet of the night to all the sounds that were lost in the heat of the sun and he began to feel that he too was perhaps a creature of the night thrust all unwanting into the light of day. He lay in the sand and looked up into the light of the moon, and thought that they would sometimes now sleep during the day and travel at night, and that they would live in the light of the moon and become night creatures themselves, like those that beat about him in the piles of dead grass and broken branches.

Upon his skin he felt the movement of the tiny black ants that came in creeping droves as they always did in search of the moisture of his body when the heat of the day had fallen away. He lay still and let them crawl upon him and over his bare feet and between his toes, and up inside the legs of his trousers and over his hands and his face. He did not try to wipe the ants away as he had learned that they would not bite, and that wiped off they would simply come again. He had learned in his time on the road to live with the black ants on his body in the nights, as he had learned to live with the sound of the creatures in the dense dead thickets of the scrub, as he had learned to live with the sharp ends of stick or gravel that pushed up through the sand and against his body in the night, as he had learned to live with the cool sweat that came on even in the depth of the nights and pasted yet more closely his worn clothing to his body and stiffened his long hair and made him seem more with each day that passed like the animals with whom he travelled.

He lay deep in the darkness of the night and watched the moon as it rose steadily from low to the east and moved out across the sky. He watched the moon as it lay low to the horizon in a shape that he had rarely seen, the moon three times its size and glowing a deep golden red, swollen and sore and fullbellied and hovering unsteadily as though in pain among the thin and distant clouds that crossed the lower sky. He looked about him, at the whitened shafts of mallee and the cleared country glowing in the night, and he felt his own face shining brightly in the light of the moon. He felt the light beating in upon him even when he closed his eyes and tried to turn down into the folds of his blanket, so he opened his eyes again and stared up at the moon and he studied for a time the dark shapes upon its surface and tried a dozen different ways of making faces from the patterns of darkness which came and went on the face of the moon, sometimes clear and sometimes lost when the moon took on a brighter glow.

He thought of Eileen, of how she told him of arriving with the wind, how on the way from Windmill Tank she had spoken of the sand blowing up behind her on that lonely track, and how the dust had risen across the sun. She knew that there was only one house beyond the dry ridges and westward of the drifts of sand, and that if they did not take her in, then there was nothing for her beyond but an end to all her living, and no going back because that way she had been, and there was nothing to go back to but what made it better to go on. She told him how she walked between the thinning trees, through the heat and climbing coils of sand, the willywillies that drove the earth before her, thinking at first with dread and then in a kind of peace that she might die along this track, and that it might be days before they found her. She would rather end like the bones of sheep she passed along the way, scattered by the dogs and the birds and the ants, than be found rotting in someone else's old green dress by the side of the road, as though she had been waiting there for someone, as though she had died hoping for one moment that some form of kindness might yet come to her out of the wind, along that lonely track.

She decided then to die far away from the road, on the peak of one of the open sand drifts that lay far to the north, where only the animals would find her, where she would take off her dress and hide it in a hollow tree because it was then the only thing she owed to anyone, and wearing it ugly and pinned and twined about her in that heat and on that track was the last debt she would ever pay. She would lie down to die with her body free and open to the night on a bed of cooling evening sand, where the winds would lay the earth across her, and she would die in quietness amid all the world's darkness, lit only by the warm light of the moon. In time when playing children found her bones, long after the flesh had been taken by the wind and the sand, when they heard the wind singing through her cage of bones, they would think of a sheep or wild dog or a kangaroo, and then of nothing but their games, shrieking and laughing up and down the slopes of sand. No person, she told him, would know her and none would ever look for her, the only person even knowing that she had ever set out along that length of track needing to hide that knowing, yet one more who took in guilt and darkness what she might have given in kindness, needing though to do it and to know it only as a sin, half hoping for the flesh of his secret shame to melt and rot and drift away, thinking, 'Yes, that was a sin. But not so much a sin, now she has blown away.'

He thought again of the man in the striped pyjamas beneath his burden of logs and broken branches, lying still and cold in the earth, but still grasping at the same bright moon. Beside him he saw Eileen in her torn green dress with its sash of darkened blood, her hands upon her breast and her hair blown across her face, stiff and silent in the cold silver light. Near them, but at a distance, he saw Joe lying naked and white except where stained with earth and horse's blood, his forehead laid open and his eyes still bright before the flash of the gun. And he remembered a story that Hannah had once told him, that if you looked too long at the moon, or if you slept a full night through with the light of the moon upon your face, you took on a special form of madness, and after a time you had a need for the light of the moon just as others lived for the light of the sun. He thought of the dogyard at night at the Ridge, and the dogs howling as his father drifted off to sleep, the sounds of the dogs lifting to the fleeing of the moon.

'So which way did they go?'

'They went off to the north.'

'That'll be Sea Lake's business then.'

'I want you to stop them. They're going to do something bad.'

'It aren't for you to tell me what to do an' what not to do, young feller.'

'You got to stop them.'

'An' who the hell are you, anyway, kid? Where you come from?'

'Nowhere, much.'

'You're not that kid they been lookin' for up north, are you?'

'Aren't nobody looking for me that I know of.'

'Hell'n Tommy! It is you! Half the flamin' country's out there chasin' all over for you and you just wander in here askin' me to go out and look for someone else! What the hell do you think you're doin', comin' in here like nothin's happened?'

He pushed his book away and leaned over the high counter, taking in the boy, the filthy clothes, the bulging canvas haversack, the battered hat and the animals waiting outside. He was a big man, with hands that had seen heavy work and the purple bottlenose of the serious drinker. The boy began to edge towards the door.

'I just want you to catch up with Cabel Singh and Eileen before Joe Spencer and his mates get to him.'

It sounded weak, in the middle of the day, with the street empty outside and not a sign of movement in the town, and the sun shining brightly on the cleared paddocks and yellow stubble all around.

'I know about you, kid. You're mixed up with that business up north. That young girl gone off, and whatever else. Word is, one of them Indian bastards done something. Or maybe done something. Like your mate, Old Sally. Not that Old Sally ever done anyone any harm, as I know of. We been told to keep a bit of an eye out.'

He edged around the counter towards the boy, who was still edging towards the door.

'We been told to keep a bit of an eye out for you, too, young feller. There's been some funny goin's on up north. That young girl an' all. Still missing, and some poor bloke gettin' burned up, up there in the desert, and some of his stuff goin' missin', and the hawker cleared out and nowhere to be found. Maybe you know anything about that, young feller?'

The boy began to make for the door and the horse which

was hitched just outside, but the big man was quicker, bringing himself around the last of the counter in a flash and taking hold of the boy's baggy jacket.

'Now. You just hang on there a bit.

'What you an' me is goin' to do,' he said, and not too unkindly, 'is take a little trip together, back up north, to see just what is goin' on. I'll talk to them on the phone tonight. An' what I'm goin' to do until then, because I can't get up there today, is put you away for the night.'

The boy struggled just a little against the grip on his jacket, and then went limp. He looked helplessly out to the horse and the dog who waited in the shade of the pepper trees that lined the street.

'You been in jail before, kid?'

The boy had not, and the policeman told him in a kindly enough way that it wouldn't be too bad, but that people had been looking for him all over the country, and he wasn't about to let him get away, because from what he'd heard they'd be unlikely ever to find him again. He said that he wasn't really jailing him but just putting him somewhere safe to be sure that he wouldn't clear out.

He called down the passage that led off behind the office, and after a time his wife came out—a redskinned woman with oily curls who waved at them with a heavy castiron frypan—and he told her that this same boy who was squirming in his hands was the one they were all looking for up north, and that he had just walked in, there and then, off the road and like nothing was happening, and that they were going to keep him there until the morning, when he would take him up north in the car. He told her that the kid would be needing something to eat, because the poor little bugger looked like he hadn't eaten for a week, and the boiled woman said nothing but just scowled at him and then at the boy and then went back with a clatter and a crashing to the iron leanto at the back of the house.

He told the boy that his horse and the pup would be looked after and fed, and that his wife would bring him something to eat a bit later in the day. He then took him out the back, one thick hand still firmly twisted into the baggy fabric of the boy's jacket, so that he seemed to hang in the air like a bundle of rags. He took his bag and things from him, and had him strip down the horse, and then led him around the house and over to the lockup, a tall corrugated iron shed nestled amid the sheds and stables and pepper trees at the back of the station. A small crowd, mostly of children about the boy's own age, had gathered to watch the law take its course. They followed the policeman and the boy around to the back, at a safe distance.

The lockup had a heavy iron door and a couple of small screened windows set very high. The door was swinging open when they arrived, and it was dark and close and there was very little room inside, because the lockup was half full of stock feed: bags of oats and pollard and chaff bags and a number of bales of hay.

'Don't get much need to use the place.'

He kicked his way into the jail, through the straw.

'Beryl usually just makes up a stretcher on the verandah for the odd drunk we get stayin' over. Don't reckon that'd be right for a little tyke like you, eh? Likely to take off at the drop of a hat, I'd reckon. Eh?'

He shook the boy, but gently, and pushed him over towards the bunk. He moved a bale out of the way and shook more straw from the blankets, and made him sit down on the bed. The boy looked about him, at the horse feed, at the iron walls, and the small high window, and he struggled to breathe against the sharp acidic smell of spilt feed and the greenish, vomit tang of chewed mousemeal, and the dry and flattened signs of generations of dead mice.

'What about the horse?'

'The horse'll be fine. And the pup. Better'n you, even. Just take it easy. Beryl will be along a bit later. She'll get you some water.'

'What about Old Sally? You goin' to do nothing? With him all busted up and everything, and his things all burned. You going to do nothing at all?'

'Old Sally comes past here and lays a complaint, I'll be onto it like a shot. Don't you worry. Nobody round here got nothing against Old Sally. He aren't killed anyone, as I know it.'

He shouldered the bags of chaff and the bales some more, so that the boy could lie down. Then he handcuffed him to the side of the bunk for a moment and began to go through his things, the filthy clothing, the crusts of food left over from what the logcutters had given him, the halfempty pack of .22 bullets, his knife and his tin mug, and a stinking bone for the dog.

And at the bottom of the sack, still rolled up in the newspapers from the Debt Adjuster's suitcase, he drew out the revolver. As he unravelled it, the bullets dropped out and fell into the dust.

'Jesus!'

He poked at it and spun the empty chambers, cocked the pistol and clicked it. He picked up the bullets.

'Where the damned hell you get a thing like that, young feller?'

'I found it on the road.'

'Yeah. Like you found a lot of things over the last few weeks. On the road. Jesus Christ!'

He looked behind him at a small knot of boys who had approached closer from their shelter beneath the pepper trees and were now peering through the door.

'You kids push off. Now!'

They shuffled off, slowly enough to assert themselves against his authority, quickly enough not to have to be told again. He peered at the boy more closely, perhaps even a little impressed.

'You plannin' on shootin' somebody, kid? You plannin' to pot this Cabel Singh feller? Or Joe Spencer and his mates? That what you got in mind? Thing like this's no damn use for anything but killing people. Close up, like. I should bloody know. You're not goin' to shoot any rabbits with a thing like this, I can tell you.'

'Wasn't planning on shooting anyone,' the boy mumbled. 'Just found it, that's all.'

'On the road, eh! Lot of things seem to have happened, out on that road.'

He looked at the boy, but without hostility.

'There's something a bit odd about you, young feller. You got some bee in your bonnet you aren't tellin' us about, eh! There's somethin' a bit wild goin' on in that damn fool head of yours.'

The boy said nothing, but just watched as his revolver disappeared from sight and into the policeman's pocket.

When he had gone, the boy tried for a time to call out, his highpitched voice sounding thin and silly against the closed door, the warm darkness and the muffling thickness of the chaff and hay. He sat on the edge of the bunk amid the reek of aged sweat that rose from the tangle of army blankets, and waited for the rest of the day to pass, listening to the yelping of the pup, which the policeman had tethered in the shade just outside, and then the scampering feet of mice. And after a time there came the thump thump thump of stones falling on the roof and iron walls, from the town kids who had come back again for a bit of sport, and then a wild yelping and howling from the pup, who was an outlaw too and had just been punished with a volley of rocks. The boy climbed up on the bunk and screamed blue murder at the kids, screamed for someone to come, and the town kids ran away.

Later there was a knocking on the door, and the scowling woman with the look of a cooked yabbie announced that she had brought his tea and that he should go back over to the corner and lie on the bunk so that she could open the door wide enough to place within a laden plate of potatoes and fried meat and an enamel mug of tea, and a plate of sticky jam pudding. This he took and ate in quick handfuls, leaving the last of the pudding for the mice and the ants.

Night fell quickly within the dark spaces of the jail, and he had nothing to do but to listen to the crackling of the cooling iron above, and far away in the distance, the sound of music from a wireless carrying to him in the night. There was no other sound, for the pup had stopped its yelping long before, and he dragged bales of straw up on the bunk so that he could listen to the wireless from the high window.

Peggy O'Neill was a girl who could steal,
Any man, any heart, any time

And I'll put you wise
So you'll recognise
This wonderful girl of mine

He took off most of his clothing and touched the sores which had begun to break out on his body, and he rubbed his ankles and toes where his outsize boots had chafed and broken the skin. He lay upon the stinking blankets and let his thoughts run out into the darkness, thoughts of a return to the home place, and thoughts of the bones of the Debt Adjuster lying out there in the desert like the bones of sheep he had found when the grass fires passed, and thoughts of the children dragging their stinking horse along the tracks. He thought perhaps the policeman was right and there was something wild going on in that head of his, and he wondered whether the wildness was in the things he saw on the roads or just in the way he saw them; but he also knew there was nothing that he had seen on the roads that did not make it wilder, and the more likely that he would never go back home. He lay amid the thick smells of the jail and watched the iron walls press in upon him and listened to the roof crack in the night. He felt the heat rise and his skin glow and the sweat run in streams about him even with the cool of the night outside, and he slipped towards sleep amid the smells and the sounds of feeding mice.

One time he had gone into town with Joe Spencer in the truck, and he walked about the town within the shadow of Joe's easy swagger and he saw at last Joe's world of girls and speeding trucks, and drinks behind the Patchewollock pub.

Late in the evening they sat about a burning log behind the Patchey pub, and Joe and his mates drank beer and threw rocks at a kero tin, and talked about guns and machines and feats against the scrub. And someone talked about Eileen because, the boy was told, Eileen could be just about anybody's because she'd blown in out of nowhere and with no family that anyone ever knew about, but she was Joe's, and Joe's by right for as long as he wanted her because there was no-one who could lump faster and straighter than Joe Spencer this side of the great lake. Joe took in his tributes in an easy way and began to pay his dues, and the boy had sat with his face bright to the fire and taking in whatever reflected gleam came his way, as Joe boasted of his doings with Eileen.

When they listened to Cabel Singh in the firelight, Joe Spencer listened as well, watching Eileen's eyes bright in the firelight, Eileen crosslegged in the dust and listening to Cabel talk. Just back from the fire a little way, always just beyond the first ring of light, Joe Spencer would lie propped up on one elbow, perhaps enjoying the stories too, but mostly just breaking sticks or peeling peppercorns and flicking them into the fire, enjoying being out in the night and near to Eileen, and the feel of the dirt and twigs and evening air upon his bare arms and the sounds of the swarming insects beaten away from the circle by the fragrant odour of the glowing cowpats. Joe broke his bits of stick and flicked them sometimes at Eileen, flicking them so that they stung like the bites of an insect, to distract her from the tales of Cabel Singh, to have her turn her head and smile at him, to draw her for one moment from those countries where she roamed with Cabel Singh.

Joe liked also to hear the soft voice of Cabel Singh, even when he didn't follow the stories, or when he could understand the stories and could see that they were wrong, because for Joe Spencer a tree was no more than lumber biding its time to become a sheepyard or a cowshed, and a dry lakebed was just a lake in need of water. For all that, he always joined them in the night, lying back a little beyond the light and watching the others drawn beyond themselves and into the worlds that lived in the glow of Cabel's embers, watching the raw glow of the fire softening upon her bare legs and arms. The boy would see, away up on the verandah, the rising glow of the hurricane lamp as the evening light died, with his parents sitting, his mother darning in the dim light, and occasionally the glow of the father's pipe, as they sat out in silence on the splintered wicker furniture, listening to the hum of the talk and sometimes laughter going on below, with Auntie Argie rocking beside them. Eventually there would be his mother's call to Hannah, which meant a call also to Eileen, and they would all say goodnight to Cabel Singh, with Joe slipping off without a word into the darkness to the shack and the snoring of Old Tollie, and he and Eileen and Hannah would make their way slowly up to the house.

Then he would lie awake and listen, lie awake until he heard her rise late in the night and dress again, measuring every step of Eileen as she crept down the corridor and eased the flywire open and crept out of the house. He would rise and follow, towards the light of Joe Spencer's cigarette which glowed amid the scrub below the dogyard; he crept after her to listen and to watch, and he would hide amid the thick boronia and broom, would lie low amid the ants and fallen bark and broken branches, with the sounds of his movement and his breathing hidden by the restless greeting of the dogs.

He would watch them in the moonlight, down beyond the dogyard, their bodies moving dimly in the darkness, the shame long gone of hiding in the darkness, watching the whiteness of their bodies glowing in the night, Eileen in seconds naked with Joe, talking in soft whispers to Joe as they lay naked in the moonlight. She arched astride him, moaning with slow pleasure as they moved together in the dust amid the twigs and the dry grass, lost in a turning coil of white bodies in the cool light of the moon, and then there was laughter again between them and the glow of a match and Joe's cigarette burning among the trees again. Soon he would see Eileen walking towards the house, Eileen moving quickly through the low trees and passing each time close by where he lay amid the bushes, Eileen doing up her dress always as she passed in the darkness and the dogs restless again and barking with her motion past the yard.

They called on Joe to tell it all, in cheers and laughter to tell them secret things of this girl who blew in from nowhere. Joe did not tell them much, but just enough to show that there was much to tell, and even the boy was pleased for the moment in the sound of Joe's easy triumphs and in the circle of flushed and expectant faces above their beer, behind the Patchey pub. It was only on the road and afterwards, beyond the laughter and the eager faces, that it crept back in silence upon them as they drove back in the night along the Baring road, with the memory rising for the boy of Eileen and Joe, watching Joe's smoke rings float and fade into the night, of Eileen's whispering and of Eileen moaning softly in the darkness, and buttoning up her dress. Joe drove on in silence, now knowing what the boy was thinking and avoiding his looks, not cuffing or joking with him as he usually did, but settling his mind by sliding back and forth, to skittle the scuttling rabbits that sped across the road.

Why did you say that, Joe? Why did you talk like that?

He sat beside Joe in the darkness, looking down the road ahead, at the unvaried passing of the trees, the light among the stooping switches that bowed across the track. He sat alongside, watching Joe, with Joe no longer joking and teasing as they slid through the drifts of sand, their minds in silence shying at the brink, both knowing of an unmapped country that ran out from Eileen, Eileen always a toppled fence and Eileen an open road, and now a place where all the words and all the tales that used to work gave out. He watched the firm hands of Joe Spencer on the wheel, now slapping the wheel to fill the desperate spaces, swerving to kill the straying thoughts like rabbits as he went. The boy looked along the long repeating passage of the truck lights in the night, and he knew then that you could let your mind run in the shadows and explore these new domains, or you could stay along the familiar tracks, but only now with violence, and hard blows. And he thought again of that last night, when Joe had struck her, the sounds of whispering in the darkness and then of harsher words, the sudden movement in the dirt and the blows to follow. He thought of Eileen pleading quietly in the darkness, half clad and writhing in the dust, pleading and struggling to her feet, limping past the boy and struggling to arrange her dress, hopping ungainly for a moment as she pulled up her knickers, and weeping softly as she limped past where he lay.

*

'Kid! You there?'

He heard a scratching upon the door, and a gentle knock, and the sound of a hacksaw working on the lock. He heard the husky voice of Joe Spencer, speaking through a crack in the iron.

'Listen, feller. I'm goin' to let you out. But you got to promise me. When you get out, you get straight on what's left of that old moke of yours an' head off home.'

'I'll go home,' he said. 'I promise.'

Joe kept on with the sawing, the scraping sound more than loud enough to disturb the people at the house, above the blurred sound of the wireless. The boy fossicked for his clothing in the darkness and gathered together the few things the policeman had left him, his own blanket, and his canvas haversack with almost everything in it except the revolver and bullets and his father's pliers. Soon Joe released the bolt and eased it back.

He felt the rush of cooler night air into his stuffy prison. Joe pulled open the door, and plunged in and grabbed him by the shirt, twining his hand in it as the policeman had before, and dragging the boy out and through the pepper trees and sending him sprawling into the dust amid the stables and yards behind. He dragged the boy down and they crouched together under the drooping branches of the pepper trees, the moon throwing enough light for them to see each other's faces, with Joe's hand still firmly entwined in his baggy shirt, his coarse whisper grating on the night.

'You promised me. Right? You go home. You take your old nag and your nitwit bloody dog and you clear out. You go west, first off, where they won't look for you. I saddled the horse an' filled the waterbag and put some chaff and some tucker in a bag. All you got to do now is get on home.'

'I aren't goin' home, Joe. I aren't listening to you any more, Joe. Not any more.'

He tried to lever Joe's fingers, one by one, from his shirt.

'What you going' to do? What are you goin' to do if you find 'em?'

'That's my business.'

'He didn't do nothin', Joe.'

'That's my business. You don't know he didn't do nothin'. Nobody knows it. Cooper don't think so. I want to hear him say it.'

'You goin' to give him the chance to say anythin', Joe? You an' all those others? Or you just goin' to hit him?'

'There's lots of things you don't know, kid. Things are bad, just about everywhere. About as bad as they get, I reckon.'

The boy slumped beside the shed, out of the way of Joe's ready fists.

'I don't know, Joe. I don't know.'

'That's why I tell you to just go home and get on with things. Aren't nothing to be got out of wandering around the country like a bloody loon.'

'I aren't goin' home, Joe.'

'He wouldn't be running if he wasn't running from some-thin'.'

'He aren't running, Joe. That's just the way he lives. All the time.'

They sat in the dust, and silently for a time.

'What I want to know,' Joe breathed, 'is what he said. What he told her. Looking out along that damned track as if she would just take off along it one day, like the way she came. With his mad yarns an' all, and moving about the place with no more sense than a damn willywilly. You tell me how come we can never find the bastard, and he's always just left.'

'He always keeps moving. That's just what he does. This time is no different. He lives over the whole place. Somehow. That's why Eileen went with him.'

'What?'

'That's why Eileen went with him.'

'Listen, you silly little prick!'

Joe leapt over and seized him by the shirt again, drawing him up close, his eyes hot in the dark.

'It's about time you got your damn head straight on one thing. That's one thing you can get straight right now, before you try blowin' anyone else's damn head off. Eileen's not with him. You got that? She's not with him. He's travelling on his own!'

'That's not true.'

'Damn right it's true. She's just gone, that's all.'

'How do you know? How do you know that.'

Joe drew the boy up close, shaking him, trying to push the information in, once and for all.

'I know. I just know it. That's all. Word is.'

'Whose word?'

'Word is, he killed her and dumped her out in the bush.'

'Whose word?'

'People reckon. Lonnie Cooper, and all. Cooper's onto him. Cooper's mates up and down the country are keepin' an eye out for him.'

'Why would he do that, Joe?'

'Maybe she changed her mind. Maybe she said she'd go off with him and then maybe she said she wouldn't. Anyway, them bastards don't think like you and me.'

'Why did he leave the dress behind? Why would he make it look like she'd been hurt?'

But Joe's answers had run thin, and all he had left was an ancient wisdom on the matter.

'Them bastards don't think like you an' me.'

'Why you chasin' him, Joe? Why you after him? It's 'cos you know she's with him, isn't it, Joe?'

Joe clenched his fist as if to hit him, but he stood up instead and delivered an almighty kick to the slabs that made up the wall of the shed, so that the timbers shook.

'Jesus, kid! Why can't yer just get on with things, like everybody else? What's it to you, anyway?'

'I don't know, Joe.'

'What did he tell you? What did he tell her, anyway? The two of you?'

The boy felt again the rush of tears, and he wiped his nose with the back of his filthy sleeve.

'Nothing, Joe. He never told us nothing.'

There was no way that the boy could answer Joe, nothing in any of it that he could talk to Joe about, and no way he could explain why he knew that Eileen was with Cabel Singh other than by looking out across the country and seeing what there was to be seen and all that wasn't, and there was no way of explaining to Joe the thoughts he had shared with the bagsewer, that this was a place where just about anything that meant anything seemed to come out of the things that weren't there; and he knew he couldn't go on for long talking to a bloke like Joe about empty spaces, because even if he tried to, after a time Joe would just get angry and thump him anyway.

*

He waited until after Joe had gone, until he could no longer hear the angry footsteps of Joe Spencer, and then finally he heard the revving of a truck that had been parked somewhere to the far side of the town. He waited until the stillness had swallowed everything, until even the music of the wireless stuttered and died, and the night slipped into a silence that was broken now and then by restless dogs.

He waited in the jail, its door now swinging open, sitting on the bunk and looking out into the night, trying to understand all that Joe Spencer had told him. Then he crept towards the house and across the creaking boards of the verandah, one slow step at a time so that the creaks sounded as no more than the cooling sounds of the house. He moved across to the rear door, lifting as gently as possible the spring lock upon its latch so that he could open the flywire door, the solid door left wide open so that the house could catch an evening breeze. He crept into the policeman's house and passed down along the corridor that ran up to the front of the house and towards the office, and there he raised the blinds so that the room was bright in the grey light of the moon. He rummaged in an agony of slow and echoing creaks among the drawers and cupboards until he found a set of keys that could open the large metal cabinet over by the window. From the cabinet he retrieved his pistol and his last handful of bullets. In a corner of the room he found his rifle standing, together with his father's pliers, and the bullets for the .22.

He passed towards the back of the house again, towards the kitchen where he might find food, and he looked as he passed into the bedroom, at the big man sleeping with his wife, as they lay sprawled in a heavy tangle of legs and sweaty sheets and shining skin and battered pillows, their thick bodies sonorous and warm within the close and odorous depths of the darkened room. He watched them moving heavily from time to time like stranded whales upon the bed, mumbling to the night and to each other in broken sighs and turning again into the pillows and the dark and sodden tangle of bedclothes. The boy crept into the room and sat on a chair in a corner. He sat and watched them as they slumbered, watched them through the night as they moved heavily against each other in the heat and sighed and moved apart again, watched them wallow and snore in the close and fusty heat of the room, its tiny flywired window admitting only fitful air, watching through the rest of the night, until he saw the first fragile shreds of dawn. And as he crept beyond the house to find the horse and pup, he decided that this would be the last time he ever set foot within a house, that his short sleep in the jail would be the last time he would sleep beneath a roof, and that he must now, like Cabel Singh, live from this time alone and on the roads.

They rode not to the west as Joe had bid, but onward to the north, following for a time the red and narrow tracks that led off from the main roads, passing through gates and along the beds of dried creeks and along the routes he knew Cabel Singh had taken, moving always towards the great saltlake to the north. He knew that Joe and his mates had gone on ahead, knowing now that Joe and his mates were moving over the country on the trail of Cabel Singh, the boy now cutting fences where they stood across his path, now cutting down the lines that rode above the fences to quiet the singing voices that crept after them, knowing when he cut that soon the whole country would be after them, but cutting anyway, chopping his way across the edge of the circle, to find at last the path of Cabel Singh.

They rode on to the north, the dog now limping badly from the shower of town kids' rocks. They rode through the long thin lines of timber that lined the tracks and fences, through thick belts of uncleared mallee and across open yellow stubble and dusty new worked fallow, and they slept in the shade of uncleared timber through the heat of the day, and rode on again through the night. They rode north towards Nandaly and turned off down the red and narrow track that led to the east and across the north of the lake and around by Daytrap, running northward towards Cocamba and Chinkapook. And after a time they mounted a cleared rise and came upon the first wide expanse of Cabel's great saltlake, breaking upon an open view of the lake that they had glimpsed just once or twice before across the sandhills and saltbush, but which now gleamed out before them, far off into the distance, running out beyond the low curve of the earth. They stopped for a time and looked out to the south, over the flat and silver surface of the saltlake reaching off and beyond the horizon, the ocean of which Cabel had spoken, shining warmer in the red and dusty light, with the dark shapes of islands in its midst that rose from the rising misty waters that flowed and eddied in the sun.

The boy pulled his hat down further over his face because the sky to the west was darkening red and the winds starting to blow more strongly. The horse stamped its feet and became restless as the sky above began to change and the deep clouds of dust began to stoop low and run out in probing fingers across the sun. He rode towards the rim of the lake, and he saw that it was here, as Cabel had once told him, that the whole dry and flaking land now found its last condition, with all the homeless shifting drifts and stranded saltpans and the rattling forests and open tracts of blasted earth gone dead and blown and flaked away, in silver emptiness.

He remembered Cabel's tales of this open sea, of an ocean in the desert where one could walk across the face of the waters, where one could make the phantom waters part and flow and close again behind, a place where those with courage and a mind to see might stroll across the bottom of the sea, and take in all the knowledge hidden there from those who never strayed beyond the saltbush beaches. And he thought of a song that Cabel taught him on O'Sullivan's Lookout, when he spoke of his journeys to the great lake, a song that he sang in English to the boy, and to his dog, whenever they rode towards Windmill Tank.

The true Guru is a sea of pearls,
And he who seeks those pearls shall find
All knowing that he needs.
The true Guru is a sacred lake
Where men like swans do come
To feed upon the precious stones.
As swans they eat all they desire
And pass their days upon the lake
And live upon pearls for ever.

Cabel Singh would smile at him when he sang his song, and tell him of the sacred books that he had studied far away and as a child, and of the sea of immensity as it was there described, and of the great saltlake to the east where he now found those precious stones. He told of how, when you rode out upon the mirror reaches of the great saltlake, all that the books had told in tales and through mysterious veils and in fantastic images took on a form of truth that you could see and feel between your toes, in the crumbling of the salt-waves beneath your feet and the slow trudge over the unmeasurable distances that flowed out before your eyes.

He said that when you rode out upon the lake, the rising waters opened out before you and eddied around you and then flowed out behind, and you stood out in the centre of a vacancy where all things you thought were real and could be touched and broken melted into rising air and shining light, the shore, the saltbush beaches and the distant trees, and all that you knew and all that you had ever known or done and all the pain and all the joy just rose and faded with the floating air. Then you were born again in nakedness, born again within the body's husk, and so again in every time you risked the saltlake's depths. For Cabel Singh had told him, on their way to Windmill Tank, that this world and such lands of dreaming met only in strange places, and almost never in the lives of many, but that such meetings might sometimes be found in the deep blue seas of untracked forest through which they passed and in the heart of the desert to the north, but mostly on the great saltlake that lay far to the east, where all 'I am' and 'I once was' and 'Now I will be' just peels from you in strips like ancient bark before the wind; and the boy would pull his hat lower and stare at the track ahead so that Cabel could not see that he did not understand, and Cabel laughed and talked of how they would perhaps cross the great saltlake one day together, where the boy would then become the wisest boy on earth.

The dust rose in the winds about them, gathering deep in clouds of red that billowed to the west. The sands began to move as they came closer to the lake, the sky now red and stooping low, and the darkness running out across the western sky and passing in rolling shadows over the lake. The boy tied his handkerchief about his face, and put a rope to the dog, and they rode on through the rising dust towards Daytrap, searching the bush and the bare plains on either side of the track for some sign of shelter from the blown sticks and savage wind. They came upon the wreckage of a stable, a frame of forks and toppled slabs that had at some time been covered with a roof of straw and broom, and which kept a wall or two of pine slabs and some sheets of buckled iron, which they could use to break the scouring winds. The boy drew his animals over, stepping across the fallen timbers and the mounds of rotting straw, across the rusted remnants of machines and down into a cavern that was formed by the wall of pine slabs, and a toppled iron manger. He drew his animals in as the darkness grew upon them, and pulled himself down, below the flapping iron and beyond the blast of earth.

He heard within the darkness another sound, the sound of a low chanting voice that rose beyond the storm, a voice that was low and muffled but wound up and down in ululation like the whining of the wind; and amid the dying light he saw another, a muffled figure crouched below the toppled manger, scarcely to be seen in the blowing sand and all the darkness of the moving earth. He saw a muffled pile of flapping cloth, already covered red in the flying dust. He saw bare legs and split protruding boots that were badly ripped and broken. In the last of the light, and through eyes slotted against the tearing of the sands, the boy saw that the figure was bound up in a long scarf or length of cloth that was wound about the face and head and whipped savagely in the wind.

'Hey!'

He cried above the chanting and the beating of the wind, and there was still no movement, no sound that ran beyond the slow muffled chanting and the flapping of loose cloth and beating of the wind. He stooped and shook the pile of rags.

'Hey, mister. Hey!'

A bony hand shot out from beneath the rags and clutched him by the wrist. It held him for a moment, and the boy struggled back. Then another hand crept out from amid the rags and took one end of the winding cloth and drew it from the face. It was a man with dark skin, much darker than the skin of Cabel Singh, with reddened eyes set deep within the bundled rags that bound his head, the red eyes peering at the boy, the lower face still muffled and the rest of an unravelling turban still drawn about his head, and the eyes the boy saw were bright and red with the scouring of the sand. The man wound away the cloth that bound his face one more turn, and the boy saw a straggling beard and crooked and rotting teeth, and much of the filthy turban now looped about his body in loose folds that flicked and streamed in the wind. He held the boy's hand, squeezing his hand with an unnecessary strength, still slowly chanting, his red eyes roaming about the boy, his voice still muffled within the shrieking of the wind and cutting sand, and his face, except for those bright eyes, fading still further in the dying light. Then he stopped chanting, and released the boy's hand, and gathered his rags about him.

'Come inside, boy. Come inside this place. I know who you are. I know about the boy who is looking for Cabel Singh. Come inside, and shelter from the wind.

'Yes. Do not be afraid. You can share this place with me. They call me Mullah the Shootcutter. My name is Mullah Singh.'

He stared intently at the boy, his raw and bleeding eyes searching the boy through the darkness, searching the strange sight of the boy with his stamping horse and cowering dog. Then he wrapped the cloth about his face again, leaving nothing to be seen but the thin line of his lips, his lips moving against the dust and wind, the tip of his tongue moving about his shattered teeth as he sang. As the boy drew the pup down into the cavern beside the man in rags, he began to chant another song, to chant sometimes in a language that the boy had only heard when Cabel sang, and sometimes in a language that the boy could understand. The boy watched Mullah Singh while he could still be seen, crouched against the toppled walls but disappearing with each moment into the piling sand; and soon all he could see were the moving lips of Mullah Singh. Through the whining of the wind, he listened to the voice that rose and fell, to the man he knew as Cabel's shadow, singing to him as though to everyone and no-one, singing his songs of dying and of lands beyond the death, that he had sung a thousand times before.

He sang of how they moved them in the darkness, long before the sun was up. He sang of how they beat them in the darkness, kicking them awake and striking them with whips, and thrusting with butt and blade while it was still the desert cold of night. In the desert cold of night they rose, all those who still could rise, and they stretched and shook their stiffened limbs, and took what they could carry. They rose and shook their stiffened limbs, to the distant sound of shooting and the beating of drums, and all around the rise of wailing voices and the crack of whips and the sounds of children crying and the desperate voices of the English officers, hoarse in the rising dust and trying to turn the cracks and beatings to a language of direction to their defeated troops.

He sang of how they moved them into lines, the Turkish soldiers falling out unshaven and still dazed and terrified from battle, as tired and exhausted as those they had defeated, beating them to their feet in the darkness of the night and into shuffling lines, to wait for the sun to rise, to wait for the call to move, amid the groaning of the wounded in their stiffened bandages, amid the ache of empty stomachs and the sounds of shouting and crying wrenched from broken lips and throats of shattered glass. He sang of the sorting of the wounded, the wounded tested with the bayonet or the boot, of the growing lines of wounded laid out upon the open earth below the rising sun, waiting below the toppled ramparts to be flung into wagons, or loaded on the barges that waited on the Tigris, their bandages caked stiff and rasping and the deep throb of infection gaining steadily on the blood.

They moved them towards the gates in shuffling lines, the city gates pocked and broken by the weeks of shellfire, past barricades strewn with ragged clothing and abandoned arms, the ramparts now festooned with the corpses of those who helped them, and of many who had not, with bodies nailed to gates or strung like ghastly garlands all along the walls, with hanging bodies turning and spilled and stiffened entrails swinging in the early morning sun, with faces hidden in long lanks of gore, and below them crowds of women and wailing children, lining the route to howl their curses upon the shuffling bandaged lines of men and those that moved them off onto the barren road that led up to Bagdad.

He sang of thousands moving through the toppled gates and through the walls of broken stone and clay, out past the broken arches and toppled walls of Kut, and through the lines of upturned earth and broken wire, the Turkish horses wheeling and rearing above the struggling ranks as they threaded their way into the desert, as they wove their way out through the shattered guns and broken trucks and the unburied stench of men and horses that lay beyond the walls. They moved out through the gates and beyond the ragged mounds of upturned earth and below the stripped and jagged shafts of ancient palms, past injured horses still writhing in the dirt and snarling dogs tearing at scattered shreds of flesh and clothing, and here and there in the half light of early morning a ragged figure battling with a pack of dogs and sifting through the piles of earth and rotting limbs.

He sang, against the sweeping wind, of how they moved them from the sight of water and all cover from the sun, away from the broad reaches of the Tigris and out in dwindling lines across the plain, and how some turned against the whip and into the cruel glitter of the rising sun for one last view of the smoking ruins of Kut. Then they walked on into the desert, and slowly to the north in long lines of dragging feet and lifting dust, goaded onwards by the Turkish soldiers with their whips and bayonets, and sometimes by the Arabs, and by their side they watched the scampering Budhoos who scavenged the sides of the rambling column for anything or anyone who might topple from the ranks. And he sang of how the Budhoos followed beside and just beyond the Turkish whips, waiting for those who might fall aside, waiting always for the wounded to drop, as they left the reeking city behind, and trudged on towards Bagdad.

He sang of how the wounded fell, how the Arabs came upon them with whips and rifle butts and forced them to their feet again, how they were chased and harried by the Budhoos who ran beside the thinning troops, waiting to strip those who fell, the bodies left to rot along the edges of the track. And he sang of how they walked for days, walked through the heat and stench of falling flesh, pushed by the bayonet and rifle butt, pushed on through cracking lips and stiffening wounds and slow torment and all contempt; and how they walked faster and stronger than most men on the march from Kut, and how when they marched from Kut, they marched beyond what most think is the normal world, and as they marched they joined with those who had passed through death and out the other side, through all forms of pain and all the graceless forms of death and all forms of disease. He sang of men who had slept amid their own shit and amid the falling shreds of flesh, who were pelted with filth in one miserable *bled* after another as they made their way up to Bagdad, who had walked through the curses and abuse and blows of children, who had walked through the long rows of women who lined the Bagdad streets and shrieked their curses at them and held up their robes and thrust their naked bodies at them in an excitement of contempt. He sang of how such men survived by living from the dead, by stealing boots and blankets warmed by the crust of blood and faeces of the dead and perhaps the almost dead. And he sang of how they walked through death again and again in the months and years that followed, in Bagdad and on the transport barges and in all the camps in which they lived and laboured in the long years to follow. He sang of how they were starved and they were beaten, and how their bodies were taken many times by the Arabs and their masters, in Sammarah and other places, and how they had watched one another fade, the cursed and beaten body falling away in strips, and he sang of how, in Cabel Singh, the five thieves fell away.

The boy then passed the last of his water to the Shootcutter, whose dry voice had now begun to rasp and fade amid the sweeping dust, and when he drank he sang at last of the lives of men who had lived through too many lives and deaths when they were scarcely of the age of men, of those who walked beyond their proper time of dying, of a husk of beaten flesh and stolen rags who became known as the Shootcutter, and of all the shapes of floating thought that live beyond the grave. And when he had taken another drink from the boy's waterbag, he then began to sing again, more softly now, the song of how they moved them in the darkness, long before the sun was up; of how they beat them in the darkness, kicking them awake and striking them with whips, and thrusting with butt and blade while it was still the desert cold of night, and again of how they rose amid the desert cold of night, all those who still could rise, and they stretched and shook their stiffened limbs, and took what they could carry.

He rode out upon the narrow tracks and through the new cover of soft blown sand, the boy pushing the old horse up to a stumbling trot, and they rode beside the low sandy ridges that ran along the north of the lake towards Daytrap, with the shining of the saltlake all around him to the east and to the south. They wound along the track that led up to the north of the lake, towards a place that Cabel called Daytrap, and along the way they met a farmer who was carrying water in an iron tank that was mounted on an ancient wagon, moving slowly along the track, with two small children with wide hats and filthy faces, riding on the tank.

'Have you seen a hawker? Have you seen Cabel Singh?'

The man told him that there was a hawker camped down by the shores of the lake a day or two ago, that he had gone down to the edge of the lake and spoken to him, a hawker who often camped there, in the stretch of timber that lay closest to the salt. The boy asked him whether the hawker had moved on again, but the man did not know, but he could tell the boy that others, too, were looking for the hawker, and that earlier that same day some young men from somewhere out to the west, and damned near as filthy as the boy himself, had called at his place to ask if he knew of the hawker's whereabouts.

He told them that no hawker had been seen in those parts for many weeks, because they had a wild and unwashed look about them, and he did not want his word to be the source of harm. The boy accepted a drink from the man for himself and for his animals, and they set off again in the direction that he pointed, the boy urging the horse forward now as fast as it would travel, moving on towards Daytrap which he knew to be the place of which Cabel had spoken, a place to the north of the lake with its crumbling cliffs and wide salt beaches, a place where he often made his camp, with a wide view of the whole expanse and the dark salt islands to the south.

Further along the road, the boy saw clouds of dust rising again in the distance, and then the sound of a motor revving high, and he saw that the dust was travelling, kicking up at speed with a motor vehicle beating through the scrub and along the track towards him, floating, or so it seemed, through a rising cloud of dust and gravel. He slipped from the horse and ran into the fringe of scrub that ran by the side of the road, drawing the animals with him deep into the scrub so that the three of them were hidden back amid the trees. He crouched low behind a bank of sand and fallen timber, holding the pup close so that it would not bark and run, watching the motion of an open truck that sped towards them through the timber and along the tracks to the east.

He saw, as he expected, that the truck was the same that he had seen before, the open truck with the wheatbags in the back, the truck now caked in heavy sprays of dark black mud, making its way in a fast and sliding motion through the impeding drifts of sand that lay across the track, raising a high column of dust as it sped towards the west. They waited within the thick scrub by the side of the road, peering through the sprays of eucalypt, and he saw the same faces that he had seen in the firelight, faces strained and reddened in the wind and dust of flight, some even seeing perhaps that he was standing with the horse by the side of the road, but scarcely bothering to look at him, the driver with both hands clasped upon the wheel, wiping his face now and then with the back of his hand and intent only on keeping his truck upon the loose surface of the track. The others beside him were silent too, not joking or laughing as they had before, but all still and intent upon the road, upon the banks of soft sand drift and the switches of mallee that swept over them and slapped the sides of the truck as they sped, the men who sat beside the driver nursing shotguns between their knees, their shoulders stooped, leaning forward, watching the winding track to come.

In the back, three more sat upon the wheatbags, Joe's mates from Patchewollock, one still smeared with the filth and blood of nights before, with added licks of drying mud across their arms and faces. With them he saw Joe Spencer. Joe's usual high colour was gone ashen, his eyes fixed upon the place in the scrub where the boy stood with his animals, his eyes fixed as though upon the boy but seeming not to see. The boy looked into Joe's eyes, and in Joe's eyes he saw only the passing timber, Joe gazing sightless at the passing timber, Joe's eyes no more it seemed than a mirror of repeating fronds and fraying bark, and the broken light that flickered through the stems and branches as they ran.

Within seconds of their passing he was running towards the lake, mounting again the horse and with nothing to guide him but the dead gaze of Joe Spencer, the scrubland that ran in the fixed eyes of Joe Spencer, thinking at last in clearness of what he had given, all his crimes and his betrayals for Joe Spencer. He broke a switch from the mallee above him and began to flog the horse, flogged it out onto the track and off into the hanging sheets of dust that lay out towards Daytrap, with the horse now, and for the first time in the weeks they had been together, taking up a slow and lumbering canter under the hot sting of the switch, the boy's eyes straining for what he knew he must now see, and the dog hopping awkwardly on its three legs, but still following close behind.

'Can't say how bad it was,' was all he said. He climbed out from the stable and brushed the dust and wisps of straw from his uniform. He looked around him at the circle of waiting faces, blinking into the bright sunlight. He held the dress in such a way as not to touch the blood.

'Might not of been much at all. Head wounds bleed a lot. Head wounds don't mean nothin'.'

He could see, though, that they expected better of him than this.

'Can't tell much about anything in there. Straw and old rubbish everywhere. Can't tell who's been in and out. Kids've messed everythin' about. Looks like some kind of bad joke to me. The stockings and gloves and all.'

The joke was lost on those who stood around the stable, the boy's mother biting the edge of her nails and Hannah still in tears, and Joe sitting over under his pepper tree, brooding and digging savagely at the earth with his stick.

He took the boy's father aside.

'Poor bloody kid. Never had much of a go, did she.'

His father just murmured that maybe they'd all have had a better go of it if they'd just given her a drink when she first turned up, and set her off along the road again. He could only tell Cooper of yet another female squall that rocked the house some days before, just after Eileen had come back from Speed with Cabel Singh, with the shouting breaking suddenly in the closed heat of the house and usual charges of carelessness and insolence and worse unleashed upon Eileen, and Eileen simply handing the insults back in kind, and Auntie Argie moving through the human sounds and the crush of angry bodies. He told of how he had as usual broken from the house and gone down to the dogyard and the company of the dogs.

'From all I hear, we'll probably just find her out along the track somewhere, sittin' in the shade of a tree an' waitin' to hear all about how much fuss she's managed to make.'

Cooper took the boy beyond the earshot of the adults around the stable, but with all the adults still closely watching him. He listened to Lonnie Cooper's questions, and as he spoke he watched Lonnie Cooper's eyes rove about, over to Joe Spencer under the pepper trees, over to his mother waiting by the stable, her face deep creased against the sun.

'I don't know nothing. About anything. About what happened last night.'

'You know, son, if you know anythin' about this business as might kind of help us sort the whole thing out, I reckon you ought to say so. 'Cause if you don't,' and here he gestured to Joe, who saw that they were looking, and gave up his digging, 'all sorts of people might get dragged in. If you know what I mean.

'I'm told that you and Joe are real good mates. I even seen you together, in town. You followin' him about. Seen him mind out for yer, kind of thing. Nothing wrong with that,

neither. You ever see him with Eileen? Do you know anythin'
much about him and the girl?'

The sun was behind Cooper and the boy had to squint and
shade his eyes when he looked up to him, half closing his
eyes when he spoke, so that all seemed like a lie. He glanced
again at Joe, looking alone and weak and beaten, under the
pepper trees.

'Cabel Singh.'

He said it in a whisper.

'What's that, young feller?'

'The hawker was the one who was friends with Eileen. He
brought her back from Speed. Maybe he knows something.'

'Ah. The Indian. This Cabel Singh feller. Spent a bit of time
with the girl recently, didn't he?'

'I went with him up to Windmill Tank. With Eileen. She
asked if she could come with him. Then he went on towards
Underbool, and we came back here on foot.'

'She tell you anything?'

The boy just shook his head.

'So, he's been hereabouts, hasn't he?'

'That was days ago. He went off to the north. Days ago. Like
he always does.'

'Yeah. Could've slipped back here easy enough though,
couldn't he?'

'Why would he want to do that?'

Cooper didn't want questions in return. Nor did he have
any idea why the Indian might want to do that. He tried for
surer ground.

'Now, what about your mate, here, Joe, and Eileen. Did she
ever go out to see him at night? Your mother…'

'Cabel Singh was a soldier.'

Cooper's ears pricked up at that.

'Who was? The Indian?'

'He'd been in the war. He even killed people. He told me. When we were on our own, one time out at O'Sullivan's Lookout. He said that there was a battle and that they nearly had to eat people. He said he might have killed someone, even though he never saw who.'

The men who had been standing about the stable started moving towards the boy.

'What's that you're saying, fella? Are you saying he was skiting about killing people?'

'I'm not sayin' he done nothing.'

'What did he tell you, son?'

Cooper glanced up and threw a knowing look around the others. 'What have you got to tell us, then?'

'I aren't got nothing to tell you.'

They waited all the same, their arms folded, forming a circle which it seemed would not release him until he gave them something more.

'He just told me once that he'd been a soldier, and that soldiers were taught how to kill people.'

His voice grew shrill, and there was no help to be had in looking across to Joe. A couple of Joe's mates from over at Patchewollock had begun to gather around, mumbling some vague and ruthless action, some future violence against the girl or anyone who sullied their strength in the name of their mate Joe Spencer.

'He knows the country. He even watches the sand drifts move. He's watched them cover things, over the years. Bushes and trees and all.'

'What's that, young feller?'

'He could come an' go without any of us knowing it. Without any tracks. Better'n an abbo. They reckon.'

Cooper straightened up and scratched his elbows in slow and ponderous thought.

'I never said he done anything.'

'Seems to me maybe we ought to be havin' a bit of a talk with this here Mr Cabel Singh,' he said.

'That don't mean he had anything to do with this. With Eileen, an' all. I never meant that.'

'Sure, son, sure. Nobody says he done anything.'

'It wasn't him. It wasn't Cabel Singh what done anything. I know he didn't do anything.'

'How do you know that, kid?'

'I just don't reckon he done anythin', that's all. He really liked Eileen. He gave her rides. I seen him talking to her. She used to bring stuff down to his camp. She'd go down there, in the nights. I heard 'em talking—often. She talked to Cabel. Often.'

'Like how often?' Cooper asked.

He followed the furrows cut by the truck that ran for miles by Daytrap, following the furrows of the truck that ploughed through the deep new sand that lay across the track, and turned at last through a toppled netting gate leading down towards the lake, through belts of loose and uncleared scrub and dry grass and unsteady soil towards the pink cliffs of soft and crumbling earth that ran across the north of the lake.

He leapt from the horse as it turned through the gate, knowing that he would run more quickly across the uneven earth, seeing as he ran a thin line of smoke rising from the base of the cliffs, and then at last the distant signs of a camp, nestled below the soft crumbling cliffs and on the edge of the wide salt beach, the familiar sight of Cabel Singh's mallee pickets and his split and open wheatsacks, set out to break the wind. The small fire within his ring of stones was still burning, but Cabel's shining pots were upturned and spilled, his wares from the cart scattered in piles about the edges of the salt, with bolts of calico and cotton prints unrolled, and gaily woven in long banners in and out the trees, with dresses and shirts flapping here and there against the butt of trees and low bushes, and other garments, hats and towels and bedsheets, blowing out across the salt, turning over and over and skidding on before the wind. Below him, the sunlight caught the glimpse of bright objects in the sand, of upturned drawers and Cabel's oddments, baubles and bangles and coloured glass, sprinkled out across the earth.

Beneath the shade of a clump of low box timber, Cabel's spare horse was tethered and waiting, flicking its tail against the thick blankets of bushflies that hung about the edges of the lake, flies that now crawled thickly upon the boy's face as he stopped to take his breath in coarse gasps at the top of the cliffs, and he beat savagely at them, clawed them away from his eyes, and searched out across the shifting surface of the lake for signs of Cabel Singh. Below, the marks of heavy wheels ran out onto the salt, the tyres of the truck making wide furrows and showers of black saltmire where it had run some distance out onto the salt and had then turned, twisting and turning back in wild black arcs and moving towards the shore. There were marks beside of many straining feet, of heavy pushing and lifting, and here and there patches of saltbush and branches that had been fetched in armfuls, where the truck had become deeply bogged in sodden patches a short distance from the shore. From the edge of the salt there led away towards the centre and towards the distant islands that floated in the mists and floating waters another set of tracks, this time lighter tracks, and the trail of horses' hooves, winding out in wide and curling arcs towards the centre, the black mud released from beneath the silver surface, flowing far out across the salt and marking a trail towards the islands and the centre, which soon disappeared in the ghostly moving waters that rose far to the south.

He ran onto the salt with the horse and the dog following close behind, the horse and dog running now because he ran, the horse slowing to the sinking of its feet within the mire but struggling after him. He ran across the thin and muddy beaches and out along the tracks, running across the breaking surface of the salt with the dog limping and bounding by his side, and on towards the wall of moving waters that ran ahead and parted as they approached and flowed around behind. He ran onto the salt, taking his breath in heavy gasps, following the muddy tracks which pulled wildly to one side and then the other as the wheels struck soft hollows and the furrows deepened, running on so that the moving waters now flowed beside them and then back towards the shore. When the boy turned to see the horse, he watched the shore behind them lifting in the rising air, the pink cliffs of clay shifting and wavering in the brightness of the air and the silver sheen that rose above the salt, the pink cliffs rising and floating off behind them as they ran towards the heart of shifting light.

They saw ahead a black shape on the lake, the boy now

calling, 'Cabel! Cabel Singh!', but seeing on coming closer that it was a cartwheel run from its hub, a cartwheel lying half upright in the salt. Beyond it the black furrows continued to run into the invisible shining distances beyond, with signs now of a deep and laboured dragging in the salt, of the wagon dragging more eerily now from one side to the other, with the mark of an unwheeled axle dragging in the salt and of horses straining deep within the brackish mire but running still in coarse unstable arcs, as in some kind of panicked motion that drove them on towards the centre and the swimming peaks of barren islands, far towards the south.

They ran on into the parting waters and the haze of liquid light, passing now as they ran thick gouts of redblack blood upon the salt, the trail running still in crazy twisting curves. At last they saw a moving shape amid the waters, the unsteady mass as of a ship that reeled and kiltered with the motion of a sea. The boy stopped for a moment, sinking to his knees, heaving and gasping for his breath, with the limping dog and the horse coming up to meet him. Far ahead, as though moving in and out of the waters, the shifting shape of Cabel's cart wheeled out across the salt.

'Cabel! Cabel Singh!'

His voice rang far across the flats but was lost on the low immensity of the waterless sea that flowed about him, was soaked up in the silence of the salt. His eyes began to stream with tears with his running and the salt that flew in the wind and clung about his eyes. He followed the moving form of Cabel's cart before him, and he ran and called ahead, now gaining quickly upon the wagon which was moving, but run all askew by the broken wheel, making its way now more slowly through the salt but only in small arcs and circles, the straining form of the struggling horses now coming into view. The boy ran on, shouting to Cabel Singh, his only answer the sound now of a shrieking horse, a horse shrieking back across the salt, as though the pain had long been there but with no-one, until the boy called out, to listen to its cry.

*So we were called by the policeman over at Berriwillock
to come and pick up this boy of ours wandering half
starved around the country with a horse that needed
attention and a threelegged yelping dog that ought to be
shot, talking of wild things the like of which no-one had
ever heard from a child his age before and waving a
revolver about that he'd stolen from some dead person on
the road, with tales following him of stolen food and
downed fences and telephone wires cut, and there seeming
to be no way, we were told, that anyone could explain to
him that he ought to be home and be looked after and not
to be roaming out there on his own in the timber country
like a rabid and abandoned dog.*

*We left the children on neighbours' farms, and we drove
across to the east and from the policeman in Berriwillock
we followed signs and hints from others until and not
before its time we saw in the distance, and making his way
over towards the great saltlake as we expected, the
wretched boy and those halfstarved animals with him,
making their way slowly through the height of the heat, the
boy dressed as always in those same heavy castoffs,*

watching us drive towards him across the plains but hardly showing a sign of surprise, not lifting his hat or scarcely raising his eyes, but looking up at us through his filth and the stink rising with each move he made and leaving it for me to wonder one more time how this daft and ragged thing could grow out of any child of mine.

The boy had just looked away from us and off towards the lake with his father trying to question him and the boy acting as though his being out there and along the tracks and on his own with those poor animals was the most normal thing in the world, as though he had not been away for days and weeks out there on his own and even up through the north where no person in his right mind ever set his foot, and then looking up at us as though he did not understand why it was that we were there, looking at us and then on to the track ahead as though we had simply come to bid him and the horse goodday while making our way on to some other place, and that now it was time for us all to be gone.

Thinking yet one more time of how the violence came upon us all, thinking again of the spreading of the darkness that ran out into all our lives from the first and always from her laughter, that ran about the boy as he came back wildeyed from Windmill Tank, and I seeing always in the unknowing eyes of others that it was my task to curb and as the mother of a family to restrain, and in watching for so long the green earth crumble and run apart before us to check and to prevent her from leaving in that way, leaving all the fences down and the earth open and drifting over us and all of us running down into the savage land from which thank God I had preserved us for so long; and she beginning to talk but like the banshee my husband always said she was, beginning to tell me tales of the dead within and moving as she always did into my thoughts and into my fears before I yet had time to think or fear. And so it was that I struck back. It was not her but all the darkness that I struck, she falling nevertheless with the blow and I striking yet again, and she reaching for the edge of the manger and the iron and then slipping back and her eyes white in the darkness not with surprise but always with an infernal knowing, saying, yes, I knew. I knew that you would strike.

Well I remember her falling heavily upon the straw and I sitting there with the coldness coming on, and how after a time I strode back to the house and lay upon the bed in all my clothes and waited for the dawn to rise and the dogs to find her and for the world which was in pieces to break upon me with the brightness of the day. And when I woke in the quiet light I wondered whether or not this was a dream or just a thought that I had, that it was but her thought and her knowing that I struck, and that the bright light would bring with it the slow and ungiving sameness that we always knew.

Then the mystery began, as the child came crying and Joe and Old Tollie coming in to tea and asking what had happened and my husband looking at me, looking at me without speaking as always, but he knowing no doubt that I had gone out late and that I had lain on the bed without sleeping through the full night, and then went on sleeping in the morning as I never had. But he said nothing, mumbling only that perhaps our luck was in, and that we might now see some peace about the place, though peace was not what I could hope for, abandoned in not knowing whether she *had dragged herself off and out into the bush or whether the Indian had come back to find her, abandoned to this day with the memory of Eileen white and in peace amid the black blood of the night, left night upon night with thoughts of the girl now moving naked to the north, moving in triumph through the broken earth and flaking trees, her arms open to him and her hair matted thick in blood, walking towards Cabel Singh beyond the snowdrift and out by Wirrengren Plain.*

Trying to tell the boy in some way without telling him all those things I did not properly know myself, feeling too that I should speak to Joe Spencer in all his pain and anger, the darkness still running out across the land in the rage and anger of Joe Spencer, yet knowing that for such an act there must always be some kind of punishment, or the whole world would lose its balance and all run back to that nature that runs cruel and all around us like blowing lignum and mocks us from the drifts. Even the priest in whispered darkness told me that the blow itself that was struck in fear and not in anger was not a sin, and I know before God that if there was a sin then that sin was in the very nature of Eileen, and the nature of Eileen is something that we now know takes life from the man who, time after time, comes in along that track like a wild seed on the hot winds from the north and that only when such bad seeds cease to run across the face of the earth will the whole earth be at rest.

So we stopped there by the side of the track, my husband and I in the truck and the boy alongside looking after his horse and dog and looking as filthy as a boy could look, with my husband looking at me, his mind moving across what I said, which was the most that I could say, that the girl—I was sure of it—was not with Cabel Singh—and I would not say why it was that I knew—and his eyes asked me how was it that I could know that she was not with Cabel Singh and I could not speak further but only call to the boy to step into the truck. But the boy just looked up at us and then at the road ahead of him which wound off into the mallee and towards the lake that was still far away, and he refused to move.

It was then that my husband leaned across and spoke to the boy as he had never spoken to him or to anyone that I knew, simply telling him to keep on his way and to find his Cabel Singh and Eileen and to do whatever it was he felt he had to do. My husband leaned across me, his body between me and that of the child, and simply told the boy to get on with his search for Cabel Singh. My husband's mind runs always upon slow thoughts that move deeply like the chill water that runs along the bottom of the river, the moving waters that one can never see because of the darkness and the deep, and I knew in the power in the muscles of the shoulder that lay across me that he would not be brooked.

We started up the truck and left the boy behind in our dust, standing by the side of the road and moving on a track towards I don't know where and my husband silent alongside me in the choking of the truck. A little further along he turned the truck around, skidding and bumping in the gravel on the edges of the road and we rolled back and past our son and the horse. The boy had not moved, and we drove past, and my husband did an odd thing that I never saw before and tipped his hat to the boy as we drove past. We moved along the unmade roads that lead back to the east, leaving the boy to find whatever it was that he had to find and to know the worst of whatever it was that he needed to know. We drove off, with the boy and his animals standing in the dust that we left behind, and I wondered then whether or not we would see this boy again, this stranger whom we had amongst us for a time, seeing again in the moving waters on the road again the things that I must now always see, the brightness of Eileen's eyes catching a start of moonlight through the slabs of the stable, and the thought coming to me and ever since in the nights of her white and broken body taken up in the arms of Cabel Singh, in my thoughts the breasts of the girl white against the scars of Cabel Singh, who left perhaps the bloodied dress as a mystery seed sewn amid the warm dung of the stable, as though he too knew that punishment must always follow the act for the world to right itself. My husband sat beside me silent in the dust and through the blue timber as we wound back across the tracks and backroads, not speaking to me as he has never spoken to me for years, smiling like the smile of stone you see upon a sleeping statue spread out on an ancient tomb, the silence behind and the silence ahead and the wind picking up our own dust and driving it back over us as we moved.

The horses struggled deep in the black mud that welled up through the crystal surface, the cart no longer moving and the horses struggling and panicking in the mire, tangled in their own harness and the dragging reins, straining to haul the sinking cart further towards the centre but now pulling hard against each other, the wagon sinking deeply to one side and now no longer moving forward, the horses only edging it in a circle, round and round the hub. Upon their flanks the white foam of sweat mingled with a foam of blood from the stripes of a whip, and from the rear leg of one of the horses, blood poured in rich thick gouts from a deep wound from a broken shaft, the broken end still hanging from the harness, and the other, sharply splintered, thrusting its way again into the wound with each plunge of the horse, moving as a bloodied piston with each motion of the cart.

They struggled and plunged, the wounded animal shrieking now across the lake, and then as the boy came closer to them, the sound of the voice and even the yelping of the dog seemed to calm them for a moment, and they settled in the mire, the red blood of the outrageous wound now

pulsing thick across the dark saltmire. The cart had come to
rest facing away from the boy as he approached, facing out
towards the south, and he saw a hand, as though of someone
waving to him from the edge of the canvas, the hand waving
gently in the still and now silent air, but still no voice, the boy
calling again the name of Cabel Singh but faintly now,
knowing there was no need to shout, knowing that he had
now all the answer he would have.

He saw him sitting upon the bench where they had sat
with Eileen as they rode up to Windmill Tank, propped up as
though still driving the cart, his eyes open but glazed and
looking forward over his injured and panicked horses,
staring out across the salt and towards the distant centre, his
arms stretched out on either side, and his body held in place
upon the wagon by tightly wound and knotted bindertwine,
his arms tightly bound on either side to the metal frame that
held the canvas covers, the thin twine drawing blood from
each of his wrists, his body still swinging gently with the settling of the cart. He leaned towards the salt, held upright by
the ropes, his head bare and his long hair falling in waves
around him, the dark lanks wet with blood.

The boy walked in circles around the cart, still sinking in
the blackness of the mud, fighting against the darkness that
rode up and spread out across the salt with every step he
took, unable to think distinctly upon this thing he wished
still not to see, thinking instead of the injured horses, one
down and weak and now at peace in the slow draining of its
blood, and the other still struggling as though seeking to rise,
struggling to raise the cart and draw it on its way, still striving
to carry its dead driver out into the centre of his sea.

He sat upon the crust of crumbling salt. He waited while

his own horse made its way up slowly across the salt, drawing its hooves carefully from the black mud, and then standing and waiting for him at some distance from the stranded cart. Even the pup was for a moment calm and quiet. Together they sat and watched the struggling horse and the corpse of Cabel Singh, still swaying with the writhing of the horse, his head and shoulders leaning out across the salt and his long hair shrouding still the steady course of blood. They watched the cart and the halfsunken horses bleeding across the salt, looked out across the lake and into the moving waters all around, and he wondered if there had ever been a pain in the world like the pain that he now knew, if there had ever been a misery upon the earth like the misery that he now saw, if perhaps all the world lived always in this new pain and that all his ways of thinking until that moment were the thinkings of a child. He looked about him at the low reaches of salt and the mesh of low salt-waves carved about him by the wind. He looked at the toppled cart and the swaying corpse and then beyond, into the haze of listless moving air that swam about him, and there was no familiar thing in anything he saw. Far above them a wedgetailed eagle and then another gathered to the smell of blood, rising high above upon unmoving wings and drifting in slow silent arcs before the unsighting conflagration of a callous but indifferent sun; waiting, as the boy well knew, with all the ease and patience of the steady rising air, to pluck the bleeding eyes of Cabel Singh.

After a time the boy rose and wiped the salt from his eyes and took the canvas haversack from his back. He drew from it the Debt Adjuster's revolver and unwrapped it from its newspaper. He loaded the pistol carefully, with just two bullets, and snapped the chamber closed and walked around to the front of the cart, trying not to look again into the dead eyes of Cabel Singh. With two hands, he raised the heavy pistol to the head of the first horse, aiming it between and just a little above the eyes, as he had seen his father do, and pulled the trigger. The heavy hammer lifted, and then the pistol bucked in his hands. The horse quivered and slumped straight to the mud, the deep red blood pumping from the hole in a rich fountain, the whole wagon lurching as the horse fell against the shafts, the fountain dying away within seconds and a pool then spreading from the head and out in a deep red arc across the crystal salt. He moved to shoot the other in the same way, the second horse, disturbed by the sound of the shot so close and the falling against it of the first, now struggling again to rise within its harness, before it too slumped and sent its fountain pool out across the salt, the arc of hot blood swinging and turning in the air as it fell, spraying the boy and his pup in thick dark horseblood.

The boy took then his knife and freed the corpse of Cabel Singh from the ropes that stretched it out across the front of the van, the weight of Cabel falling forward upon his body, falling about him far heavier than he had expected, and he struggled and floundered in the soft black mud to lay the body back, fighting to clear the blood and salt and sweat that entered his eyes, pushing the body back in the van so that Cabel Singh would lie deep amid the remnants of his stock. He leaned over and across the body, lying half across the body of Cabel Singh, and he wiped what blood he could from the face, the blood that had flowed from Cabel's wounds, and he arranged the body among the last of his familiar things, the bolts of calico and tablecloths and drapery. He lay the body with hands folded upon the breast, adjusting the sleeves of Cabel's coat so that they covered the livid ropewounds to his wrists. He took a sheet of calico and laid it across the whole.

From the bottom of the cart he took the tin of kerosene that Cabel always carried to fuel his lamp in the nights, and he splashed the kerosene across the body, over all the things in the cart and over the sides of the cart itself, until all the kerosene was gone. He took matches from his canvas bag, and threw a match into the cart, and then another, and he waited for a moment until the blaze had fully caught, aided by the heat and the soft fanning winds that had begun to blow across the salt. The kerosene burned at first with a rich and oily aromatic smoke. Then the things in Cabel's cart, the cloths and papers and the thin plywood walls and canvas of the cart began to catch, and the smoke grew lighter and rose from the cart in clouds, the blaze beating noisily against the stillness of the lake, catching in climbing starts of flame the paintwork of the cart, the canvas falling away in glowing patches, the outline of Cabel's body soon etched out amid the rising smoke and flame. He took the bridle of his horse and drew it away to a distance, calling also to the pup, who was still circling the wagon and sniffing at the dead horses, and licking at the pools of blood upon the salt.

From there he walked alone and now as though alone for the first time, striding back into the floating waters and making his way step by step and slowly along the jagged wagon tracks that wound and scraped across the salt, past his own steps traced out in recent pain, the dog turning always back towards the burning cart, but then slipping again into step with the boy, hopping alongside him as for weeks on the road it had trudged beside him, adapting to his pace. They stopped for a moment when the boy came to his hat, lying black and upended on the salt. They stopped and turned to look at the wagon as it crackled in the heat behind them, the wagon already lifting in the rising air and burning as a pyre upon the waters, the black smoke thinning high above them in the bright unstable air. And it was then that he thought one more time of Eileen, thought at last of what Eileen had said, the last of what she told him on the track from Windmill Tank, as they had sat together upon the darkening rim of drifts, and looked towards the distant palms, and the windmill on the Ridge.

It was towards the middle of the day, with the high heat rising all about her and her straw hat shading her amid the sprays of mallee that fanned the route, her arms and legs bare in the cotton sundress. Again she felt the sweet sting of gumnuts and burrs and broken sticks upon her skin as she sat crosslegged in the sand, with the sun climbing and the sandflies piping and the sweat running in streams inside her dress. She had wondered in the reckless daze of midday heat if she might leave her bag and hat and all she had been given, and move off one more time towards the drifts and wild country, move off again like the wild goats and live upon the soaks and roots and wild honey, or try her gentle death amid the drifts.

Then he passed and saw her with no surprise as though he knew that she would one day be sitting in the sand beside his track, and he held out his hand to her. Upon that road, amid the slow padding of his dog and the twitching of the horses' tails, against the flies and the creak and clatter of the slow wagon with its hobbles swinging and its clashing pans, they began to talk, speaking just a little and soon as she had spoken to no-one, of the life that was before, and then more strongly to the strengths of Cabel's silence, of casual kindness and of causeless cruelty, of a child making no sense of the kindness or the cruelty but living yet in the mute hope of the healing body that remakes itself in the running of sweat and the flowing of blood, and thinking always and against all betrayals of perhaps the next day and perhaps the next place with its green shaded places and singing windmill as the place she might call home.

He told her tales, and this time of a man called Cabel Singh, and as he spoke she held his arm and ran her fingers along his skin and touched the hand that held the reins, and he talked to her not as before his fire in the nights but this time of a knowledge of pain and of broken walls and youthful bodies taken, and of bodies torn apart. She also spoke, and this time in words that she had never used or never put together in such ways, or perhaps she did not speak at all, for he seemed to know her thoughts as she knew his. They talked together of the heat and distance, and the track ahead and the dry lands that lay behind, and they took their joy in the sun gleaming on the sand drifts to the north, and in the light breeze that sprang up behind them and ran their dust about them as they moved. They saw a living in the motion of the winds and moving clouds of dust, a wisdom in the trackless seas of bushland that ran off to the north, saw that the past was just another country among a thousand countries they might cross, and that they had no need of this fragment that people called Eileen or of this broken shard called Cabel Singh, which was not today what it was yesterday and which will not be known tomorrow, that their own story was just one among a thousand stories they might not choose to tell. Time beyond time, she told how she would come with Cabel Singh along that track like a thistle seed on the hot winds from the north, and out again from time and anger and beyond the wire and iron and harried earth and scars of trees and tethered dreams and all the tracks and fencelines of constrained desire, and for the strength and knowledge that it gave each time would ride again into blue seas of untracked and untenantable forest and out across the silver flood of moving waters that part and circle in the floating air. They would run north by Pheeny's Tank and Monkeytail and laughing through the forests of the dead, along Nowingi's broken dreamlands and down by Carwarp to the waters of Kulkyne. Together they would ride with no thought between them beyond the thought that lifts the bark from trees or tears the lignum from the earth or echoes in the sounds of birds, and they would blow like rolling lignum past the still and unseen waters of Timboram and Wahpool and on beyond the floating earth of Tyrrell Downs, through the winds that break about Nandaly and the tall stacks of Pier Millan, eastward to the ocean kingdom, where they would walk upon the silver parting waters, and all the land about them would rise and fade and float apart and with it all their names and all their doing. And one day there would be no Eileen and Cabel Singh, but only travellers in stories, nothing left of them but tales of wanderers that move always and have no end but only a beginning; and Cabel Singh and she would meet always in stories that began *before ever they began, and would not end at that time when they met their ending.*

He left his hat behind him on the salt, and strode on across the crumbling surface towards the low banks and pinkgrey cliffs that lay beyond the mirage waters, and as he moved closer towards the shore, the tops of the cliffs began to appear through the shifting haze. As he walked he threw away his canvas haversack and unbuttoned his heavy coat, which was soaked and dripping still with the blood of the horse or perhaps it was the blood of Cabel Singh, and he let it fall, a dark and tangled blemish on the salt. He then pulled off his shirt which stank in the sweat that had coursed about his body under the heat of the coat, which dragged like hooks upon the scabs of the sores that had broken out upon his body, and he threw it away so that it too lay as a dark blot on the salt behind them. As he moved closer towards the cliffs the airy waters trembled and parted and ran off behind him to the south, and through the parting haze he could see upon the cliffs and amid the windtorn trees the shape of moving figures, the outline of trucks and carts moving about, the black stickfigure shapes of people walking about the cliffs and making their way down towards the beaches, but with most just waiting above and upon the heights, for they would now be able to see him, moving beyond the seas of floating light. They would now see him walking towards them, and far behind him now the clouds of black smoke that drifted upwards and out across the lake, amid the brightness of the vacant air.

He saw people collecting there, more people now than he

had seen for weeks, from Daytrap itself and Chinkapook and from up at Nandaly and down the Chillingollah road, people who had perhaps already heard the story of the boy and his pursuit of Cabel Singh. They watched but did not move from the shade of the straggling trees that clung to the edge of the cliffs. As he came closer he loosened the twine that held his castoff trousers with their baggy cuffs. He let them drop and kicked them off across the salt, and then at last the heavy boots that he had now worn for weeks with their torn seams and dragging rope and the flapping sole that had mocked at him for days. He walked onwards towards the watchers on the cliffs, the teacher perhaps from the little school that he had passed, and no doubt the policeman and perhaps his wife from Berriwillock and perhaps even Joe Spencer and his mates now sober and in deep remorse, and perhaps even someone who might know something, he thought for just one moment as he walked without his boots and in a full nakedness, a nakedness which despite the sores and sweat and flow of blood drew all the brightness of the salt to the whiteness of his body, his body blazing in the white shock of reflected sun. He felt the crumbling crystal of the saltcrust upon his feet and the uneasy softness as the black mud forced its way up between his toes, and his dog still hopped alongside him and the old pony to the rear, and all the three were clad only in the blood of the horse or with the blood of Cabel Singh; and he wondered in his last moments upon the lake, before he crossed over the saltbush beaches and strode fast and tall towards those waiting on the cliffs, if there might not be someone among the watchers who would know something, who might have heard the still voice of Eileen.